AN IGNORANT WITCH

WITCH KIN CHRONICLES, BOOK 1

E M GRAHAM

For Carmel – the last one standing.

CHAPTER 1

Benjy had fallen in with the fairies up on the barrens, but I didn't know that then. I thought our worst problem was the ghost of Nan Hoskins, Alice's Great-Grandmother who'd been dead since before either of us were born.

Her old rag doll sat in the shadows of the chair, its wispy brown wool hair and the embroidered mouth half undone with the years. It stared vacantly ahead with mismatched button eyes, and an ancient stain covered the lower part of its face like a scar. It was ugly enough, but it didn't look haunted.

"It's not doing anything," I pointed out, turning away.

"Dara, of course it's not – now. When I left this morning, it was in the upstairs hallway."

"Maybe Sal ..." Alice's sister was fifteen and unhappy with the world, so I'd suspected they might have a poltergeist infestation.

She shook her head and spoke over me, not letting me finish my thought. "No way. We left at the same time, I walked her to the bus stop, I know she didn't touch it. In fact, she won't go near it since all this spooky shit started happening."

I drew a deep breath, sending mental feelers out all around for some evidence of supernatural activity, and tried to switch into the Alt world.

Being a half-blood witch, I have the ability to see both the regular everyday world, and the supernatural, orAlternative, world. It's sort of superimposed on our dimension, or maybe more like, lurking underneath it. To switch back and forth, it's as if I have a pair of those glasses which shade to dark in bright light, only I do it in my mind. Sometimes I can see both at once.

I tried not to flip too much as the Alt world is a scary place to be. And I especially hated to do it in Alice's neighborhood, because there were vampires and all sorts of other nasties living in those parts. They gave me the creeps.

I shivered. Despite the warmth of the September day outside, it was freezing cold in that dank house. Narrowing my eyes to slits to prevent the full onslaught of Alt, I tried to just sense any supernatural presences. Alice started to speak and I hushed her with my hand, for something was coming through and it was centered in the old rocking chair.

A form was materializing for me, a skinny scrawny old woman glaring at me as she knit so furiously I could hardly make out her hands. She was rocking back and forth to keep time with the clicking of the needles, and she was agitated.

My heart sank. This wasn't a poltergeist, a scary bundle of mindless energy, but a real ghost. A very angry one, judging by the hatred in her eyes. Still, I had experience with ghosts, perhaps all this spirit wanted was to tell her tale. Perhaps I could help her resolve whatever issues she was holding onto, and help her towards the light.

"The chair is moving!" Alice shrieked in my ear and broke my concentration.

I opened my eyes again and there it was like I had pictured it in my mind's eye but without the terrible specter in it, just the rag doll going back and forth, staring at me with malevolence.

"What's going on?" She was beside herself and clutching me hard. Still the chair rocked seemingly of its own volition, creaking on the old wooden floor.

"Get behind me, Alice," I said with a firm calmness I was only pretending at.

"Is it Benjy?" She was almost sobbing as she scuttled around, placing me between her and the chair. "Is he dead?"

"Benjy? What does he have to do with it?" I shook my head. "No, whatever it is, it's definitely not your brother." I took a step forward, and nothing changed. Emboldened, I stepped again.

With that, the doll flew into the air and launched itself into my face, the black button of its right eye becoming tangled in my long hair. Alice screamed once more as she ran out of the room like a shot, leaving me trying to tear the doll from my head – it no longer felt like a limp ragdoll but a small animal, all hardness and muscle and teeth. We struggled, the creature determined to do its worst, clawing at my face and ears as if it was a rabid rat.

Finally, I won out and wrenched it off me through pure force of will, flinging it to the floor where it lay senseless and limp once again with a few strands of my hair in its fist like a trophy. I looked back up at the chair and in my fear and outrage forgot to put on my Alt blinders.

The malevolent old bat in the chair cackled with glee when she saw the scratches on my face. A wind was starting to whip around the room, taking papers and dust and the petals of silk flowers up in its maelstrom, even the heavy drapes were stirring. I could feel myself being pushed backwards.

"Who are you?" I was yelling at her. "Go away, leave Alice in peace!"

Like that was going to work, ever. The thing just kept cackling and rocking away while she sent me a stream of psychic spite so powerful it felt like acid being thrown at me. My hair was whipping in front of my face, blinding me.

I tried something I'd seen in the old movies Edna and I used to watch sometimes. With one hand clutching my hair to keep it out of my face, I stepped forward and let her have it as I held up my other hand.

"In the name of God and all that is holy, leave this place!"

Did I mention that Edna was an atheist and hadn't let me go to church as a kid? She wouldn't even sign me up for Youth Camp, she hated organized religion so much. So God could be forgiven for not being on my side that day.

"You! You get out of *my* house!" The cackling had stopped now and the entity was no longer gleeful. A terrible rage overtook her ancient wrinkled face but the roar could have come from the depths of hell itself, and the wind rose to hurricane speed as the lamps and end tables went flying and careening around the room. I ducked as the cable box detached from the wall and flew past my head.

There's only so much you can do to help a friend, so I was out of there in half a second flat, banging the front door behind me and not stopping till I found Alice underneath the highway overpass across the road, huddled into the shadows of the concrete. She was crying, yet even through her tears she could see how shaken I was.

"What is it in there?" She was whispering as she scuffed at the weeds and grass growing in the cracks at the pillar's foot. "What's in my house?"

I shook my head, reluctant to tell her my guesses, but she had to know.

"It's an old woman, and she's really angry. An old wizened woman, but she scared me. A lot." I leaned against the concrete and stared at the foot bridge crossing the river. The smell of diesel and rot wafted up on the gentle fall breeze.

"Oh."

This made me look back up at Alice, for that one sound held a lot.

"You know something about this, don't you?"

"Yeah," she said. "Maybe. Did the old woman ... did she look sort of like me, the way I'd look a hundred years from now?"

I nodded slowly. Yes, the specter did have that look of Alice about her, come to think of it.

"It's Nan Hoskins, it's got to be," Alice said, her voice as mournful as the gulls crying over head. "Shit. Gran always warned us this would happen."

I blinked as I tried to process her words.

Alice was unique, for she was my only real friend growing up. The children of the Kin, the arrogant elite with full witch blood in their veins, they hated me because they thought I was lesser and unnatural. On the other hand, normal people could sense that I had one foot in the supernatural, and they didn't want anything to do with me because they thought I was too strange.

But Alice? She never seemed to notice my weirdness, and for that I'd always been grateful. Now, I was beginning to realize there was more to her than I'd previously thought.

"Gran always said her mother-in-law was too nosy to die," Alice continued, with her hands shoved glumly into her jacket pockets. We were heading toward the foot bridge over the river. "Should have seen it coming. At her wake, when everyone was sitting around having a good time on the rum, she sat right up in her coffin and gave them the old hairy eyeball. Gave them all some scare, I tell you. They still talk about it."

I looked over at my friend, appalled. Dead people sitting up in their coffins? Jesus, and I thought *my* family was strange.

She caught my look. "Well, they were in a hurry to bury her, I guess," she said in a defensive tone. "She died just before the May 24th weekend and everyone wanted to head out around the bay for the first week of summer. They didn't bother with the undertaker's stuff, just put her in the coffin she'd bought on sale twenty years before and had the party."

"Wait now." I stopped mid bridge. "You can buy coffins on sale?"

"It may have been secondhand," Alice mumbled. "I don't know the details. Anyway, the doctor said it was rigor mortis setting in, nothing spooky, they were just in too much of a rush to see her off."

We both stared down the river toward the port. It was quiet there, away from the noise of traffic, but I became aware of a sniffling sound. I looked toward Alice. She had her back turned away from me and her shoulders were shaking.

"If it's your Great-Grandmother's ghost, I'm sure we can do something about her,' I offered inadequately as I placed my hand on her arm.

But that didn't soothe her. She began to cry aloud in deep, wracking sobs. I took both her shoulders in mine as I turned her to face me.

My friend couldn't help but 'pretty-cry' even when she was sobbing fit to break her heart. The minute I start tearing up, my eyelids swell up like a duck's and the tap in my nose turns on. But with Alice, the redness in her eyes just made her gray irises turn silvery and luminous.

"What is it?" I waited until I finally got it out of her.

"It's Benjy. He's disappeared too, on top of all this. No one's heard from him in two weeks. Mom said he's probably gone back to the mainland without telling anyone, but he would have told me."

Benjy was her older brother, and he was a skeet. Heavily into drugs and booze, not too particular about how he got the money to buy these amusements, he'd been bad news ever since I'd known him. But he was her older brother. They were close and she loved him.

"You know what he's like," I said, trying to reassure her. "If one of his buddies was driving up to Nova Scotia and it sounded like a good party, he'd hitch a ride with them and wouldn't think to tell anyone in the spur of the moment."

"But he should have sobered up b ynow, sent me a text or something at least."

True enough. "You think something bad happened to him?"

"Yeah, Dara, I do." She was silent for a moment. "I think he's gotten himself into a pile of trouble finally, and he can't get out of it."

CHAPTER 2

"So that's why you asked me if he was the one haunting your house. You're worried that he's ..."

With his life style, it could be a distinct possibility that he would meet with an early demise. He was always the worst kind of trouble maker during his life, and there was no way he would go gently into the light just because he'd stopped breathing. But Alice didn't need to hear that.

"He's not dead! No way, he can't be...." Again looking at me with those big eyes, desperate for comfort. She delicately wiped her nose on her sleeve.

"Course not. He's just being more Benjy than normal. He's probably living it up somewhere, having the time of his life. When the booze runs out, your brother'll come back."

We walked to the end of the footbridge and in to the wasteland by the old train station. My assurances to her rang hollow. 'Where did you see him last?'

"He was headed up to the Southside Hills for berry picking, to the family patch. No one has seen him since."

I know what you're thinking – big tough guy hoodlum like Benjy Hoskins doing a pansy thing like picking berries? Well, this is Newfoundland, and everybody does that. You want blueberry jam for your morning toast? Then you provide the berries, they're free for the taking in the scrublands and the barrens. Besides, her family had a spot up on the Southside Hills behind their house, they'd been going there for generations ever since old Nan Hoskins stuck her flag in the dirt and declared it her own. No one would dare steal the berries from under that old harridan's nose even after she'd been dead for twenty-five years. Reputations die hard in this land.

But those cliffs which loomed over the city of St. John's – they were a dangerous place if you didn't know them, and maybe even if you did. Full of bogs and gullies and beaver dams, rabbit trails leading nowhere. A person could get lost pretty easily up there.

Benjy could be lying up there with a broken leg unable to move, or may even have fallen over the cliffs into Freshwater Bay on the other side of the mountain, where the sucking surf would take his body deep into the currents never to be seen again till he was vomited up by the ocean at Cape Spear, or washed up on the shores of Ireland.

Worse than the physical dangers, though, were the fairies. Personally, I avoided the area, it had always smelled wrong to me. I felt the first ripple of fear for Alice's brother. My steps faltered.

"No one's gone up to look for him?"

"Mom and Aunt Trish went up for the berries when he never came back, and they didn't see any sign of him. They were complaining because he took the good bucket, the red one, and didn't bring it back."

Just as Newfoundlanders carefully keep the best berry patch locations secret, so they treasure their berry pails. The best are old salt-beef buckets, the one-gallon ones, although others do at a pinch. The trick is the pail has to be big enough to hold the most amount of berries you can get, but not hold so many it's too heavy to carry back. It's got to have a comfortable handle and preferably a lid that doesn't get lost, one you can snap into place so the berries don't spill when you bring the harvest home over the hills and rocks. Yeah, we're a strange breed, but we know our buckets.

"I wouldn't be worrying about him so much if it wasn't for the doll," Alice continued. "It's all too strange."

But the fairies. I sighed deeply, right from the pit of my stomach. I couldn't tell Alice about my fears, and not just because she wouldn't believe me. She knew I could see ghosts, but even though she was my only friend, I'd never told her about the other stuff. About being a half-blood witch, and Alt, and magic. About the fairies on the hill, or the vampires living down the road from her, or the dwarves who worked in the old tunnels.

The thing was, I wasn't allowed to tell her or anybody else about all that, as part of the agreement with Dad. There was a faction of the Witch Kin in those parts who believed that impure blood was an abomination, and I'd only survived this long because Jonathan de Teilhard was my natural father. As his illegitimate daughter, he supported me financially with the stipulation that I had to suppress the magic side of me and generally stay under the Kin's radar.

This was after Mom disappeared. That still hurt. I tried not to think about it, but I blamed his wife Cate.

Alice broke into my thoughts, and I gladly turned away from them. She'd decided to come home with me till her parents got off work, as she didn't want to be home alone. Understandable. We continued up Topsail Road to my house on the hill.

"What I don't get is, if it is Nan Hoskins, why show herself to you and not me? I'm her own blood, after all."

"I guess it's because I can see ghosts," I said. "And talk with them."

We paused at the bottom of the long dirt driveway leading to Richmond Cottage, the family home for me and Aunt Edna and, until ten years ago, Mom. The iron gates had long since rusted away and weeds were taking over as I was the only one who ever used it. Edna and her boyfriend drove in the back way off Shaw Street, the old tradesman's entrance to the estate. It was a lot easier to keep shoveled in winter.

"Are they all like Nan Hoskins? The ghost in your house doesn't sound creepy."

"Nah. Most ghosts are peaceful, or sad. Sometimes they don't even know they're dead, sometimes they're just really confused. And Maundy, well, she tries to bully me, but she's harmless." Not like the fury of terror in Alice's house.

I'd always been aware of Maundy, I think we first met when I was three years old and I wandered into her room. In life, she had been the niece of my great-great grandfather, so I don't know what that makes us – four times removed? Five? I could never figure it out.

"Hey, your ghost," Alice said, brightening for the first time that afternoon. "Maybe she can help with Nan Hoskins."

I shook my head. "No, she's way too self-involved. She won't even leave her room."

We'd reached the top of the long driveway and went round to the back door. Edna's battered red Civic wasn't there and the place was locked up secure. Not that anyone would ever try to break in – the old mansion was way too spooky looking, and besides, there was nothing worth stealing in here – but her boyfriend Mark was a cop, and he was always on at her to keep the place locked. She must finally be taking heed.

As I waited for the kettle to boil, I thought aloud to Alice.

"You know, I've been in your house dozens of times," I began.

"Hundreds."

"Yeah, maybe. So why is Nan Hoskins only showing herself to me now? She died before we were born."

She gave a shudder. "It's weird. You never saw her before at all?"

I shook my head as I poured the hot water into the mugs. Her house had always had a creepy feeling, but I'd assumed that was because it was so dark, huddled at the foot of the Southside Hills as it was and never getting sunlight in there. I honestly hadn't thought it was any more haunted than other houses of its age – you know, with the residual emotions that hang on in any family home over the years.

Alice squeezed her teabag and dumped it into the bowl which held other used bags, long since dried out. I needed to make a trip to the composter.

"I don't suppose you can get rid of her?" she asked in a tentative voice.

"What, like an exorcism or something?"

"Whatever it takes."

"That's a little harsh, isn't it? She's your great-grand-mother."

"I don't care, I want her gone."

"Maybe she's appearing now because she wants to tell you something."

"Oh, yeah? And what did she say to you?"

Alice had a point. Nan Hoskins was more like a screaming demon than a spirit with a message from beyond.

"Gran always hated her, she made no bones about saying how happy she was when Nan finally kicked the bucket. She died before I came on the scene, but they lived together for years in that house, right from when Gran married into the family."

An idea struck me. "Where's your Gran now?"

"Living in St. Pat's, the nursing home. You think she can help?"

"Maybe," I said. "Why don't we go see her after classes tomorrow?"

We made arrangements to meet in the library the next day, then Alice went back down the road to meet her mother after her shift at the drugstore. I took my tea up the back staircase to my bedroom to sit and ponder in my favorite spot, the window seat overlooking the large unkempt garden.

This mansion, or house, or 'cottage' as it was formally known as – it's like a Tardis house, if you've ever watched any of the Doctor Who series. It looks real cute and small on the outside to someone looking up from the road below, but inside it stretches on forever. Part of the trick is caused by the long floor to ceiling windows at the front of the house. They give the optical illusion of a compact space within, and it's only when the viewer draws closer that they realize the main entrance is dwarfed by the French windows which are a good fifteen feet high. We didn't use those front rooms any more, they were impossible to heat in winter.

In fact, much of the house was closed off permanently those days. I used to love wandering through the library and drawing rooms as a child. Yeah, there were residual ghosts all around there, too, but it was pretty clean of supernaturals. It had been a happy home at one time.

Likewise the gardens had been left to revert back to their natural state, the ancient oaks and chestnuts providing a solid wall against the world. The vegetable plots at the back had long since become an unexpected urban woodland for the neighborhood kids. The City was always on at us to fence it off, but what was the harm?

My favorite place outside was the statue garden off to the side of the formal drawing room. The French doors once opened onto this courtyard walled with cedars and with a single fountain in the middle. The copper fish was all green now and no longer spouted water, while the garden doors were nailed shut, but I could still gain access through the old garden gate. It was like another world in there, and it was all mine.

I had only ever shared that space with my older half-sister Sasha. We used to play hide and seek down there among the statues when Jon, our father, would bring her to visit, and we used to play magic games down there too. All that ended though when things came to a head between Mom and his wife Cate.

Dad had a traditional marriage, arranged for optimal alliance and merging of two big houses. This is what the Kin do, and it's one way they've held on to their power through the centuries. Mom was the mistress he fell in love with. After all the fighting began between Mom and Dad, well it was about that time Mom went away and never returned. I wasn't allowed to play magic anymore after that.

As I sat on the cushion of my window seat and looked down upon my old domain, my mind was working hard. The sudden appearance of Nan Hoskins was a puzzle, and the fact that she chose to show herself right after Benjy's disappearance was not a good sign. The two events had to have a connection. But what was it?

CHAPTER 3

I hung out at the library for a few hours, waiting for Alice to finish her lab. She was such a nerd – I could never convince her to skip her time with the microscopes and algaes and what not. Unlike myself, of course. I planned to have a long and undistinguished career of professional student, doing only enough work to prevent them from kicking me out, compliments of my dearly dreaded Dad. It was the closest I would ever get to a trust fund, unlike his other, legitimate children.

The Newfoundland Studies section was always where I gravitated to. They wouldn't let you go behind the desk and browse through all the stacks of old papers and books, only staff were allowed back there. I sometimes idled with the thought of actually getting a job there, just for the privilege of hanging out behind the scenes, however I never got round to filling out the application.

A search in the computer showed a few mentions of the Southside Hoskins clan in the archives. Yep, they had been parishioners of the old St. Mary's Church, the one torn down in the 'sixties along with a bunch of houses in order to widen the road.

I came upon an old article from the time of World War II that discussed a new shooting range on the Southside Hills. The writer seemed quite outraged that the local people were disregarding the bans and traipsing all over the fenced off area to pick their berries that fall, heedless of getting shot by the troops doing their rifle practice. Hah – I'd bet Nan Hoskins was leading that brigade of scofflaws. No one would dare shoot her.

While I was poking around the electronic records of the archives, my thoughts moved on to the reign of Nan, along with her family's secret blueberry patch. As an outsider, I'd never been allowed to accompany Alice on the yearly excursions of berry picking, but that had never bothered me because I could feel something creepy happening up on that mountain.

And I don't mean the vampires in that big scary house with the turrets and gables down the street from Alice. This feeling came upon me the few times I'd ventured up the path by the Fort Amherst lighthouse at the mouth of the harbor, the path that led straight up the hill to the Southside Barrens at the top. Physically, it looks like the top of any large hill or mountain on the Avalon Peninsula, I guess – all rocks and bogs and scrubby pines growing in the direction of the prevailing winds, and completely open to the sky above. But I always knew there was something very, very wrong up there.

The tops of those hills felt like fairy. You know that mucky, sticky feeling like honey that's almost dried on your skin and won't come off no matter how much you lick it? My skin would feel dirty and grimy just being up there. And the hills smelled of fairy too, to me at least. Normals probably wouldn't catch it, would think it was just the poo plant down the road wafting up in the summer breeze, but I knew for a fact there was no smell like fairy.

Think about the forgotten package of hamburger meat at the back of the fridge leftover from when it rained on the day of the barbeque that time, or the rat who expired unseen in the bedroom wall. Think about the salt flats on the Bay of Fundy mixed together with the street gutters in Mumbai. Or better yet, visit a dead whale beached on the shores of an abandoned outport, and that will give an idea about the smell of the fairies.

People have the wrong idea about the fae, I blame Walt Disney and urbanization. Too many people don't live close to the land anymore. They're so busy living their lives surrounded by concrete and lawns and their SUVs with GPS and AWD, they can't see the world outside their narrow scope. The fairies have been around since time immemorial and folk were justly afraid of them throughout history.

I will tell you they are not cute, or pretty, or sweet or anything nice. They don't float around on little wings spreading magic dust to grant wishes or to make you fly. Fae are a rotten crowd who are just plain mean with cruel withered hearts, and they excel in torture.

"Hey." A bag plonked down on the table next to me, making me jump. "What're you looking up?"

Alice bent over for a better view of the screen. "Really? Fairies in Newfoundland." She made a scoffing sound and rolled her eyes.

This from a girl whose dead Nan was terrorizing her.

"Haven't you ever heard the legends?" I quickly exited the screen and gathered my stuff.

"Nobody talks about that foolishness anymore," she said. "C'mon let's go before Gran goes back to bed."

We made our way out the glass library doors.

"I can't promise you much, you know," she warned me as we crossed the campus in the direction of the nursing home. "She's a little, uh..."

"Senile?"

"Dementia is what they call it. Losing her memory, about the recent stuff, anyway," Alice said. "She seems to be living in her youth, or at least years ago. She thinks I'm my aunt."

St. Pat's was a big nursing home, formerly run by the Catholic Church until Eastern Health gobbled everything up. I don't know why her grandmother ended up here because Alice's family had always been Anglican. Still, the staff were really nice, and it had a gorgeous chapel right inside the nursing home itself.

Alice pointed out her grandmother down the long corridor. The woman was headed for the center lounge where the TV blared, and we hurried to catch up to her. Even this early in the evening she was dressed in a flannel nightie sprigged with roses with a shapeless pilled cardigan over it for warmth. Her feet were clad in thick socks and sneakers to prevent falls.

"Hi Gran," Alice said to her.

The old woman turned to peer at her visitor, a puzzled look on her face.

"Debbie?" she asked.

"No, Gran, Debbie's my aunt. I'm Alice."

"Hmm." Gran was reserving judgement on that, and looking very suspicious too.

"Come sit, Gran," Alice coaxed her and settled in next to her on the vinyl covered sofa. "I wanted to ask you about Nan Hoskins."

"She's dead."

"Well, we hope so, but..."

"Come back, has she?"

We looked at each other in amazement. How did the old lady know?

"It was too good to be true, I knew it at the time," Gran muttered, barely audible over the television game show.

"What do you know of it?" I approached her and asked carefully and loudly. "Why would Nan Hoskins come back?"

"Well she never left, did she? Even when she sat up in her coffin and scared the hell out of everyone, even then I could hear her cackling away, for all the doctor said it was rigor mortalization or whatever they call it."

"She's come back, and Benjy has disappeared," I said.

"Who's Benjy?" The old woman raised her voice.

"Your grandson."

Alice reached over and turned off the volume on the TV. The silence reverberated around the concrete walls of the large room.

"Well, that's not good then." She looked out the window, right across town to where the lowering sun was lighting on the windows in the old tower overlooking the harbor. "Where'd he disappear to?"

"He went berry picking up to Nan's patch, and no one's seen him since," Alice said softly.

"Just goes to show, doesn't it?" the old woman said with a scowl.

"What do you mean?"

"The fairies have broken off their promises. Who'd trust them anyway? She was that arrogant, she thought she could bully them too."

I knew it! I thrust my arm into the air in a silent victory cheer behind Gran's back. I knew there were fairies on the Southside Hills. "Tell me more about the fae," I pressed the old lady as I came round to her side.

She gestured me closer and whispered in my ear. "Have you got a bite to eat? They don't feed me here. I'm starving to death I am."

I hauled out a Hershey bar from my knapsack and quickly unwrapped it for her, looking doubtfully at the tightness of her nightie as I did so. She sure didn't looked malnourished. "Tell me about the fairies and the broken promises."

Gran was too busy stuffing the bar into her mouth to answer, and I realized why when a nurse swooped down on us.

"You're not giving her chocolate, surely? Don't you know she's diabetic? You trying to kill her?"

This was as good as a declaration of war for Gran, who screeched as the bar was taken from her hand. "They're starving me here, haven't had a bite since yesterday! Help me for the love of God, I'm wasting away!" She lashed out with her hand, missing her caregiver's head by only inches.

"Now Mrs. H, you know you get a good three squares a day and more here." The nurse ducked then grimaced at us as if we were to blame for the scene. "Come on back to your room and we'll give you a nice pudding with your meds."

Gran was having none of it, although by this time she seemed to have forgotten why she was upset.

"Help me Debbie! They're going to kill me, I tell you," she hollered as she tried to wriggle out of the nurse's firm but kindly grasp.

The soothing sounds from the nurse did little to calm the old woman as she was slowly but surely led away from us, her protests echoing down the long empty corridor.

Alice stood up with a sigh and hitched her backpack onto her shoulders.

"We won't get anything else out of her today," she said. "Come on, we might as well get the bus home out of it."

There wasn't much conversation between us as we waited at the stop in the drizzling rain. I could tell Alice was miserable, dreading to go back to her haunted home to see what new horrors her dead Nan had in store for the family.

CHAPTER 4

That night, I tried to think what I could do to help Alice and her family. She'd reported that things were rapidly getting worse in her home. It wasn't just the doll creeping around, now doors were slamming back and forth, and it sounded like Nan Hoskins was clomping up and down the stairs in army boots all night long. Her great-grandmother was ramping up the offensive.

Despite my powers, I had no idea how to be of assistance, for I'd had no formal training in the supernatural. Unlike my fullblood siblings, my education in those matters hadn't been deemed worth bothering about. Dad didn't have enough guts to formally acknowledge me to the rest of the world, even though everyone knew who my parents were. In his circle even back then, mixed blood kids were deemed mongrels and a lesser species. Things had only gotten worse over time.

I knew enough to know that I didn't know anything, and had spent the past ten years or so pretending to the rest of the world that I knew nothing at all. Most of what little knowledge I had gained concerning magic and the supernatural world had come through books, fiction mostly, and I'd found out the hard way that a lot of this wasn't reliable.

Anything else I knew had been learned through my experience of the Alt world, through my forays and experimentation. I had told Edna none of that of course.

As I'd said to Alice, I couldn't even turn to Maundy for help, for that kid hardly even realized she was dead. Not being a part of the Witch Kin community, I had no one to turn to.

Sasha might have helped me, once upon a time. But we'd grown apart after her mother put her foot down, right about the time Mom disappeared. My half-sister was the only one I could play magic with, back then. We used to do fun stuff, like divert the water from the fish fountain to splash over each other, levitate the garden chairs – you know, kid stuff. But there's no way I would approach her these days for she and her friends had made it clear during high school that I was *persona non grata*.

So I had no one to turn to for advice. Except my father. My heart sank at the thought, for there was one thing I hated in this world and that was asking Jon for assistance of any kind. Yeah, I accepted his support cheques no problem, but that process was removed from the man himself – the money was automatically dumped in my bank account every month and I could continue to despise him and to sneer at him from afar.

I made my own money for spending of course, babysitting for Jane. She was a single mom of three who had dedicated her entire life to doing everything right for those kids of hers, and managed to do this without a boyfriend or any other visible support except Social Assistance. Those kids were all breastfed then went on to diets of organic kale and gluten free everything, poor things. But she looked after her own needs too, and that's where I came in. Every so often, she would pump the baby's milk into bottles and I would look after the littles while she went down to George Street, maybe looking for Baby Daddy number four.

The kids loved to see me coming because I don't believe in childhood without chocolate, but I swore them to secrecy. She marvelled at how much they loved me.

Children need to have treats and fun in their lives. I remember how Dad used to let me find chocolate coins in his suit jacket pocket, always acting surprised when they appeared, swearing to Mom they hadn't been there when he left his house that morning. That was back when Mom was around and we were a family in our own weird little way.

But Dad. Asking for his help meant being in his physical presence, and that prospect scared the crap out of me these days. The last time I'd seen him face to face, a few years ago when I found that book of spells hidden in our house, he'd been so furious when he swooped down to remove it, I think I still have PTSD. But that's another story.

I needed back up, someone to hold my hand to give me courage.

"Edna," I said the next morning as I walked into the kitchen. Best to get her before coffee, before her brain turned fully on. "I need a ride."

"When are you going to get your driver's license, Dara? Mark has offered to teach you loads of times."

"Not this morning, at any rate." We both looked up to see Mark stroll into the kitchen, dressed in what I call his plainclothes uniform, the suit he wore when he went undercover. Well, when he tried to go incognito, anyway. He still looked like a cop in any outfit, he couldn't help it, but I wasn't going to burst his bubble by telling him that. "I'm working today, but any other time I'd be happy to give a lesson or two."

I hadn't even known he stayed over last night. Those two were nothing if not discreet.

"Can you give me a ride out to the east end?"

"Take the bus." Edna poured herself another coffee, and to take the sting out of her refusal, poured me one too. The morning newspaper was spread out in front of her and she prepared to dive in.

I sat across from her, eyes boring into the crown of her head. "I need to go see my father."

One blue eye peeped through the mass of curls.

"I have a problem," I continued.

"Financial?"

"No, it's more..." I couldn't tell her what the true nature of my problem was, not with Mark standing five feet away, filling a mug for himself.

Edna understood what I was getting at. She lifted her head fully and shook it. "Don't do it Dara. Don't give him the chance. You know how upset you get every time you see him."

"But..."

"He hurts you. His kids hurt you. And then I have to pick up the pieces. Stay under the radar."

Mark stepped out of the room, perhaps to give us space in what might be turning into a family argument, or perhaps for some other reason of his own. He walked lightly for such a big guy.

"But Alice needs help," I whispered to her. "Her great-grandmother is haunting her house."

"You know the terms of the agreement!"

Yeah, the agreement. Dad was fully aware that I had supernatural powers, that he himself had given me those powers with his contribution to my genes, and that's why he had agreed to support my education so I wouldn't be tempted to go halfassed into the Alt-world and embarrass him.

My side of the bargain was that I would subvert that side of myself, turn my back on my abilities and embrace the Normal world.

You see, the Witch Kin of St. John's controlled everything and had done for centuries, ever since this brand new world and its riches had been discovered. The Normals who lived outside that tightknit circle saw only the families of old-money ruling from their seats of high power in the government and church and merchant circles, and some of them tried their darndest to break into these spheres. They didn't know it could never be, for the Witch Kin was the most closed of societies.

Quite frankly, I figured Dad was embarrassed by me, perhaps he was ashamed of his affair with my mother which had produced this half-blood. The money he paid for my support was peanuts to him and I guess he didn't care if he had to pay it out for the rest of my life, just so long as I didn't rock his precious boat.

"Right, there's always the money to think of." Yes, I was bitter that she supported him.

"Look, Dara, I'm not saying this for my own sake," Edna continued in a low voice. "Sure, it's great that his money helps pay our way. But I can live without it, I could... I could get a job or something. I'm thinking about you."

I must have looked pretty sulky, for she sighed and got up, coming over to place her arms around my shoulders.

"He's right," she said quietly. "You need to turn your back on all that. You can't fit into their world, being a... a..."

"Half-breed."

"Yeah. You know how cruel they are. If he finds out you're dabbling in any of it, well, I'm worried about more than the money being cut off."

She didn't bring up Mom's disappearance all those years ago, but I knew without her saying that that's what was on her mind.

"You're never going to tell me what happened to Mom, are you?"

"If I knew, I would tell you," she said, her voice low and fervent. "You know that we never found her body. I couldn't prove anything, and besides..."

"Yeah, the Chief of Police in the Royal Newfoundland Constabulary is always one of *them*."

"It's not that way anymore, but still..." I could see her nodding in the mirror on the sideboard.

I twisted my head up to look at her. "Does Mark know about that side of the city? About the ruling classes of Kin?"

Her boyfriend Mark was not from here. Also, he was with the other police force, the RCMP, the Royal Canadian Mounted Police. They looked after everything the RNC didn't want to touch. The outports, the bay towns, Labrador. Mark was originally from up north and had been posted to a lot of places in the country before ending up here.

I didn't know if Mark knew about my magical powers or the existence of the supernatural world, but I'd once overheard him telling Edna about a strange experience he'd had under the Northern Lights with a shaman when he was growing up in the Yukon. Maybe his mind was open to all that stuff, yet I still couldn't allow myself to broach the topic when he was around. Dad had me so scared shitless that secrecy was second nature to me by now.

She placed her index finger over her lips. "It's not something I talk about with him," she said, then returned to her seat and her coffee. "So, that's settled. You're not going to go see your father."

Mark cleared his throat at the door to the kitchen. How much had he overheard? I was beyond caring by this point.

"I, uh... I was hoping to speak with you, Dara," he said in that very kind voice of his. "I'm glad I caught you this morning."

He came and sat between the two of us. "There's a lot of weird stuff happening out there, these days," he continued, cocking his head towards the outside world. "Especially at night. At this time of year."

"I'm twenty years old, Mark," I said, beginning to bristle. "I'm not some little kid. I can take care of myself. The students are back, and they go downtown and get drunk. I can outrun anyone who tries anything on me."

Like, really? He felt a need to give me a 'talk' this early in the morning. I like Mark, I really do, maybe even love him because he's just what Edna needs, but I could do without this fatherly side of him.

"No, I'm not worried about you," he said, a little taken aback at my tone. "I actually wanted to ask you about it, get your take on things. You know, the weird graffiti and symbols that are appearing on the alleyway walls?"

Now it was my turn to be surprised. Yes, I was aware, and I'd seen what he was talking about. Hex signs, runes, other symbols or letters or hieroglyphics I didn't recognize, these were all being sprayed and painted onto the more hidden of the backstreet lanes downtown and even on the older stone churches. I'd assumed they were from a new generation of defacing doodlers, ones brought up on the paranormal stories which were so popular.

"I've seen them, yeah," I said. "Why? They're in St. John's, not your territory."

"Normally, no," he said. "But we've got a task force on the go, one working with both law-enforcement agencies in the province, and I have a feeling these are a central part of the investigation."

Now he had me flabbergasted. "What's going on?"

"It's not just the graffiti," he said. "But I have a feeling it might be tied into things. It's like there's some kind of ... I don't know how to say it. There's something wrong going on, I feel it in the air. I can't put my finger on it."

Yeah, I knew what he was talking about. I'd felt it too. It had been a horribly hot summer, and it was as if the endless weeks of heat had caused a rot somewhere, the over-riding humidity in the air had sparked something evil to burst its spores and spread like a dark miasma over the city. And I had thought it was just me and my half-witch imagination.

"For example," he continued. "This graffiti has certain religious arcane overtones to it. And that woman who opened up the so-called magic store..."

"Magic store?" This was the first I'd heard of this.

"Yeah, down on Duckworth Street. What's her name, Zeta? What a loony tune. I have a feeling she might be behind some of this. At any rate, she's not helping matters."

An actual storefront that dealt in magic. I was growing excited. Perhaps I didn't need Dad's help in dealing with Nan Hoskins's haunting.

Mark was still talking. "We can't help but feel, especially in the light of other... evidence, things that have surfaced." He was watching me closely.

"What other stuff?"

"You know a body was found the other day, over on the mountain behind Portugal Cove?"

I nodded. That had been a weird story, a body found in a small dale in the barrens up there. The newspapers had been asking questions of the police ever since the woman was discovered, but no information was given out. She had been a visitor, not from the island. One of the local radio stations had interviewed the owner of the B & B she'd been staying at, who'd told them her name was Tracey and she'd been here looking into her roots, but none of the family she was supposedly related to wanted anything to do with her.

A strange tale, and one to occupy the bored press when not much else was happening in the way of politics.

"This didn't leak to the press, but it was the strangest thing, the whole set-up." He leaned over to me so close I could see the little flecks of hazel in his normally dark brown eyes. "There were similar symbols chalked onto the rocks all around the site of the death. We could barely make them out, the weather has gotten to them of course. And there was no cause of death that we could find, just weird burn marks all over her body, on her hands, and her navel and the top of her head."

"Did she, I don't know, get scared to death or something?" I wondered aloud. "Was she being tortured?"

He nodded. "That's the general consensus," he agreed. "However, we've brought in an expert on arcane subjects, because you know what the strangest thing of all is?"

I shook my head.

"Despite the burn marks, there was no trace of accelerant on her body at all," he said. "Nothing flammable, no evidence. It was as if she was burned by lightning."

I could feel the hairs on my arms prickle. Lightning. Or magic? I searched his face to see what he suspected, if he had any thoughts, any suspicions about my own birth.

"And you want to know something even more disturbing?" His eyes were totally holding mine now. "When we found the body, it was in perfect condition, barring natural deterioration and the fact that the corpse had been lying exposed to the elements since the death. No wild animals, no foxes or coyotes, no crows had been picking at her. Not even the gulls."

He sat back. He was right, this was creepy and totally unnatural.

Something weird was happening around the town, I'd been feeling it for a while. Maybe it was the shifting weather patterns, maybe the increasingly strong winds were stirring up something best left forgotten. Or maybe it was unsettled magic.

CHAPTER 5

I couldn't help Mark out with his investigation, but I still needed assistance of my own. I wasn't going to get to Dad's house with Edna's help, that much was obvious but I could still check out Zeta and her store. This might be grasping at straws, for Mark said she was a wing-nut which could mean one of two things. Either she really was a crackpot, a delusional human desperate to believe in magic and all things super-natural, or else she was the real thing. A renegade Kin wanting to open up the supernatural powers of everyone, going out on a limb to defy the conventions of the craft. I thrilled at the thought of such boldness in the face of the Kin, and the more I thought about it, the more excited I became.

Today was Saturday, no classes for me. Alice was gone off on a boat-tour with her nerdy classmates, something about a walrus being spotted on the shores further down the coast. Walruses don't live in New-foundland normally, it must have got stuck on an ice floe off Greenland and floated down. She'd offered to take me along, but I'd declined. I get sea-sick in anything bigger than a canoe on a pond.

I set off walking downtown. I usually love this time of year, just before it turns to autumn. It's a time for new starts, new beginnings, despite the impending death of summer, or maybe because of it. This past summer had been the hottest on record, days and days of hot weather so humid it pressed all the good out of you. I was glad to be coming into the cooler weather.

At first I just wandered, enjoying the fresh air. The old core of the city, with its original winding lanes and alleys and slums – much of that has been cleaned up, widened, straightened or just plain bulldozed down over the years, but much still remains. Dead end alleys, hidden corners and passageways just off the main drag – there's lots of places for the forgotten side of life to lurk and thrive if you know where to look. The cardboard shelters, the unplanned nooks strewn with broken glass and needles and smelling of piss and worse... These are the evidence of the seamy underbelly, and all those hidden walls are ripe for graffiti.

It was in Birdshit Alley that I first noticed the graffiti, along that small angled staircase connecting Duckworth and Water, the one that never sees the sun. It's shaded by a forgotten inner city forest growing in a fenced off empty back lot, a natural place for the starlings to congregate, so much so that you can't hear yourself think at sundown when they've all come home to roost. And underfoot... well, that's how it got its name.

The old stone and concrete walls lining this alley are also a natural place for passing graffiti artists, and after every summer there's fresh work on show. It's usually just trash stuff, stupid tags and dicks and things. But not this year.

This summer the art had taken a different turn. It consisted of a single symbol, hand painted over and over again, repeated until the black mat paint almost covered over all the colors of the previous years so that hardly a square foot of the windowless wall was untouched. Or I should say, it was two symbols merged into one. There was a simple Celtic knot, a continuous line defining the corners of a circle. I knew that symbol well – I'd seen it many times on the heavy silver chain around my father's neck. It was the symbol for the Witch Kin.

Inside the square at the very center of the circle was a simple cross, or plus sign, like the international symbol for the Red Cross. By itself among the Witch Kin lore, this was the symbol for purity.

But juxtaposed as it was with the Celtic knot, there could only be one meaning.

It made my blood chill just looking at the repetitions painted over and over again, like a chant increasing in volume and pitch.

Purity of blood. Purity of *magic* blood.

Being a half-blood who grew up around Witch Kin kids, I knew there was prejudice in this town, always had been. The Kin were like that. But mostly it took the form of petty snubs to keep the halflings and non-magic Normals in their place.

But this graffiti. Even though it was on an alley wall hidden from view from the light of day – this was in your face, a simmering pot of hatred about to boil over. The matte black paint covered the wall like bacteria on a rotten carcass ripe to split open to the air.

I reached out my hand toward the paint, and the magic leapt out, burning my finger. Turning tail, I fled back to the sunshine and bustle and normality of Water Street and tried not to think about what I'd seen, and about what Mark had said about the dead body.

·····•·••····

The store I was looking for was located down on the west end of Duckworth, above the rum joints of George Street in one of those old rickety wooden buildings.

'Zeta's House of Magick', it was called, and it promised to have spells for every need. Was this a sign that the Witch Kin were opening up their ranks to the Normals, cashing in on the interest in all things supernatural? Not bloody likely given the writing on that alley wall, but I had to check it out.

I walked into an atmosphere of incense and spices which covered up the smell of ancient mice and wood rot, and it was like entering a storefront in a Harry Potter book. Almost.

It was a tiny space. The shelves were crammed full of all sorts of arcane looking objects with handlettered signs describing the wares. I rifled through a basket of glass evil eyes from Greece, then my fingers wandered over to the books on display, where every subject under the sun was covered in a mishmash of colors and titles, with no apparent organization to the lot of them. Runes. Shapeshifting. Unicorns. A large poster of a pretty fairy sitting on a bluebell, fairy dust all around her, was on the wall above. Next to the books sat a display of Harry Potter flavored jelly beans. I sighed.

I could sense some power around the room, but it was hard to tell where it was coming from in the jumble, for there wasn't much real magic here at all among all this second-rate plastic stuff. Disappointed, I was about to leave again when a clatter of beads from the curtain under the stairs announced the arrival of the store's proprietor.

She wafted over to me, a tall blonde woman with generous proportions, dressed in flowing skirts and scarves and her hair all frizzed out. She looked to be about Edna's age, although it was hard to tell through the heavy makeup.

"Welcome to Zeta's House of Magick," she said in a ringing baritone and she strode forward with her hand out to shake mine.

I hate touching strangers, so I held back, and merely nodded.

"How may I be of assistance?" She looked me up and down, then put her fingers to her temples and breathed deeply, as if tuning in to another frequency. "Ah, I sense you are a seeker."

"Yeah, right..."

"Are you a witch?" She threw this at me so quickly I almost lost my balance.

Could she sense my half-blood? I automatically glanced around the space but of course we were alone.

"If you are searching for answers and find yourself here, you may be a witch," she told me. "Sometimes people don't even know they have magical powers. Do you have a longing deep in your soul for the unknown? Do you feel disconnected to your true purpose? It is my role in this life to help searchers find meaning in their lives."

She made a grand gesture with her arm towards a hand-printed cardboard sign hanging on the wall behind the cash. It listed all the services Zeta could provide and it was a very eclectic, wide-ranging menu, from spells and incantations, to potions and therapy.

"Take this," she continued, pressing a business card into my hand. "We hold classes every second Thursday night here. We encourage all who are open to the supernatural to attend. Coffee and muffins provided, ten dollars entrance fee."

"What – witch classes?"

"We delve into all things of the other world," she said loftily. "I also help to find solutions for life's problems through spells and other magical accoutrements, all of which are available for purchase."

"Are... are you a witch? A full-blood witch?" No way, I didn't believe it for a minute.

"I am a witch," she announced proudly. "The daughter of a line of witches, in a tradition stretching back hundreds of years."

In my experience, real witches didn't advertise to all and sundry about their magical blood. Did her family know about this?

"What Kin do you belong to?" I found myself whispering this, I was so unused to discussing this out loud.

"Kin? All witches are my kin, all women of power."

"No, I mean, your father's house." Contrary to popular New Age philosophy, the Witch Kin were all very patriarchal in their organization and always had been. Although women of powerful families like Cate kept their own last names when married, lineage went through the father's family.

"My father?" she asked, her face blank. "What does he have to do with it?"

That's when I knew she wasn't the real deal. Not at all. I sighed and turned to go.

"Wait!" she said, with a note of desperation in her voice. "You came in here for a reason. What are you searching for?"

I faced her again, thinking hard. If she would only shut up and leave me alone, I might find the source of the magic I sensed among all the flotsam on the shelves.

"My friend has a ghost terrorizing her family," I said. "I was wondering if there was anything we can do about it."

She made a great show of thinking deeply, shutting her eyes tight and breathing in noisily.

"Yes!" she exclaimed as her eyes opened wide again. "I have it! The very thing." Zeta went behind the old wooden counter and turning her back to me, began taking down canisters and jars, opening them up and measuring tiny amounts onto a scale, humming as she went.

I took the opportunity to scan the tiny store again for the magic I had sensed within. A slight whiff drew me to the back corner of the store, over near where the beaded curtain hid the stairs to the cellar. It was there, in a basket full of oddments of metal and wood. I dug in, searching with my fingertips till I felt the unmistakable tingle of magical power close by.

And then my fingers brushed against it, a warm metal like a disc or an old coin, but when I took it in my grasp it burned me, the heat searing through my fingertips like lightning. I dropped it quickly and brought my hand up to my mouth.

What was that? I was shaken. There was no physical damage to my hand despite that it was still stinging, but in that instant of the burn I had felt something else, too. No, not felt, but had seen and experienced, as if I had been transported momentarily to a scene of darkness, too terrible to even contemplate. It had been a place of sadness and grieving, and it felt like a memory too intimate for comfort. I stepped back from the basket, for I wanted no part of that magic, whatever it was.

But I knew who had owned it.

"Okay, that'll be twenty-five dollars."

"What?" I straightened up and faced her, still confused by my reaction to the old coin in the basket.

"Taxes are included." Zeta crossed her arms and set her mouth in a grim line.

"Twenty-five dollars! I'm not paying that much. How do I even know it'll work?"

She held out the tiny sachet, not more than two inches square and made of rough cotton. "I made it up specially for you, it's a custom spell. That doesn't come cheap, you know," she said. "Besides, I give you the incantation and all the instructions are included, everything you need."

I blew the hair from my face with a puff. Alice was really going to owe me for this one.

Zeta placed the sachet and a preprinted sheet of instructions into a small paper bag.

She paused then spoke again. "There's a twenty percent discount on everything in the store if you buy a membership..."

"No, thank you," I said as I hauled out the cash from my wallet and took the package from her. I could hardly believe I was doing this, but I needed to get out of Zeta's store and away from the terrible magic of that coin. I could feel it calling to me, wanting me to take it and use it and change my life forever. It scared me.

"It's guaranteed to work, as long as you do everything correctly," she called after me. "Read the small print. And don't forget about our Thursday evening gathering..."

I let the glass door slam behind me. The woman was a fake, and I had the rotten feeling I'd just been had. She had no more magic in her than... than Mark did! Zeta had made it obvious that she didn't know the first thing about the Witch Kin, let alone Alt Town or the supernatural which surrounded us. But... that coin...

It had been owned by my mother. I needed quiet time to process this.

I almost walked right into a couple of people on the sidewalk outside.

"Oh this is desperation, isn't it?" That hated drawling voice.

I looked up at the tall slim figure dressed all in black, her long shiny hair framing the face which hadn't aged a bit in the past ten years. Cate, my father's wife, and she was sneering at me. Dad was by her side and had stopped in his tracks, looking up askance at the store's sign.

"Magic should be left to those who have it," she said. "Half-bloods have no business dabbling in things they don't understand." She flicked her hair and made to move on.

Dad stayed where he was. His gaze slowly came down from the sign to me, and his eyes hardened. Darn! Of all people to find me outside a magic shop. And worst of all, the magic inside wasn't even genuine, except for that single disc of metal hidden in a basket of hardware. He turned away without even speaking to me, and followed his wife into the old Saddlery that sat on the corner above George Street.

I could feel my cheeks burning as the rush of tears blurred my vision and I rushed blindly down the concrete steps to the street below. I kept running till I hit the iron fence surrounding the harbor.

CHAPTER 6

My inner world had just tilted on its axis, yet outside it was still a bright mid-September day, the wind was calm and the sun glinted off the water in the harbor, what I could see of it between the huge ocean-going vessels lined up at the wharves and the tall iron fence.

Dad was on my mind. I know I always put up a big front about him, pretending not to be hurt by the disdain he showed me and the meanness of his other kids, but actually it gutted me. Usually I could keep those feelings hidden even from myself, squashed way down inside me but I lost it right there and then. I was overwhelmed and got lost in my misery and sorrow at Dad's treatment of me. Maybe it was the run-in with him and his wife, maybe it was the peacefulness of the harbor that did it, maybe it was the mournful cries of the gulls as they hovered overhead.

I must have been really caught up in my angst that day, forgetting to put a damper on my Alt-thought, for when I turned around I found myself in the middle of it, barely teetering on the edge of a long finger pier.

Did I tell you about Alt-town? Well, Alt-town is sort of like a Gothic-punk version of St. John's, only laid over the present in a mixture of the past. You couldn't be certain, before you visited any spot in Alt-town, where you were going to end up.

For example, on Harbour Drive where I had been standing just moments before, all that road had been built up over time, reclaimed I guess you'd say from the water, with room enough for hefty parking lots behind the buildings. This was a recent development over the past century. As the years passed, the government and merchants had filled in the harbor with rock and rubble to extend the space, enabling them to put a wide road in behind the businesses that used to sit at the water's edge over the original beaches, along with the parking lots.

But once upon a time, those old merchant stores and warehouses were built right on the beach, and each one had their own wooden finger piers sticking out into the harbor where their boats would rest and their back doors, the loading doors, opened right on to these piers.

In Alt-town, there's no rhyme or reason to what stays or changes according to the modern version.

So in that flash of a moment, I found myself in Alt-town, in the same geographical location, but teetering on the edge of the rickety wooden pier in Baird's Cove. One step in the wrong direction and I would have ended up in the filthy sludge of the harbor. It was already filling my nostrils with its stink.

I had to act fast while trying to keep my balance, forcing my mind to shut down the curtain to the Alt and bring me back to the normal world. It worked, fortunately. It doesn't always. I leaned against the cold iron fence of real time, grateful for its presence as I caught my breath. That was a close one.

It took me a moment to calm down, but when I had, I realized something else weird was going on.

You know when you can feel someone staring at you, you just know it because of the way the hairs on the back of your neck prickle? I felt it then at that moment, and something more, like someone or something was trying to push into my mind, past the steel curtain which normally keeps me out of the Alt. It's not a good feeling.

At first I could see no one close that was giving me special attention. Only cars going by, late-season tourists from the big cruise ship thronging along the sidewalks heading for their buses, a couple of business men in suits leaving their cars in the lot across from me. They wouldn't be bothering with me in my hoody and Mom's old jean jacket. I was invisible to them.

But over there, sitting on the low concrete wall by the Eastern Edge Gallery. There he was, shades covering his eyes as he lounged with his legs stuck out and facing right towards me. He was long and lean, clad in jeans and a scuffed leather coat and a white t-shirt as if he was James Dean or something.

What the frig you looking at, A-hole? I thought in my mind.

I saw that. He answered me, I swear he answered me, even though his lips didn't move.

With that, he unfolded himself and stood up and began to saunter across the road as if he didn't have a care in the world. All the time his eyes were trained on me. Cars slowed down for him. In fact, it was as if time itself slowed down for him. He reached me and stood too close, looking down at me.

"I saw that," he said again, but this time aloud. I could tell by his accent he wasn't from here.

"What?" I shrugged one shoulder and turned to leave.

"I saw you shift into Alt."

"You nuts or something, buddy? I don't know what you're talking about." I sounded way more calm than I was feeling. Only witches and supernaturals could see the Alt, and if he was a witch, then that meant he was a compatriot of my father's, perhaps a friend of Sasha's. And that meant Dad was going to be plenty pissed at me when word got round to him, which it would. I could see my pseudo trust fund evaporating before my eyes, and that was actually the least of my worries.

It wasn't just my dad's embarrassment about me that kept me quiet about my half-blood status. Throughout the centuries, the Witch Kin has always felt uneasy about the presence of half-bloods in the general population. I don't know why they would feel threatened but, well, for example you remember hearing about the witch hunts? Salem and all that?

They weren't actually searching out the witches. The Witch Kin were, and have always been, the ruling classes, and you didn't see any of them getting burnt at the stake. The Royals and the aristocracy thrived during that period. No, the infamous witch hunts actually started as a scourge of the half-bloods, a movement that got out of control when the Normals took up the torch. A lot of blood was shed back then.

Admittedly, things seem a lot more civilized these days, but it's just not a good idea to advertise your half-blood status. There's still a hell of a lot of prejudice around these parts.

"What are you? Who are you?" He moved to block my exit and placed his hand on my jean jacket shoulder. This guy was going to be trouble.

"Let me go or I'll scream," I warned him, shaking him off.

"No you won't," he said, with all the assurance of a formally trained witch, the knowledge of centuries of entitlement behind him. "I'm not going to hurt you. I'm just curious."

He held his hands up in the air to show he meant no harm.

"Who I am is none of your business." I stood and faced him off, wishing I was a mite taller than my five foot six against his six feet plus and broad shoulders to boot. "I don't have *any* dealings with your sort."

"Hey, I'm just new in town," he said, taking a step back at the vehemence I threw at him. "Don't lump me with all the others up the hill." He jerked his head in the loose direction of the east end.

He paused and looked me over again.

"I get it," he said quietly.

"Get what?" I really, *really* wanted to turn tail and run away from him as far and as fast as I could before he caused my whole world to crash down around me, but something made me stay.

He removed the shades to reveal green eyes so shot with gold they seemed to glow.

"I'm a half-blood too."

Now I was good and floored. He was a half-blood and was admitting it to a total stranger? Christ, he was braver than me, that's for sure. Unless it was some kind of ruse.

I grabbed his arm and forced him to walk along the waterfront with me, away from any prying ears or eyes.

"Are you nuts?" I repeated myself, this time in a whisper. "Don't go shouting it from the rooftops or you won't last long in this town."

A fellow half-blood. I'd never met one before, at least, not one who admitted it freely.

I waited until we were sitting at the Harborside Park down by the waterfront, hidden from view by the rose bushes and other greenery. The park was otherwise empty.

"This isn't the sixteen hundreds, you know. We have nothing to hide, or to be ashamed of," he said. He seemed amused.

Now I could place his accent. He was from the other side of the pond, and by pond I mean North Atlantic Ocean. Ireland, or Scotland. That was a distinct burr in his 'r's.

"No trouble to tell you're not from here," I said as I rolled my eyes at his innocence.

"I think we started off on the wrong foot. Let's have a do-over," he suggested, then stuck his hand out. "Hi, I'm Hugh Sabiston, and I'm a half-blood witch."

He still had that note of amusement in his eyes. Those mesmerizing green gold eyes.

I shrugged and took his hand.

"I'm Dara," I said.

"No last name?"

"None that you'd recognize," I said. "The part of my name that wasn't given to me is de Teilhard."

"Ah." He nodded without saying more, simply looked out through the narrows to the ocean beyond.

"Are you really a mixed blood?" I had to know. He held himself too well, had too much confidence in his voice and his walk. Hugh acted more like a witch, a fully trained witch who had taken his rightful place in society. But that couldn't be, not if he was a half-blood as he claimed.

He didn't answer my question, not straight out. Instead, he started to tell me about where he came from and his family.

A little island in the Outer Hebrides, off the coast of Scotland. There were many like him there; in fact, everyone in his early school years had some sort of mixed blood in them. There was a whole island of them.

"And none of them full-blood? No one policing who marries whom, in order to keep the lines pure?" I was shocked.

"Don't be ridiculous," he started to say, then saw the expression on my face. "Oh, right. It's still that old-fashioned here, isn't it?"

Now it was my turn to nod and be silent.

"But I don't understand," he said. "If they don't acknowledge their bastard offspring, where were you taught?"

"Through the regular school system, like most people," I answered. "My father's other children, they're the ones who got to go to finishing schools, not me."

"No, I mean the craft, who taught you the craft?"

"What craft is that? Dad said he'd pay my way through university, and I plan to be there for the rest of my life. I don't intend to learn a trade."

"I'm not talking about plumbing, you nit! Witch craft, where did you pick up that?"

"Oh, no, I don't know any witchery," I denied, then said in a rush exactly as Dad had made me swear to it. "I'm not a witch and I don't know any witch craft."

Hugh had replaced his shades as we were talking, but now he removed them again to search in my eyes. He looked long and hard before he spoke.

"I saw you shift into Alt," he said.

Hadn't we already had this conversation?

"Yes and you saw me shift out again pretty damn fast once I'd realized what I'd done," I pointed out to him. "I almost got a dunking in the harbor. One of the dumbest things I've ever done."

"Exactly."

I waited for him to explain what he meant, but it seemed he was waiting for me.

"I agree, it was stupid," I said, getting exasperated. "I usually keep a tight grip on the Alt stuff, or I might get lost in it. I was just... a little emotional at the time, and forgot."

"And my question was – where did you learn to do this?"

"No one taught me anything! It's against their rules."

He stood up abruptly, taking me with him. "I'm starving. Let me buy you lunch, preferably someplace quiet, because we need to talk."

I led him straight up the hill to my favorite go-to pizza place, and up to the booth section which was empty.

This way we could both sit with our backs to the walls without fear that anyone would overhear us.

Hugh made me go all the way through my short life story, about Mom and Dad, and Mom's disappearance. About how Edna continued to bring me up in their old family home and refused to admit that Mom was dead. About my experience as a half-blood witch and how Edna had made me swear not to tell anyone, not to show anyone my powers. I didn't mention about me telling Alice, because I couldn't risk getting Edna in shit with Dad. We only paused when the waiter was nearby. Hugh was firing questions at me rapidly as he dragged the whole story out of me, and this brought us right to the last bite of his pizza.

Finally he sat back, staring at the dregs of beer in his pint.

"Why? Why all this interest?" I was finally able to ask a question myself.

"I don't know where to begin," he answered, shaking his head. "But I'll try. In my primary school, on the island, you realize we were taught both curriculums simultaneously."

I raised an eyebrow in query.

"The regular school system, as you put it, and the craft," he replied impatiently. "We all had magic blood, so it was considered the most efficient use of time."

"You mean, they teach witch craft to little kids? Like, it's not something extra after they graduate?" This was the first I'd ever heard of such a thing.

"Yes," he said with a dark look. "Your ... siblings, your father's other children, they've all received this education, you know."

"No, I didn't." I thought for a moment. "Is that why they're such smug jerks?"

He chuckled. "Possibly. Anyway. Alt shifting is a course in itself, usually given only to the more gifted students. One has to go through rigorous training before Alt is even considered, as it's thought to be too hazardous without the right preparation beforehand."

He looked at me for my reaction.

I had to give him something. "Wow."

"You don't understand what I'm saying, do you?"

"Nah, not really."

"You claim to never have received formal education, yet I saw you – I saw you! – flip back and forth to Alt like a gymnast."

"You think I did it wrong?"

He puffed out his cheeks and blew a sigh. "No! You did it perfectly! Except for the part of not knowing where you were before you flipped, which would have earned you a fail for not performing your prior due diligence check, I might add."

"So this means..."

"This means, my dear Dara, that you are an extraordinarily gifted witch."

"But I'm just a half-blood."

"That makes no difference at all, despite what they tell you."

"But the line is diluted in me." I continued to argue for my limitations yet he was having none of it.

"It's the magic in the blood that counts, not the genes."

"Well. Imagine that." I thought a bit further, then came to a conclusion. It was all too much for my head to handle. I rose to go. "Doesn't make much difference, as far as I can see. I'm still a half-blood in the eyes of everyone who matters, so I'll never be allowed to be educated in witch craft. I'm better off if I just continue what I'm doing, and stay under the radar so that the Inquisition doesn't sniff me out."

"Fine," he said, his eyes narrowed at me. "Spoken like a true Normal. You keep doing what you're doing, then, and just pray you don't accidentally switch over into a dragon's den when you're out hiking someday. You just keep on hiding that light until someone else happens upon you, someone with far less good intent than me."

Hugh stood to go too, after first laying a few twenties on top of the bill. Before he strode out the door, though, he turned and flicked a card on to the table.

"In case you change your mind, I'll be in town for a while yet."

And then he was gone.

Shit. I should have asked him what to do about Nan Hoskins. He probably could have helped, but it was too late now. Now the only thing I had was that stupid spell from Zeta, and I knew already that was worthless.

CHAPTER 7

Mark came by for supper again. He was a nice guy, and I liked him even though he was a cop. A good looking man for an old guy in his fifties, I suppose, but he was perfect for Edna. Mark had a pretty heavy workload with his job and didn't have a lot of free time, which meant that he wasn't always hanging around my aunt and getting in her way. Edna was free to be her weird little hermit-slash-writer self most of the week, lost in the characters of the various novels she had on the go at any one time, and he would come by on the odd day to take her out into the world and keep her in touch with reality.

He didn't need her, and she liked that. So that made it strange that he was with her two days in a row. However, I fully intended to make use of him, to pick his brains over the lasagna to see if he could help me on the Benjy front. We didn't bring up what he had been discussing that morning.

"So," I began, giving him time to start shovelling the hot cheese and noodles into his mouth. "If some-one went missing, what should you do?"

He swallowed and looked up at me. "You'd file a missing persons report, of course. With the RNC, if it's a person from St. John's. Why, what's on the go? One of your friends?"

"Nah," I said. "Well, my friend's brother, actually. He was last seen heading off up the hill to pick berries a couple of weeks ago, and no one's seen him since."

"A couple of weeks? They can't be too worried about him, then, if they haven't taken any action yet. How old is this brother?"

"In his early twenties. They did go up the South-side Hills to look for him, and didn't see any sign of him, so they just figure he went off on a party somewhere."

"Does this brother make a habit of that?"

"Yeah," I said. "He does. It's just... he hasn't been in contact with Alice yet, so she's worried."

"Who we talking about?"

"Benjy Hoskins."

"Oh, well, that one," Mark said, dismissing any concerns at the mention of the name and tucking back into the lasagna. "Good riddance, I'd say."

"Mark! That's her friend's brother you're talking about," Edna said as she drifted back into the conversation for a moment. You never could tell with my aunt. Sometimes she looked so spaced out, you were sure she was stuck in whatever fantasy land she'd been writing about that day, but then she'd surprise you and show she had been there all along.

"Benjamin Hoskins is more trouble than he's worth," he stated as he pointed at me with his fork. "And he doesn't even live in my jurisdiction. He's usually the RNC's problem, although we've had dealings with him too."

"He's okay," I muttered. I remembered having a crush on Benjy when I was thirteen. He was cool and cute and actually gave me the time of day even though I was just his little sister's friend. I still had a soft spot for the guy, I admit, despite his lawless ways.

Or maybe *because* of his badness. Who knows?

"Oh, yeah?" Mark said, warming up to his topic. "Tell that to the little old couple out in Maddox Cove his crew terrorized for the sake of one hundred measly dollars. Tell them 'he's okay'. Tell it to the parents of the kids he's hooked on meth. Tell it to..."

"Alright, already," I said. I couldn't help but roll my eyes. Mark's a good guy, like I said, but he still thinks I'm fifteen years old and that he has to act like a father to me on the occasions when he sees me.

Truth be told, I don't actually mind him getting on like that, because it's sort of comforting in a weird way. Not that I would ever tell him that.

"Stay away from Benjy and his crowd," he said. "I don't ever want to see your name coming across my desk."

"Oh go on, Mark," I said, a smile on my face now. "You'd love to bail me out. Think of the scolding you could give me."

"Don't tease him, Dara. Act like an adult."

"But seriously, Mark, normally Benjy would contact Alice eventually. Despite their differences, they're pretty close."

He looked up at me again, his eyes watchful, the cop in him sensing something was up. "What are your feelings in the matter? Do you think something bad has happened to him?"

I nodded. "Yeah, there's something wrong, but I don't know what." I couldn't explain more than that. Couldn't say anything about Nan Hoskins coming back from the dead – if she had ever left, that is.

"Well, wait and see," he said. "I'm sure he'll turn up. But tell you what, I'll make inquiries next time I'm at work."

"I appreciate that, Mark. Thanks." But I had a cold feeling that whatever had happened with Benjy was going to be under the radar of the RCMP.

·······

The next afternoon, Alice appeared at my house still all flushed with being on the ocean the day before, and with something like excitement in her voice.

"How was the walrus?"

"Oh, just fantastic," she said, and she proceeded to give me all kinds of technical details about the length of his tusks and the color of his hide. I only listened with half an ear, as I usually did when she went into her science mode.

"But even better – I got a text from Benjy!"

"That's huge and wonderful news!" I squealed and gave her a hug. Thank God for that. If the idiot had gotten himself killed, my friend would have been lost.

She was so excited she didn't even bother shaking me off. "Want to see it? He says he's having the time of his life with some new friends he met up with, and he asked me to come join him, says they all want to meet me."

"Where is he?"

"Umm," she said. "Well, he doesn't say. Typical Benjy!"

She flicked through her phone. "But, the weird thing is, he's not talking like Benjy. These new friends must be a big influence on him."

"How do you mean?"

"Just read." She handed me the phone with his text open.

These fine ladies and handsome gents request you to join me in their celebration...

I stared at the words. Handsome gents? Request? This didn't sound like the Benjy I knew. He tended to communicate in grunts and one syllable words only. I handed the phone back to her with a sinking feeling in my heart. This smelled bad.

"But they must be good for him, right?" She chattered on, happy for her brother and with all memories of the nightly hauntings forgotten for the moment. "And hey – you can still see the walrus, he's parked himself on the rocks across Freshwater Bay. Why don't we take a walk up by Fort Amherst and up the path, and you bring your binoculars. You'll have a great view of him!"

"I hate going up there," I said. It wasn't just the climb straight up the hill. I've already said, there's a lot of creepy things up on those hills, even though the east end of it over by the ocean, down Fort Amherst way, that's not so bad.

"Oh, come on," she said, stretching out the words. "I really, really want to do this."

"Why?"

"I just do," she said. "I haven't been up the hill all summer, what with the extra classes and labs I was taking. I just have the urge, that's all. We'll ride our bikes over to the path. It won't take any time at all."

I stopped to think. I hated that hill, but if she just wanted to go to the top, down at the end over the water, that might be alright. As long as I stayed in sight of the ocean, I found, I could handle the stink. I'd read that just as fairies hated iron, they also couldn't stand to be near salt water. Made sense when you thought about it, for nurses use saline to cleanse wounds. Fairies didn't like getting cleaned up.

"Alright," I said. "Let's do it."

It didn't take us more than fifteen minutes to whiz down Old Topsail Road and past her house and down the three kilometers to the lighthouse. For a skinny girl, Alice could really go when she wanted.

We parked the bikes next to the breakwater, locking them on to the chain link fence, then turned up the path.

She jumped up that route like a mountain goat, leaving me to scramble along below her, stopping every so often to admire the view (i.e. catch my breath). When I finally reached the top, I found her on the edge of a rock face, arms wide open to the ocean, breathing deeply of the glorious salt air.

"Don't you just love it up here?" She paused, then looked over to me. "No, you don't, do you? You never did like it here. Why is that, anyway?"

"Maybe," I said, finding a big boulder to sit on, still breathing heavily. "Maybe I hate the friggin' climb."

"Yeah? I think it's something else." She was laughing. "I think you're scared of the fairies!"

I stopped breathing for a moment. Was she nuts? If any Newfoundlander knew one thing about being in the wilderness, that was to not mention the fae. You were as good as inviting them to take you by saying their name out loud. Even in all the folklore books I'd read, they all stressed that.

"Shut up, Alice."

"Fairies, fairies, Dara's afraid of the fairies!"

She laughed again and skipped along a rabbit path which led to Freshwater Bay on the other side of the hill. "Come on, get the binoculars out! Let's see where that walrus is."

I looked around nervously then followed her.

We sat near the cliff's edge, our feet almost dangling over the breakers and boulders far, far below. It sounds more dangerous than it was, honestly. There were lots of little bushes and scrubby trees to hang on to if you thought you were going to fall. But it was a clear day and the rocks were dry, so it really was perfectly safe.

She concentrated on focusing across the water to the next headland, and then down at the base near the waves where she'd seen the walrus. She searched and searched, but was coming up with nothing.

"He's gone," she said.

"Maybe he moved further into the bay for shelter?" Despite the fine weather, the waves were rocking pretty high. She turned to the right, intent on inspecting every inch of the coast line.

"Nope. Nope," Alice chanted after looking at every little cove and nook and cranny. Then she stood up, the better to examine the shore of the cliff we were sitting on.

"Careful," I said.

"It's no good," she said. "He's probably buggered off back to Greenland. Too bad – you might never have another chance to see a walrus here again."

She still had the binoculars up to her eyes as she swept back towards where we were sitting.

"Oh, my, God."

"Do you see him?" By now I was leaning back against the sun-warmed rock, enjoying the heat coming off it, and was reluctant to move.

"No, but... I see something else."

I opened an eye. Her attention was caught on something, but she was focused inland. Alice paused and looked up from the binoculars, fixing the location of whatever she'd seen.

"Come on." Her voice was terse, and she leapt off the rock headlong into the bushes, not even searching for a path.

No way I was going to do that, thank you very much. Up here, and on any barrens, it only made sense to stick with the tried and true trails or a person might disappear into a boghole or something equally dangerous. Alice was well aware of the hazards, yet she hared off through the wilderness as if the hounds of hell were on her tail.

I tried to keep her in sight as I ran along the ocean side path. It wasn't hard, because I could hear her floundering through the low trees and could catch glimpses of her blue vest.

Looking up past her, I finally saw what she was headed for. Just beneath a large lichen covered boulder silhouetted against the blue sky on the next hillock over, nestled quietly among the golden dry grass there sat a glint of red. Red, the color of blood. Or the color of a prized pail, the kind that Alice's Uncle Jerry had brought back from Alberta all those years ago. The Hoskins's family berry bucket.

This stunk, and I don't mean metaphorically.

CHAPTER 8

"Is it yours?" I asked this hoping it wasn't, but knowing the answer would be positive.

She nodded.

"I don't understand," she said. "Benjy would never, *never* frig off and just leave the bucket here for anyone to take. It's more than his life is worth."

She realized what she'd said and whimpered, clutching her mouth as if to take the words back.

"Alice, is this near where your family berry patch is?"

"Sort of," she said as she surreptitiously glanced to the right, down the hill towards the city. "But I didn't tell you that, okay?"

"No problem." I loved eating berries but hated picking them, so the Hoskins's family secret was perfectly safe with me.

"But I got a text from him!"

"You did," I agreed. "So he must be alive... somewhere."

Things were beginning to click with me. Benjy's strange description of his new friends in words he would never use in a million years, not even if he went back and finished high school. The red plastic bucket left forgotten to the elements on this hillside. The smell which permeated the whole place and overcame the freshness of the salt air from the ocean not five hundred meters away.

Could fairies live in such close proximity to salt water? Looked like they could. This made me wonder what else the folklore books had gotten wrong. I needed to warn Alice, but she was already exploring the cleft in the rocks below our feet, the space unseen between the boulders till we climbed right on top of it.

"Maybe he fell down this hole," she said, her tone feverish. "Maybe he's lying down there with a broken leg and he's... he's delirious from lack of water or food, that's why he sent that weird text."

"Wait, don't go there..." Jesus, did she not have any sense at all? She was supposed to be the smart one.

Alice had already disappeared into the rock.

"Oh my God, Dara." I heard her voice faintly as if from a long distance away. "Come down here. It's absolutely frigging amazing."

I had to get her out of there before it was too late. If she saw Benjy and the fairy folk with her human eyes, she might be lost forever, but it meant I had to go into Alt mode in order to be safe, to be able to see through their enchantments. I took a deep breath and plunged after her.

And oh – it was beautiful. The crevice between the boulders opened up into a large space, as large as a ballroom there beneath the granite of the hill.

It was bright as sunlight down there from their fairy lights strung up all over the walls. And these weren't the roughhewn rock walls you might expect in an underground cavern, no, these walls were made of finely shaped stone and wood. The scene before us was a grand celebration, the musicians playing off in the corner and the fine ladies and handsome gents all dancing in the center, their gorgeous gowns competing only with the beauty of the elegant folk.

Tables laden with food lay off to one side, all manner of old-fashioned food like jelly trifles and great slabs of roast beasts. The mead was flowing, and gentle laughter tinkled over the mesmerizing music. A great chest of gold sat in one corner, overflowing with coins and jewellery, glinting in the soft light.

And off to the other side – oh dear God. I hoped Alice couldn't see around that corner, to the large four poster beds where the naked beautiful fairies were taking their pleasure with no shame, for all their world to see. That might be Benjy there, lying amidst the bodies, writhing in ecstasy and getting a lot more action than he ever did in the town below.

I had to turn it all off and tune into Alt, and quickly. When I opened my eyes again, I took a moment to let them adjust to the new gloom that lay before me, lit only by a few burning pitch torches. Where I had seen tables overflowing with delicious foods, now sat cauldrons bubbling over with the greasy soups of roadkill and weeds that the fae had scavenged, too lazy to hunt for themselves.

The golden chest was now of moldy wood, yet the gold within still glittered from the light of the rough torches which hissed as moisture dripped from the ceiling. Lichen grew up the damp walls.

Where musicians had played, there were only ancient beings slaving at the rock, quarrying with picks, crying with despair. They may have been human beings once, but too much time in the land of fae soon broke down any aspect of humanity, turning them into worse than mute animals, tortured as they were.

The fine folk themselves were revealed for what they really were, horrid little goblin-like creatures, filthy and matted as they nastily poked and teased their slaves, and bade them carry out their most depraved instructions.

And where the fine beds with their billowing silk hangings had been were rough straw mattresses, filthy with excrement and worse.

Benjy lay among them tied and tortured and screaming in pain, though he believed the hurt he felt was pleasure. That was the abominable way of the fae, they could totally manipulate and mess with how humans perceived the world when under their spells. Jesus, what a sight.

"There's B..." Alice began, but I shoved my hand over her mouth, and with my other hand dragged her roughly back through the crevice we'd come through. If the fae knew we'd invaded their hall, we'd both be goners. She fought me the whole way.

Outside, I paused a moment to sit on her chest, preventing her from escaping back down the fairy hole and to her doom. I kept my hand over her mouth while I explained what was what.

"All that you saw down there was a lie," I hissed. "It is not pretty, they have enslaved poor souls and used them horribly. We need to get away, and quietly. Believe me on this one, I know what I'm talking about. Got it?"

Her eyes were huge as she nodded. God bless her, she was smart, after all.

I removed my hand and helped her up, and led her back on the long path, over to the Freshwater Bay cliffs, then skirting the ocean till we reached the safety of the lighthouse at the bottom. There's no way I was going to cut through the bush, even if it was the land of Nan Hoskins.

We climbed through the hole on the wire fence the government had erected, the one to prevent people from getting too close to the crumbling concrete of the World War II bunkers. It was a dangerous place, and not just physically – yet as it was still bright daylight I knew it was safe enough from the trolls who dwelt in those mossy damp places. I just needed to get as close to the clean salt ocean as I could after the experience up the hill.

"I saw Benjy," Alice finally said, her back against the lichen covered concrete. "He was... hmm, enjoying himself."

"You think you saw him," I corrected her. "Let me tell you, I could see what they were really doing, and it was very painful."

Her eyes filled with tears. "How are we going to help him?"

"*I'm* not going back down there," I told her.

She said nothing, but a teardrop fell onto the rock by my hand. A moment later, it was joined by a second one.

"Jesus, Alice, you got to be kidding me?"

"I don't know anyone else who can help, and we have to get him out of there."

Benjy. Handsome Benjy, recipient of my first crush. Shithead Benjy, petty criminal and seller of drugs to kids. Addiction-addled Benjamin Hoskins, beloved brother of my best, my only human, friend. Yes, even his life was worth saving from the fairies, but it wasn't a job I felt able to do myself.

I had no choice. Much as I hated the thought, I really was going to have to ask Dad for help.

·············

Why didn't I phone Hugh? He had offered his assistance, after all, and I knew he meant it even though he seemed so pissed at me when he walked away.

I didn't contact him because, despite his big words and his claim to education and his assured manner, he was still a half-blood, no better than me.

This situation called for a real witch, one with the power of mature years and the full blood of the Kin.

I timed my visit to arrive before his Sunday dinner with my siblings. Dad was a stickler for tradition and once a week they made a habit of having the family meal, with him presiding over the long table and the four kids, probably with their respective boyfriends or girlfriends these days, and that horrible witch Cate at the other end of the table.

She was such a pretentious bag.

How do I know so much about them? Well, Dad used to love me, and I was actually a part of his life, back in the early years.

His was an arranged marriage between powerful houses, as many of the marriages of the Kin are. But somewhere along the line, he met Mom, and he fell in love even though she was just a Normal. I came along, and he loved me too. He didn't visit often, he couldn't I guess, but I have enough memories of him before I was ten years old, laughing with Mom on the cut lawn outside our house, and on picnics down at Bowring Park. He would bring Sasha, my half-sister with him sometimes, for she was only a year or so older than me.

He loved me so damn much, he even brought me to his home some Sundays for the family dinner, which took nerve, though I bet he didn't tell Cate who I really was. Yet she must have had her suspicions because I remember her sitting at the end of the polished table, fatly pregnant with the last of her whelps and glaring at me over the pudding.

His kids were okay then too, friendly and accepting like little kids are, and we spent some great afternoons doing cool things with our powers. I was the middle child in the group, which might explain why things became awkward when Cate found out my true identity.

This was before the fights and arguments began between my parents, and not long after Mom disappeared from my life and Dad turned his back on me. I'd always blamed him for her abrupt departure, but thinking back on it, Cate might have had something to do with it. The kids had all hated me since then too. At any rate, I'd never been given an explanation for it.

I put on Mom's old jean jacket and wrapped her long blue floaty scarf around my neck for courage before leaving. Like with her, that indigo blue really brings out the color of my eyes. I rode my bike rather than ask Edna for a drive, for the less she knew, the better. That way she could honestly say she'd forbidden me to go there if anything bad happened.

I finally pushed myself up Portugal Cove Road to Dad's homestead which glowed greenly in its enclosed estate right in the middle of the east end of town. It was perfectly situated to lord over everything close by.

I paused outside the closed gate and looked up to where the gothic mansion loomed over the city, up on top of its own private hill. Did I really want to do this? The picture of Alice as I'd last seen her, big gray eyes filled with tears, came to my mind. I sighed, and reluctantly started pushing my bike up the lane.

It had been years since those long-ago visits, but not much seemed to have changed on the estate. More cars in the driveway, and a new pool house and other toys of the rich scattered about. Shouts of laughter came from the direction of the tennis court – my siblings must be enjoying the last of the Indian summer. I left my beat up old bike behind a shed, taking advantage of the landscaped shrubberies to hide it out of sight, and I tucked my helmet beside it.

Now, if I knew Dad, he was probably hiding in his study prior to dinner in order to stay out of the family dramas. That's what I would be doing if I was him. I crept around the side of the house towards the French doors leading to the garden from his nook and peeped through the glass. Yes, there he was, at his desk in front of the computer. I tried the handle, but it was locked.

Something must have alerted him to my presence, maybe the shifting of the shadows, and he looked up directly into my eyes.

He hadn't changed at all, I realized now. I hadn't noticed the other day when I ran into him downtown. The same touch of light gray at his temples, the strong chin, those dark hazel eyes. He was exactly the same except... he wasn't looking at me with hate. No trace of the usual dismissiveness, no sneering.

As he gazed at me, he looked softly vulnerable, if one could dare to say that about Jonathon de Teilhard.

But it didn't last long, not once he realized who I was. With two great strides, he was at the door, unlocking it even as he searched around the garden to make sure I hadn't been seen. He pulled me in, snapped the locks again and drew the curtains against the afternoon sun.

"What is the meaning of this?" His voice was a sharp whisper. "How dare you?"

"Hey Dad, nice to see you too," I said, pretending to be way more laid back than I felt. Fake attitude often helped cover up the quivering inside.

He merely stared at me, the thunder clouds gathering. All that anger was suddenly too much for me to bear. Couldn't he be even a little happy to see me?

"I need your help," I said, looking down at my right toe which was busy scuffing his expensive Turkish carpet.

He said not a word in reply as if I didn't deserve an answer.

"Someone I know has been caught by the fairies up on the Southside Hills." I was begging already, so much for my bravado. "I need to help him get away."

"Not my concern."

"But they've enslaved him and..."

"How do you know what they're doing with him?"

"Well, I saw, didn't I? First it looked all lovely and fun and glam, but then when I..." I caught myself quickly. He didn't need to know about my forays into Alt. "Then I looked again and I could see what was really happening, and it was horrible and..."

"You went there?" He cut in and spoke over me. "You entered the fairy hall?"

"Yeah, I had to chase after his sister, Alice, my best friend, it's her brother, and I needed to get her out of there before they got her too..."

I stopped. Oh, shit. By the look on his face I had really done it now, broke one of those basic Witch Kin rules that everyone was supposed to know, just like the ones about which fork to use at a dinner party, but how was I supposed to know which rules I was breaking if no one would even tell me what the stupid goddamned rules were?

He went back to his desk and sat with a heavy thump, then motioned me to take a seat opposite. He buried his face in his hands. After a moment he looked back up to me.

"Jesus Christ, Dara, are you telling me that you not only went into the fairy hall and got out again, but you saw them, I mean really *saw* them for what they are?"

I could only nod. My eyes must have been huge as I sat staring at him, waiting for the ax to fall. But at that moment I didn't care what he did to me – he could cut me off without a cent if he wanted. Alice needed my help.

But when he began speaking again, it was like another man had taken the place of my father.

"I pay you money every month," he began. His voice was gentle. "And I'm prepared to continue paying out that money every month of my life, and it is for one reason. Do you know why?"

He'd meant this as a rhetorical question, but I was so upset I didn't see that.

"Because you hate me, and never want to see me again," I blurted. "I know this. Look I'm sorry, I wouldn't have asked, I wouldn't have come here at all, except that it's Alice that needs your help!"

He shook his head and sighed a deep one.

"You've heard about the body found in the woods the other day?"

I nodded yes, puzzled at this apparent non sequitur. That was the one Mark had told me about, and they had no leads on the murder at all, they only knew the victim's name.

"What I am about to tell you isn't to go any further," he said, his face more emotionless than I've ever seen it. "Not to your aunt or her friend. And don't ask me how I know this. But that woman was a visitor to the province. She was a half-blood who came looking for her roots."

I didn't want to hear this, and he didn't want to tell me, but he forced himself to continue.

"Of course, none of my Kin were involved in this incident," he said. "But, I'm trying to tell you that old sentiments die hard sometimes. And with certain economic factors in a downturn, well, some other Kin are looking for scapegoats."

He crossed his arms with the shirt sleeves rolled up just so, and adjusted the tie he wore even on Sunday.

"I pay you that money to keep you safe, to keep you from using and developing any powers you have," he said. "That is the condition. Too many people... too many know who and what you are already."

Including Cate, I realized. It was on the tip of my tongue to blurt out the question I'd never gotten a chance to ask. What had he and Cate done to Mom?

CHAPTER 9

"And I've been thinking," Dad continued. "Perhaps I should actually send you away."

"Banish me, you mean. Get me out of sight."

He looked me directly in the eye. "That's one way to put it."

A knock sounded on the heavy oak door. He jumped up to answer it before the person outside could enter, and he shielded the room from their view.

I was too busy with my thoughts to pay attention to whichever of his brats was presently seeking his attention. He was not going to help with Benjy. In fact, he was prepared to sentence Alice's brother to a lifetime of slavery and torture under the fae by sending away the one person who could help him. The one person who cared enough to do anything.

And here I was sitting in Dad's home office, hastening his intent to get rid of me. I cursed my stupidity in not listening to Edna. The less he was forced to think about me, or even remember me, the less likely he would be to send me off to God knew where.

Dad closed the door and returned to his throne behind the desk where he resumed staring at me, stroking his chin while he did so as if in deep thought. He opened his mouth to speak again, but before he could get a word out, the door opened quickly, catching him off guard.

"I just forgot one detail," Hugh stood in the door-way, holding out an old book as he spoke. He glanced round, surprised to see another person in with my father. "Lord, sorry Jon, I thought you were alone. This can wait. Cheerio, then."

He gave a quick silent shake of his head to me before he closed the door again and disappeared. I think he was telling me to pick my jaw up off the ground and pretend I didn't know him, pretend I wasn't shocked at the sight of him in my father's house.

....

I left Dad's house the way I had come in, sneaking through the garden door, my head buzzing all the way.

What the hell was going on? Did Hugh realize the danger he was in? A half-blood in Cate's den – that could not turn out well.

If he actually was mixed blood, that is.

Mark had told us the details of the girl's death, the body found out in the wilds behind Portugal Cove, way up on the top of the mountain where the glaciers had long ago scoured the topsoil off the granite head. Well, he had filled Edna in on the more horrible details after I had left the room, and I eavesdropped. Not my fault if they didn't have the door closed all the way, was it? He didn't usually talk about what happened at his work, but on this occasion he was so horrified he'd had to let it out.

Along with the burns, she had been tortured severely before she found release in death. She was in such bad shape, they couldn't tell if she had been raped.

The police suspected a ritualistic killing of some kind. Although maybe three months had passed since the girl's death before her body was found, Mark had said there were still faded chalk markings around the site. The RCMP had brought in a specialist folklore investigator who had suggested some relation to voodoo, but the cops had laughed at that. There wasn't a big Carib population around St. John's.

According to Dad, witches were responsible for the death of that poor girl, but I knew the only other clan around these parts was Cate's family. The wedding of my father and his wife had been the contract of the century, a merging of the two great families, the final unification of the Avalon Kin. But they were still two unique factions, despite the hype.

Hugh was playing with fire if he was hanging out at that estate because although my father had a powerful grip on the Kin, witches were a moody crowd.

Unless... unless Hugh had been lying about his status. I was beginning to suspect his honesty. There was no way on earth the St. John's Kin would accept someone whose family tree wasn't well known.

And if he was lying, well, that really wouldn't surprise me. That's just the sort of behavior I learned to expect from full-blood witches like my half-siblings. Lying to me in order to expose me, not just for mockery this time, but for a deadly game of cat and mouse.

And Dad – what was all that about threatening to send me away for my own safety? As if he cared that much. Hugh must have told him about my little spasm on the waterfront, and Dad was only worrying about his own image within the Kin.

Yet, no, Hugh had pretended not to know me, so it was unlikely he'd told Dad about meeting me.

As I coasted in free cycle all the way down New Cove Road, I wondered where my father might banish me to. The wilds of New Zealand, maybe, or to the deepest heart of Africa where no one knew the de Teilhard name.

Even though I was twenty years old and long past the age of majority, if he said I had to go, I really didn't have much choice in the matter. It wasn't just the money aspect. I could turn my nose up at the monthly allowance, but he still had the unique ability to make my life hell even without magic. So the best thing I could do was just remain under the radar for as long as I could until he forgot about banishing me.

Hugh.

Crap. I didn't know which story was real. And I was no closer to getting help for Alice and her brother. With the fairies, every day counted. Benjy might be enchanted into thinking he was having the time of his life, dancing, making love, eating sumptuous feasts, but in reality he was enslaved, beaten (and worse) and eating muck. He would quickly fade away until the fae got bored with this new toy and he would become like the shades I saw slaving at the rock walls in the hall.

Nobody deserved a fate like that, not even Benjamin Hoskins.

·············

I realized, as I made my slow way up King's Bridge Road, that there was no living being I could ask for assistance in saving Benjy from the clutches of the fairies. Yeah, I toyed with the idea of getting Mark on my side. After all, cops were trained to be unimaginative and there was a slight chance that this lack of imagination would help him see through any enchantment... No, I was just clutching at straws, there.

And Zeta? Don't make me laugh.

No, my only hope was Nan Hoskins. Despite the hatred she'd shown me, this specter might be persuaded to help her own great-grandson, if I could just get Alice to stay in the room with me.

I shot along Water Street in the sparse Sunday evening traffic, ignoring red lights and other rules of the road in my haste. Alice's mom would be gone out to Bingo by now, and her father would probably be at 'Bar'. Yeah, the tavern probably had a real name, but the neon sign in the window only said 'Bar', and that was all the little hole in the wall needed to communicate to those desperate enough to go there. Tucked under the overpass on the other side of the river from Alice's house, it was a charmless place but the beer was cheap. Yes, there he was, toddling up the slight incline, right on time.

My bike bumped over the foot bridge and then I was at Alice's. No need to lock up the bike as I dropped it by her back door, ran up the steps and rushed into the house.

"Alice? Alice!"

There were movements from upstairs.

"Dara?"

"Come down, we need to talk."

"I'm writing up my lab reports," she said as she turned the corner into the kitchen rubbing her eyes. She was in pyjamas already, and her hair was stuck up any old way on the top of her head. "What do you want?"

"Are you alone in the house?"

"Mm, I think so," she said. She stuck her head back into the hallway and screeched loud enough to be heard up on the third floor. "Anybody home? Sal?"

Alice cocked her head. "I think Sal's here, sounds like there's music coming from her room, but she won't bother us."

It would have to do.

"Listen, I need you to explain to your great-grand-mother that she has to talk to me."

"Oh, no, I'm not going in that front room. Forget it. You go talk to her yourself. Leave me out of it."

"Alice," I said with great patience. "She is the only one who can help me help Benjy."

I didn't bother telling her about my visit to Dad, or even about Hugh. She wouldn't understand, and it was too long a story.

"She's a ghost, and she's stuck in our living room," Alice said. "How can she possibly help?"

"Look, we don't have a choice."

I made her sit down at the table and I began to tell her the bare bones of my life story, about the witch stuff and being half-blood and that's why I could talk with ghosts and see through the enchantments of the fae. Then I told her everything that I thought I knew about those so-called 'little people', which was only what I'd picked up from reading and listening to stories.

"Benjy is in a dire situation," I said finally. "I have no one to turn to for help, and no way of getting more knowledge about what to do. Nan Hoskins is the only one who might be able to give me a little more info, something I can use to get him away from them."

I could see from her face that she was upset. Who wouldn't be? Ghosts and fairies and witches – it was probably an overload of fantasy that her science brain couldn't handle.

"I always knew you were weird, Dara, but this is too much."

She pushed away from the table. I was losing her.

"You don't believe me? Do you remember seeing Benjy this morning?"

She shook her head firmly. "That didn't happen. I dreamt that. You were in my dream, you made me leave him there."

Needless to say, I was flabbergasted at this response. My last ally was turning her back on me, and it was *her* brother I wanted so desperately to save.

"How about Nan Hoskins? Do you believe she's haunting your house?"

She looked like she was going to burst into tears. "No, yes, I mean... I hate this! I can't sleep. I need to do my lab reports. If I can do them, I'll be okay. They're real, not like this foolishness you're filling my head with!"

And she turned and fled back up the stairs. It was just me then. I followed her out to the hallway, and paused at the parlor door.

"Nan? Nan Hoskins, can you hear me?" I narrowed my eyes to allow the Alt vision.

The rocking chair in the corner began to rock almost imperceptibly. It could have been a trick of the light.

"I know you don't like me, Nan," I said to the empty chair. "But Benjy needs your help. Your great-grandson. Can you just show yourself, so we can talk?"

I could see a distinct wavering of the light over the chair, but she still wasn't appearing. I sighed. Damnit. I was going to have to go into full Alt and face her down on her own turf.

Closing my eyes, I relaxed my mind and let it happen. Fortunately for me, Alice's house existed in Alt town too, probably because of the old lady herself. When I opened my eyes again, she sat glowering at me, her needles still furiously knitting.

"Benjy's been taken by the fairies," I told her. Might as well be blunt. I wanted to be in and out of Alt as fast as possible.

"Not my problem," she said. At least this time her voice was normal, not the horrible demonical roaring she'd given me last time.

"But he's your descendant," I said.

"He's a bloody hangashore, that one," she said. "That's the Smith blood in him, he's none of mine. They were all pirates and Catholics."

"You mean to tell me, that you're going to let your great-grandson rot inside the hill up there, not a mile from your house, and you're not going to lift a hand to save him?" I pointed dramatically in the direction of the hill in the back of Alice's home.

"Not the Southside Kith?" The old ghost screeched as she dropped her knitting. "They would never dare."

I had touched a definite sore spot there, and quickly moved to take advantage of it. She knew of the fae up the hill, that was for sure, and by the sounds of it had developed a relationship with them over the years. Her daughter-in-law was right, Gran hadn't just been a senile old woman rambling when she spoke of Nan and the fairies.

"Yeah, the Southside Kith," I agreed. "Not very respectful of them, is it?"

I leaned against the doorjamb and crossed my arms.

"We have an agreement. They would never harm a Hoskins."

"Well," I said slowly. "Problem is, you're dead now, so maybe they think that voids the contract."

"I don't believe you. You Witch Kin are all the same, you're a lying cheating crowd and you always were."

"No, Nan..." I was taken aback. "I'm not a witch. I'm not one of them."

"Don't be lying to me, I can smell the de Teilhard off you a mile away, even dead as I am, so you claim."

"I'm a half-blood..."

"You all think you're so special with your bloodlines and purity," she spat out, not listening to anything I had to say. "You think you have the monopoly on supernatural blood, eh? Let me tell you, there's more of that sprinkled through this town than there is Normal. Did you know that? And from lines far older than your Anglo-Saxon pretenders. Look at me, I've elf blood from the original pre-Celtic tribes. Diluted a lot over the years, yes, but it's a far sight better than being a witch. And you never saw me going around, flaunting it in everybody's face."

Wow. I could see how Witch and Normals could mate, but elf and Normal? This was a day of discoveries, to be sure, and something I needed to think about later, when I had time. When I was out of Alt and Benjy was safe.

"So what was this agreement, Nan?" I didn't have much time. I could feel the Alt taking a hold of me, a chill growing at the base of my spine. Like I said, you don't want to spend too much time there, it can cause changes.

"The berrypatch," she said. "They agreed I could have that and they would never harm one of mine."

"Okay, but what were they getting out of this deal?" Despite my cool demeanour, I was impressed. This tough old bird had the nerve to go up against the fairies, she must have had elf blood in her, after all, or at least some kind of supernatural element in her genes.

"Never mind that."

"Come on, you expect me to believe this? The fae would never make an agreement with a mere human unless they thought they were getting a better bargain."

She was reluctant to tell me, but I eventually got it out of her.

"I would send them the odd ne'er-do-well," she admitted. "The ones no one would miss anyway. The drunks, and the murderers, and the ones who diddled with little kiddies. I was doing my bit in cleaning up the town." She stuck out her chin and looked me in the eye, daring me to judge.

Nan Hoskins had been a one-woman vigilante team and all for the sake of a few berries. No wonder her very name had struck terror in the hearts of the locals. Too many people must have disappeared after she 'had a word' with them.

And possibly, just possibly, the fairies had been confused when they found Benjy on the hill wandering too close to their hall, with the smell of drugs in his body and the stink of sin on his soul. They might have thought Nan had sent him there, a present from beyond the grave.

Still, he had to be rescued.

"Can you go up there, Nan? Explain to them that it was a mistake, that he's one of yours?"

She looked at me, all the fire gone from her ghostly visage. "I'm dead, so you say. I can't leave this house."

"Can you at least *try?*"

"You think I haven't?" she snapped at me. "You think I want to be stuck in this house with that god awful TV going all the time?"

Nan Hoskins shook her head then continued in a broken voice. "It costs too much for me to leave the house. Won't do it."

"What can *I* do, then? Tell me, because I really haven't got a clue."

She sat all hunched over, her mouth screwed up. "You'd have to give them something in exchange. Someone. Or make another bargain with them. That's the only way of it."

Great. I'd have to become a fairy pimp in order to save Alice's asshole brother. Not happening.

She sighed and looked about her. "I knew something was wrong, just knew it. But that idiot family of mine, they wouldn't pay attention. Too stunned, every single one of them."

"Well, they think Sal brought a poltergeist into the house," I said. "On account of her age and her angst. They were going to bring in a priest to exorcise you."

"A *Catholic* priest? In *my* house?"

I nodded, but I was inwardly wincing. I may have said the wrong thing. Back in her time, there had been strife between the two denominations of the Christian church, the Catholics and Protestants, and sometimes violence too. These prejudices died hard.

"By the Lord jumpin' Jesus!" With this the storm began again, the wind rising and whirling the papers and books which had been tidied, and whipping the drawn curtains up and shaking loose the accumulated dust and cat fur. I slipped out of Alt, and then out of the house, leaving Alice and Sal to deal with the rage of Nan Hoskins themselves.

I couldn't do what Nan had done. There had to be another way.

Could I go up there and reason with them? Use logic with the fairies, like that would ever work.

Not that evening at any rate. I was so bushed I couldn't pedal the short distance up Old Topsail Road, and ended up pushing the bike home. I just couldn't see myself leading poor drunks and addicts up the path to the fairy hell, so the only advice I had been given wasn't acceptable.

Or was it? Didn't Nan Hoskins mention the possibility of making another bargain with the fae before she went off the deep end at the thought of a Roman Catholic priest in her house?

But what could I offer that the fairies would ever want? I had to go back to the books and dig a little deeper into the folklore.

CHAPTER 10

The closest source at hand was in the old library in the house. All these ancient leather-bound books had been kept safe behind the built-in glass-fronted book shelves for years and years, and the entire wall was covered by them. I remembered a particularly thick volume which was dedicated to Victorian thoughts on the little people which might help a bit.

Lying on my bed that evening I had the music from Aunt Edna's old ghetto blaster on bust. Yeah, really retro, right? But that old AudioLogic was a bomb, the best sound ever for all those eighties and nineties CDs in the family collection. David Bowie might be my favorite, followed closely by Freddie Mercury. Well, but that all depended on the day, didn't it?

Edna was gone out with Mark so I figured I could play the music as loud as I liked.

Anyway, I got totally lost in that old book, full of secondhand tales of visits with the fairy folk. They were really high maintenance neighbors apparently, if you had the bad luck to live near a den of them. They were always spying so you couldn't badmouth them or even speak the truth about them behind their backs or they'd do something dreadful to your children and your cow. And you always had to refer to them as Ladies and Gentlemen, or the Fair Folk, even though they were nothing of the kind. A shiver ran down my spine as I remembered the wording of Benjy's text.

I was so engrossed in this, it must have taken a while for Maundy's pounding on the walls to make its way through my consciousness. Talk about high maintenance neighbors.

"Stop that racket!"

Jesus, she was a ghost, she could tune it out if was bothering her so much, and I told her so.

"The vibrations are killing me!"

"So come in here and turn it off," I yelled back at her. At which point she began her heavy sobbing routine for she never, *never* left that room and nobody understood her.

We eventually agreed on some cheerful Buddy Holly and rockabilly. At least she didn't subject me to the hits of the 1890's or whenever it was she lived. She was a weird ghost.

It didn't take me long to dive back into it, but the next time I heard knocking I got really pissed off.

"What is it now?" I yelled out, but almost jumped off the bed when the door opened.

It was Hugh. How the hell did he get in?

"The back door was unlocked," he said. "I did knock and ring the bell. Hope you don't mind."

Mind? I was floored. The sight of him all tall and exotic, still in his faded blue jeans and scuffed leather jacket, his dark hair tousled. He had a motorcycle helmet under his arm to complete the drop dead gorgeous pose.

But like the Fair Folk, he was completely false. A witch in half-blood's clothing, so to speak, because anyone who hung out at Dad's house was no friend of mine. I turned my back on him and stared at the headboard.

"Why are you here?"

"Just wanted to have a chat."

A chat. Right. He must have told Dad, who sent him here to tell me I had to leave town. He wasn't fooling me. I kept my back to him.

"Yes, that is correct, but only partly. It's a good idea for you to go away. You *need* to." He winced as a new song began to racket through the room, and reached over to turn the music down.

I *needed* to help free Benjy, but mostly I needed to learn to clamp down my mind away from this witch. I hadn't spoken those words aloud, he had bloody well been inside my head and... and seen, or heard my thoughts, or something like that. How dare he? Why did he think he had the right to be so invasive? This guy was good – too good surely for the half-blood he claimed to be. Only a full witch could read minds so easily. Frigging witches, they were all so arrogant.

And I tried to block my thoughts from him, I pushed around in my mind, looking to see where the breach was and how to close it off. I don't know how I did it, it was like drawing a thick iron curtain all around to shield my head, I guess it was more instinctive than anything.

"Sorry, I didn't catch what you think you really need to do. And I must say, you're a really fast learner," he said, pretending to admire my skill, but I knew he was just trying to butter me up for reasons of his own. The Kin are like that, so false in every way. "Good defensive blocking. This your first time you've ever done that? A little rough in the delivery, but you show great promise."

I whipped my head around and glared at him. He didn't need to patronize me on top of it all.

"So your father and I, we were talking about you, hope you don't mind."

"You told Dad about the other day?"

"No, he brought up the question of you, actually. And I agree with him, I think it would be good for you to go away, perhaps to my island for the winter? That would be a great start. A fantastic opportunity for you, really, but I didn't tell him that."

"What, spend all winter in the Outer Hebrides? That's so far north, the sun doesn't shine for months. You have got to be kidding me."

"It's not quite that bleak, but on the other hand, the Aurora Borealis is stunning."

I didn't know how long I could keep this mind block up – I guess those muscles were weak from never having been used. I needed to get rid of him so I could think in private.

"I'll think about it."

"Really?" Hugh looked surprised, but in a pleased sort of way. "It is important, not just for your safety. You'll find it a different world there."

Yeah, a cold world, ten times worse than this world right here in St. John's. As if.

"Alright," I lied. "Now go, I have work to do."

He looked with interest at the old book lying open on the bed. "What's that you're reading then?"

I tried to block his view with my arm. "Just some stuff for a folklore course I'm doing."

"Fairies?" His eyes narrowed in suspicion. "Please tell me this is theoretical work. Your father mentioned a run in you had... You're not equipped to handle those folk."

This was *so* not his business. "You think I'm nuts? I'm not going near them."

He was quiet for a moment – I couldn't feel him probing my mind but I wasn't about to relax my defences. Then he nodded decisively. "All right. The sooner we get you out of here the better."

We? He was working with Dad, he was, which meant he wasn't on my side, no matter how much he pretended.

"See you later. Don't slam the door on your way out." And I turned my back on him again.

After a moment I heard his footsteps on the stair, then from a distance the sound of the back door closing. I jumped up and ran to the bathroom at the back of the house to watch him depart on the motorcycle. Man he looked good on that Harley, good enough to eat.

But then he ruined it by looking right up at me and waving good bye. Bloody witches.

CHAPTER 11

Of course I'd been lying about my plans to not visit the fairy hall, and I had a feeling he knew it too. But I had a full day of classes Monday and besides it was wet out, so there was no clambering around the Southside Hills for me that day.

Nothing scheduled for Tuesday, though, at least nothing I couldn't skip, so that day I rode my bike down to the lighthouse and climbed back up the hill. I suppose it would have been faster to cut up through Alice's back yard and find my way from there, but I couldn't chance having her with me again. I needed to do this alone, and I needed all my wits about me which I couldn't do if I had to go hauling her out of the crevice again.

It was a good thing she forgot to bring the berry pail back with her the other day, because that was my only marker to the fairy hall. Up here on the barrens, all the hillocks looked the same.

I sat on the rocks outside and debated which was the best way to go about finding them. I sure didn't want to have to go back down inside there, the smell was bad enough out here.

All the folklore said that to avoid alerting the fairies to your presence, you should never say their name, instead refer to them as the 'Good Folk' or some other misleading misnomer. So it should be easy enough to grab someone's attention.

"Fairies! Hey, fairies, anyone around?"

Not a peep. Were they all asleep? It was chilly up there on the hillside, and I wrapped Mom's scarf around me tighter.

How did fairies cope with our winters, anyway? I assumed they had come over from England and Wales, way back when, and those countries had much better weather than Newfoundland. Hey, the frigging *moon* had a better climate than this place. But really, in England, they didn't have as much snow or ice or freezing winds, so how had the fairies adjusted? Did they hibernate like the bears did?

If one of them ever showed their faces outside the crevice, I might get a chance to find out.

"Hey! Anyone there? Yo, fairies, I need to speak with you." Still nothing. Had I imagined the whole scene the other day? If they were waiting for me to go see them in their den, they were out of luck.

"Stupid asshole fairies anyway," I muttered. I was getting sick of this game.

But at least that did the trick. When I looked up, a fine gent stood before me, dressed in velvets and silks with slippers that curled up at the ends. He stood not more than two feet high, but placed on the rock above where I sat, he still managed to look down his nose at me.

I knew this would be tricky, and I was prepared. In order to block any enchantment which might seep through my defenses, I had to keep one foot, or eye, in Alt, while the other remained fully in the physical. Sort of straddling two worlds, so to speak, but with nothing to anchor me. It was best done while wearing shades, so Mom's round John Lennon retro sunglasses remained firmly on my nose.

Yes, I admit it, I wore a lot of Mom's old stuff, for a few reasons. The main one was to keep her close to me, to keep her alive. The other was that she had really cool, classic taste and I was now just about the same size she was when she disappeared.

"What manner of half-breed is this who speaks so contemptuously of my race?"

Frig this little shit and his pretensions. He was a nasty dirty fairy and had no reason for putting on airs. I cut to the chase.

"I want Benjy back. Let him go."

He trilled a little silvery laugh, but the Alt side of me could hear the wet wheezes in his lungs. He was an old one, then, or at least not well. He stroked his unwhiskered chin as he thought.

"Benjy, Benjy... Let me see. No, I don't think we have a Benjy here."

"You do too, you liar, I saw him in your hall the other day."

The facade slipped a little, and the stink was tremendous. "That was you?"

"Yep. I saw him, and I saw what you were doing to him."

"Oh, of course, Benjamin, I remember now. Such a delightful playmate." He was all sickly sweetness and light again. He bent down to whisper at me. "I think he's having too much fun to leave. Why don't you come down and speak with him? Maybe you'd like to join in with the play? You've always liked Benjamin that way, haven't you Dara?"

How the hell he knew my name and my past crush, I'll never know.

"No, not happening," I told him. "Look, I think you made a mistake taking him down your suck-hole. He's one of Nan Hoskins's crowd. She is really pissed at you guys."

"Why, how interesting! And why hasn't dear Nan Hoskins come to speak to me directly, herself?"

I opened my mouth to answer, but he did it for me.

"Because she's dead," he hissed. "She's dead so the contract is over. I owe her nothing."

"She's still here though, at her house anyway," I said. "People are still avoiding the berry patch and your hall just on the strength of ingrained fear of her, dead or not."

"Did she tell you *she* was protecting *us*?" He laughed that horrible cut-glass trill again. "Too amusing for words, my dear."

This was my first inkling that I was fighting for a losing cause. Did that old bat Hoskins actually lie to me? Perhaps the terms of the agreement were not what she had specified.

He saw my doubt and raised the stakes. "We've hardly had any new blood for a good twenty years," he growled at me. "Our Benjamin is all the sweeter to us for that, and we'd be loath to see him go."

"Look, I don't know what sort of bargain I can make with you in exchange for Benjy. I'm not going to supply you with more unsuspecting humans, no matter how degraded they are or deserving of the hell you can offer them." Yes, I was as desperate as I sounded by this point.

"So she didn't tell you the real terms of the contract?"

"Obviously not." I hated being at this disadvantage. "But she did say I could strike some sort of other bargain with you. Who are you anyway?"

"I am Oberon." He drew himself up another half inch and his velvet robes sparkled with diamonds in the sunlight.

Oberon. I vaguely remembered the name from high school English class, and then it came to me. Of course, our Shakespeare studies. I laughed in his face.

"No you're not! The king of all fairies wouldn't be living in this shithole of a rock in Newfoundland in the middle of the Southside Barrens and so close to the salt ocean. What's your real name?"

This let the air out of his tire.

"You can call me Thursk," he said.

So he wasn't going to tell me his real name – fair enough. There's a lot of power in a name.

"Well, Thursk," I said, trying to get my tongue around the unfamiliar sound. "You know my position in the matter. I want Benjy back, and I'm prepared to do something in return for you, but only within reason."

"What could I possibly want from you that I couldn't get myself?"

"I don't know, but you should think hard before I get the de Teilhard witches on your case."

His eyes widened slightly at this.

"That's my dad," I added.

He sat himself down on the boulder, with his shoulders drooping. The glamour wavered, then disappeared, and I saw Thursk for the truly pathetic creature he was. I shifted slightly, trying to get upwind of him, anything to ease the stink.

"There is something we need," he said, his sharp little teeth catching at his bottom lip as he spoke, causing him to speak with a bit of a lisp. "You're right, I'm not Oberon. Oberon banished me from the Eden that is the homeland many years ago, sending me and my family across the ocean. The salt water! Not all of us survived that treacherous journey, how could we? The salt ate at the very fabric of our beings."

"If salt is so corrosive to you, why didn't you move inland, away from the ocean? There's hundreds of miles of wilderness out there in the center of the island. You don't have to remain here on the coast."

"We stay because we live in hope, hope that dearest Oberon will forgive me my trespasses (they really were so trifling) and allow my clan back into the fold. We perch here on this rock and wait for his summons."

He coughed wetly.

"You don't sound well," I noted as I tried to shift further away from him without hurting his feelings. I didn't need sick fairy germs on top of it all.

"I am ill," he said as he gave me his most doleful face. "We are all ill. Worst of it is, the youngest of us is the most vulnerable, and she is almost... dead."

"You have a sick baby?" I'm not a big fan of kids, but jeez... our cat had kittens once, and one of them got ill, so ill that we couldn't help it. It died. That was the saddest thing I've ever lived through. Besides, of course, Mom's disappearance.

He darted a quick glance at me, then gave another heavy sigh. "Do you know of any human babies?"

"I'm not getting you a human baby!" I told him. "I said anything within reason, and that is *so* totally unreasonable."

I made as if to get up and leave to show him how serious I was.

"No, no, no," he said quickly. "We have no use for a human baby! Nasty, puling things, they are. What we need is... mother's milk. The milk that only a loving human Mum can provide."

"Ah, gross," I groaned, trying desperately to wipe that image from my mind, this horrible little creature suckling... Oh, God. "Would formula do you?"

"No, absolutely not," he repeated firmly. "Only true milk."

"You want me to persuade some human mother to come all the way over here to give you some milk from her boobs. It's not going to happen, I can tell you that right now."

"Not so hasty my dear friend," he wheedled. "There may be a way around this dilemma. I understand that humans now have the habit of, I believe it's called, *expressing* milk into bottles?"

I thought of Jane, and how she would often ask me to feed the littlest one from the bottles in the fridge when she was gone downtown partying. It was also useful for her to be able to give the bottles the next morning with the alcohol still in her system. I nodded, slowly.

"One bottle, that's all I need," he said softly. "You see, once the youngest of us has been made well, so all of us will thrive. A half-pint of milk... that's all it would take. Such a simple thing. Such a small thing, to mean so much... and I'm sure I could persuade your Benjy to return to your world with you."

I shook off the glimmerings of glamour he was trying to throw on me. "I don't know what a pint is, but I might be able to get you a bottle."

He smiled beatifically at me, once more transformed into his fine gent self.

"I said *might*, don't get your hopes up too high. And I want your assurance that he'll be freed."

"The man has free will, as do all men," he said, all trace of his speech impediment gone. "But I promise you, I will do my utmost to convince him. He *might* want to leave."

What more could I do? I didn't trust Thursk, not one bit, but this was my only hope to free Benjy. I was babysitting tomorrow night for Jane, and that would be my opportunity.

I hated this, okay? But we needed to save that jerk Benjy. The baby wouldn't miss one bottle of milk.

CHAPTER 12

Mark dropped in that night to tell me he had started looking for Benjy. I hated to see him put all that energy into looking for Alice's brother now because he wasn't lost anymore, or at least not lost in the 'missing persons' sort of way. But I couldn't very well tell him that Benjy was stuck in a rabbit hole with a bunch of fairies.

"So, he hasn't shown up in any hospitals or morgues in Atlantic Canada," Mark said. "And he also hasn't been arrested anywhere in the country."

"That's good news," I agreed.

"But you know what the weird thing is? There's no record of him leaving on any flights or ferries, even the St. Pierre one."

St. Pierre and Miquelon are two tiny islands on the south coast of Newfoundland, still owned by France. Benjy had been down there a bit before in order to smuggle cheap booze and cigarettes up into Canada.

"Hmm," I answered, trying not to squirm.

"So he must still be on the island," Mark said. "Any idea where he might be holed up to? Perhaps a friend's cabin?"

"It's a big island." I shrugged. "He could be anywhere, I guess. I'm not actually that worried about him, I'm sure he'll show up again."

"Not worried?" Edna broke in. "Dara, the other day you were begging for help. What changed?"

"Well, he sent Alice a text to say he was okay," I mumbled. "He just didn't say where he was."

This news was met with a momentary silence. Then Edna started in at me.

"Thanks for letting Mark know! He wasted valuable time looking for your friend. You should be a little more thoughtful..."

"S'alright, Edna," he said. "I'm sure Dara's been pretty busy."

"Sorry Mark," I said, looking down at the table.

"That's okay," he said. "Anyway, it doesn't hurt to keep an eye on his sort. You never know what he'd be up to next."

I felt like such a shit, but I had other things on my mind now too.

Although I hadn't shown it at the time, it had really creeped me out when Dad told me about the dead woman being a half-blood. Mark had said her body was found amidst arcane runes and symbols and I couldn't help but notice on my walks that the Witch Kin purity graffiti was spreading, seeping from the dark alley like pus from a wound to spread ever further into the daylight until there were representations of the merged symbol right out in the open. There, on the boarded up window of an empty Water Street storefront, and yonder on the stone fence below the old Anglican Cathedral graveyard. Then finally, on the very wall of the Court House itself.

And no one was cleaning it off.

Over the next day, I also had an uncomfortable sensation of being watched, as if there were eyes on me every time I left the house. I would turn quickly to try to catch whoever it was, but there was never anyone there. I suspected it might be witch craft, so I sent out mental feelers hoping to latch onto something that was aimed in my direction, but those searches turned up nothing.

I told myself it just had to be Hugh and Dad keeping a strict eye on me, making sure I didn't go upsetting any of their apple carts doing magic or anything else like that. I hated that they didn't trust me not to meddle in supernatural activities, or rather, I hated that they thought it was their business what I did. Neither of them was willing to lift a finger to help Benjy when they so easily could. I had no choice in the matter, so it wasn't really my fault what happened next. It really wasn't.

I kept up the mind blocking to stop Dad and Hugh from spying on me, not that I was doing anything the next day except skipping classes and hanging out in the library, trying to bone up all things fairy related.

I ran into Sasha in the library, or should I say, I saw her and stuck my head deep back into my books and ignored her. She was usually cool with that.

But not that day. The new guy she'd been hanging round with for the past few months chose to sit at the table right across from me and she joined him, though I could tell she was reluctant. Seth, from Montreal, that was his name.

He was a witch, and he was also a French Canadian so the glamour practically dripped from him every time he shook that luscious head of black hair. His eyes held liquid dark like the deepest wells. I could tell she had a major crush happening, and really, who could blame her? He was a magnet for the eye, and a girl just wanted to drink and drink of him to sate a thirst she didn't even know she had.

He looked up and saw me staring, and once caught, I couldn't let go of that gaze.

Seth turned to whisper in Sasha's ear, all the while holding me captive with his eyes. Then it was her turn to look up at me, the hate and jealousy and something else coming off her like darts. She gave a fake laugh and draped herself over him.

I felt like a specimen on one of Alice's petri-dishes.

"That's the one," she murmured as she shook her head. "The mongrel."

He continued holding me with his gaze while his hand slipped over Sasha's left breast and his red lips parted. God, was he going to start feeling her up right there in the middle of the library? And she, the ice-queen, was letting him. Unbelievable.

Seth said something else to her, and she laughed again, but with a slight tremor running through it like fear.

"God, no," she said, her smile forced on her face. "Why would we bother?"

Seth's eyes never left mine the whole while and I felt like a rabbit caught in the headlights of a car. I watched as he licked those perfectly shaped lips of his and kept his hand on her breast. That's all, he didn't move it an inch, but I could see her breath catching.

I hate to admit it, but mine was too a little. He was hot, Sasha's new beau.

The room was growing very warm and something deep inside me was responding to him, something dark perhaps last felt in a nightmare or a wet dream, the kind forgotten in the light of day but that lingered deep within, below the conscious mind.

His eyebrows flicked up as if to invite me to join them and I almost found myself getting up from the table.

What the hell?

I had to nearly physically wrench myself to break the spell between me and him, and I looked again at my sister who was stuck to his side like a fly in a spider's web. Was that ecstasy on her face, or terror?

"You are such a creep," I muttered as I grabbed my books and prepared to leave. "Both of you. Freakin' witches."

I could feel his eyes still burning into my soul as I ran out the door.

....

Wednesday evening was babysitting night, and I planned to slip a bottle of Jane's milk into my knapsack before she came home again. I was sure if I told her what it was for she'd be okay with it because she was pretty laid back and New Agey like that. Still, I held back because the fewer people who knew about all this supernatural business the better.

The two older kids, Tiffany and Braden, were bouncing around me the minute I got in the front door, hanging off my jeans and trying to get a sneak peek into my knapsack to see what delights I'd brought.

"I'm so glad they love you," Jane said. "I don't know if I could trust anyone else with these kids. You make my life so much easier."

Trust. *Jesus.* "What can I say?"

"You know, it's funny. I would never have pegged you for someone who likes kids, Dara, you always seemed so grumpy and moody when we were growing up."

Jane was a few years older than me. She had been paid to take me up the road to St. Mary's School back when I started kindergarten. We'd walk a meandering path through the old graveyard, and she'd make up stories about the pretty fairies and pixies and other beings who dwelled there in her imagination amongst the trees and gravestones. The stone angel was her favourite. I had tried to tell about Maundy, the ghost in our house, but she cut me off and scolded me for trying to scare her.

We all said our chorus of good-byes to her as she slipped out the door in her stilettoes and short skirt and into the waiting cab. Then it was treat time. They especially liked Mars Bars, those sickly sweet gooey confections, and I'd stocked up on a bag of Hallowe'en minis.

After they had gorged and we'd played some video games I brought with me, I heard the baby stirring upstairs so I got a bottle ready in the microwave, following Jane's instructions to the tee. I was about to bring it upstairs when a knock came on the back door.

I couldn't see anyone out the window, but then the knock came again. I admit I wasn't thinking, I figured it must be tiny Mrs. Jones from next door. Eighty years old and under five feet tall, she was always dropping in to Jane's on any excuse because she loved babies.

So, I undid the double locks and opened the door, and there were two frigging fairies in front of me. Not Thursk, these were younger ones, all decked up in their fancy togs.

"Good evening, lady," the male said as he cocked his top hat boldly. "I believe you have something for me?"

"No way!" I held the bottle up and back behind me and hissed at him. "You're not getting this till I know that Benjy is free. I told Thursk that!"

"I regret to inform you of this slight change in plans, so sorry if this inconveniences you."

I made to shut the door in his face but they pushed past me roughly, almost knocking me down. Who knew those horrible little creatures had such strength?

The other jumped up in a flurry of silken skirts and grabbed the bottle out of my hand and then they both disappeared into the house, so fast that if I'd blinked I would have missed it.

Running after them, I almost tripped over Tiffany who had come out to see what was happening.

She stood in my way with her little hands on her hips. "Who was that? They smell bad. What're they doing in my house?"

I gently maneuvered around her, all the while pushing her back into the living room.

"Stay in there and keep the door closed," I told her. "Hold tight to Braden. If that thing gets a hold of you there won't be any more chocolate tonight."

She did what I told her to, banging the door on her way.

Taking the steps two at a time, I ran first to the baby's room, but she was still in there, asleep again and no sign of the fairies except a lingering malodour despite the open window. Had it been open before? Jane believed in fresh air for health reasons. I checked every other room and all the closets, even the linen closet at the top of the stairs, but I could see no one.

The fairies had disappeared. I searched with my mind, too, but could feel no overt trace of supernatural in the house. I leaned against the rails in relief, whatever had just happened, it looked like all was well now.

Except that the little shit had stolen the bottle of Jane's milk and now I had no bargaining chip against Thursk for Benjy's freedom. I clumped back down the stairs, thinking hard. Would Jane notice two bottles missing? She probably would.

I rechecked the littles, they were safe in front of the TV. I gave them a couple more sweets to help Tiff forget the incident, and then it was bedtime.

Strange that the baby hadn't woken up again, for she liked her feed regularly and on schedule. I got another bottle ready for her and brought it upstairs, and that's when I discovered the true extent of the damage wrought by the visitors.

I don't know what alerted me, for the baby looked the same as she had not half an hour previously, soft red curls barely covering her head as she slept peacefully on her tummy. But there was something not quite right about her, and when I picked her up she was absolutely flaccid, no muscle tone whatsoever.

Yes, I dropped her back into the crib, bottle and all, unmindful of damaging her for I knew what had been done. Not only had the fairies stolen the milk, they'd stolen the baby and left a sickly creature in its place.

"Shit shit shit!"

I'd really done it this time. Unless I was wrong, Jane now had a changeling in her nest.

CHAPTER 13

"Edna, I need help!" My hand was shaking so much I almost dropped my phone. "It's the baby – she... she..."

"What is it? Is she breathing?"

"Oh, yeah, I guess, but she's..."

"I'll be right over. Do we need an ambulance?"

Jesus, what would they make of a changeling baby in the Emergency Department? That would be fun to explain. I groaned.

Edna was speaking to Mark. "Honey, call an ambulance to go to Jane's house on Warbury Street. Sick baby!" She turned back to the phone. "Okay Dara, we're on our way."

I went down and unlocked the doors for them. They arrived at the same time as the ambulance from St. Clare's Hospital up the hill – our society takes sick babies seriously. We all ran upstairs to the nursery – me, Edna, Mark and the two paramedics.

And saw the baby on her back suckling at the bottle, giving off little gurgles and grunts, happy as could be, though I could swear there was an evil glint in her eye as she looked up at me.

"Looks okay to me," the first ambulance attendant said. "What were her symptoms?"

"Uhh, she was unresponsive," I began.

They all looked at me with doubt.

"And she felt feverish!"

They checked her out, then gave her the thumbs up. I was subjected to a short lecture on the care of babies and wasting valuable public resources. I wasn't even the one who called for the ambulance, that was Mark, but they didn't tell him off, did they? No, it was all my fault. Jerks.

And then of course, Jane had to be called back from her evening out, and to make matters worse she found the empty Mars Bars wrappers scattered all over the living room next to the video game.

In one single evening, I had totally screwed up any chance of bargaining to get Benjy back, possibly lost Jane's baby and definitely lost my job. I didn't even get the opportunity to lift a second bottle of milk. Sometimes it sucked to be me.

··········

I thought things were the worst they could be, and there was no one left to turn to for help. I had to get the baby back (if it was indeed a changeling), and I had to free Benjy from the fairy hell. Dad was really the only person who could help me out of this jam, but he would banish me to some icy rock off Scotland if he knew the truth of what I'd done, and I just didn't trust Hugh. Crying didn't help at all.

Yes, I thought things couldn't get worse, but then Hugh tracked me down.

I was riding the Number Ten Metrobus to the university the next day, because I might as well go to class. If I flunked out, then I really would have to do plumbing or something like that and work for a living for the rest of my life. I was soaked from having walked up the hill to the bus stop. It was a dark gray day, rain drizzling down the windows of the bus. A hurricane was brewing, the TV said, making its inexorable way up the eastern seaboard from the Carolinas.

So one moment he wasn't there, and the next he was sitting on the seat beside me. His leather jacket wasn't one bit damp, but his black umbrella was dripping onto the floor. Didn't he realize that umbrellas were useless in this climate? He'd find out soon enough.

"I've been watching you. You've really put your foot in it now."

"Nosy bastard." Bravado was all I had left.

"This is precisely the kind of thing that happens when witches are left untrained," he began to lecture.

"That's not my fault!"

"I agree," he said, his voice surprised. "It's *not* your fault that no one has admitted you have power and taken you in hand to learn how to control it. However, you're smart enough that you should know not to dabble when you're in over your head."

I stared out the window. The wind was starting to whip up the leaves on the trees which hadn't yet begun to turn color. If it really was a hurricane coming, these same green leaves would be ripped away *en masse*, their wet weight taking the oldest branches down with them, and it would be messy and dangerous out there in the heart of the storm.

"Don't ignore me," he said to the back of my head. "This is serious shite. I want to know how you think you can undo it all."

How much did he really know, I wondered?

"I'm talking about the fairies who have been following you around," he said. "Your little foray up the hill must have stirred up the hornets' nest."

Okay, so maybe he wasn't aware of the worst of it, about the changeling or the bottle of Jane's milk. Unfortunately, this didn't help lift my burden one bit.

"What do you think I should do?" Yes, I was hedging a bit, to see exactly how much he knew.

"Well, give back to the fairies whatever you took from their hall, for a start," he said. "Hopefully, that will get them off your back."

I turned to face him, hurt at being unjustly accused. "I didn't take anything from them!"

"You have something they want," he said. "Or they wouldn't have come down off the hill. I saw them yesterday, following you around. That's a long distance for them to stray from their den."

"I don't have anything they want," I said to him again, as miserably as I felt. "They already took what they needed. I probably won't be seeing them again."

He blew out a long breath, and I sneaked a glance up at him. Those cheek bones were sharp enough to cut your heart on. In fact the whole package of Hugh was really something for although he wasn't glamorous the way Seth was, there was something solid and strong and clean about him. He was larger than life, like a model in a magazine or an actor on the big screen. Too bad he was way out of my league, and a shithead witch to boot.

"Look, I obviously don't know the whole story, and I don't think I really want to," he said. "Just tell me something. Are you in danger, personally?"

"Me?" I paused to think about it. Other people were in danger, and the baby was totally my fault. But I personally was safe, and it seemed rather unfair. I shook my head. "No, I don't think so."

"Right then," he said, his voice firm, but his eyes were taking on a kindness that seemed misplaced to my guilty mind. "You need to get out of this town. Now, before anything else happens."

"No!" I didn't realize I'd shouted till I saw other people lift their heads in my direction, so I lowered my voice to a whisper. "No, I can't leave here."

There was far too much at stake. I had to undo what I'd done and fulfill my promises.

"Your friend in the fairy hall?"

I clamped back down on my mind, and nodded. Of course, Dad had told him about Benjy.

"Forget him, he made his own bed. He's not your responsibility."

"This is none of your business," I told him. "Subject closed."

We got off the bus outside the Arts Building. My first class of the day was Folklore, and we were looking at the history of Fairy Lore in the province. Boy, I could really ace my final essay for this one if I dared, using primary resources even. Too bad I couldn't do any such thing, my prof would never believe it.

Hugh opened his umbrella to walk the short distance to the building. I almost warned him about the uselessness of such an attempt, but decided to let him learn the hard way about brollies and the Newfoundland wind. Serve him right.

But incredibly, the umbrella stayed right side out. It was as if Hugh was now the center of the storm, the peaceful inner spot. We walked to the building past the cars and the rose bushes with nary a drop of rain getting on us.

"How'd you do that?"

"You could, too. Easily. If you'd just go away for a bit of education like I suggested."

I probably glared at him as we entered through the main entrance.

"Well look what came in out of the rain," a cool voice greeted us.

Sasha again. My older sister, number two of Cate's litter, was waiting right inside. She looked just like her mother, long straight dark hair and dark eyes, a flawless skin and not an ounce of fat anywhere around her muscled torso. She was gorgeous of course, and doing her degree in Economics while a member of the rowing and rugby teams, definitely a force to be reckoned with. Sasha was no doubt eager to join Daddy darling in his business empire.

But something about her made me look twice. Beneath the sheen of witch glamour, there was something murky around her edges, as if she was carrying a heaviness, and I could swear there were dark circles beneath her eyes, under the artfully applied makeup. But it was gone a second later when she narrowed her eyes at me. Just a trick of the light.

She hooked her arm around Hugh's and looked at me with all the superiority of a full blood witch to a half-breed.

"You've met my friend, then?" She emphasized the word friend as if she was pissing to mark her territory. Jesus, she must still be rankling over that weird episode the day before with Seth in the library. But she didn't need to worry, I wanted as little to do with that false witch Hugh as possible.

Sasha kept hold to him, anchoring him down so he couldn't follow me.

"Remember what I said," he called out to me as I made my way up the stairs.

"Sorry, not happening," I called back. "I'm staying right here."

....

In class, we were discussing the latest assigned reading, which I hadn't actually gotten round to, but no matter. *Fables, Fairies and Folklore* was a slim volume published in the early 'nineties, and three of its chapters were second or third or fourth hand accounts of human interactions with the fairies.

I quickly read through them before class began. There were some common threads to my experience, like the fairies living up on the barrens away from the coastlines behind Conception and Placentia Bays, but some of the stuff just sounded foolish.

According to these stories, I had put myself in danger by talking with the fairies, even just by acknowledging their presence. One man in the story was kept captive by them for merely wearing green inside the fairy circle where he happened to stray, and because he spoke with them, they could keep him as long as they wanted. Green was the color of the fairies, apparently. They tied him down, enslaved him, and whipped him, trying to get him to eat their food so they could keep him under enchantment forever.

That made sense, for I remembered how Thursk had tried his damnedest to get me to come join their party. I wondered why, if I had spoken with him, that didn't immediately put me in his power like the man in the story.

It had to be my witch blood, diluted though it was. This realization floored me, for I had never viewed my accidental heritage in any way that was positive before. My eyes opened just a little to what Hugh had been trying to tell me.

I leaned back in the chair, the class around me totally forgotten, and placed my hands inside my hoodie pocket as I tried to absorb this new self-knowledge. A paper bag crinkled under my touch. Zeta's spell, I'd forgotten I was carrying it around with me. The sachet inside the bag was completely lifeless – not a tingle of magic came from it. It couldn't chase a fly out of Alice's house, let alone the ghost of her great-grandmother. It was useless.

Whereas I had power. Real, supernatural power.

CHAPTER 14

This realization was an eye-opener, that's for sure. I had never before understood that I held actual power. It was an uncomfortable thought, yet thrilling at the same time.

It was like... my whole world shifted right there and then. Here I was, sitting in a second-year Folklore class while the ponytailed prof intellectually discoursed on the finer points of fairy lore and magical thinking among the poor ignorant people of times gone by, the superstitious idiots of this island who had believed such outlandish things. He, the pompous come-from-away who thought he knew everything, dissecting the living soul of those people with his sharp razors of logic and not seeing a thing in front of him. Not seeing the real live witch sitting right before him.

What the hell was I doing with my life, searching for answers from the likes of this man? I could have laughed; it all seemed so simple in that moment of time. How could I have lived this long without understanding who I truly was? And I had been searching for answers all this time, I realized, delving into books which hinted at anything supernatural.

Yes, my whole world had shifted ninety degrees. And with this new understanding came responsibilities.

I realized I wanted to take Hugh up on his offer for further education, I knew I sorely needed this. Yet, at the same time, there was no way I could run away to the Hebrides and leave the mess of Benjy and the baby behind. I needed to learn more about harnessing my power in order to help them, but I needed a crash course.

I sat the rest of the class totally wrapped up in my own thoughts, and only realized I had bitten three nails down to the quick after the class was dismissed. I needed Hugh's help, but could I trust him? Perhaps he was telling the truth about being a half-blood after all, but still, he was too close to Dad and Sasha for my comfort.

In the little sitting area down on the first floor of the Arts Building, I grabbed a dark roast and searched my knapsack for Hugh's card. I knew I hadn't tossed it, it had to be there somewhere. At last my fingers found it and I withdrew the crumpled cardboard, blowing off the pastry crumbs which had left grease spots on the front of it.

But what to say to him? I'd changed my mind and wanted to learn, but he had to teach me everything he knew right there and then. I had a feeling he would never go for that. Despite the fact of the company he was keeping, he seemed too upright, too righteous even, to bend the rules.

If I even hinted at the shit I'd caused, he'd probably get my dad to pack me up and send me far, far away up to his precious northern island, and Benjy and the baby would be lost forever.

Perhaps I could convince him to impart a little knowledge, just enough to tide me over, if I promised to go along with his advice. Yes, I could claim that I needed to finish this semester, of course, he would see the sense of that. A girl couldn't live on witchcraft alone, right? She needed to have direction in life and a human education.

Okay then. So the next question was – what did I need to learn in order to be able to rescue the baby from the fairy's clutches? There, I drew a blank. I knew so little about the craft that I didn't even know what I lacked.

It was all Dad and Cate's fault that I found myself in this peculiar situation. If Dad had taken responsibility for his action of sowing his seed so lightly into a human; if he had had the guts to go against Cate and his community and made sure I knew how to use my powers properly, instead of just throwing money at me and hoping I would go away; well then, I wouldn't be in this boat right now, would I?

I was going to have to wing it. There, Hugh's number was punched in, all I had to do was tap to dial.

But before I could do that, I was interrupted by Alice.

She sat in the affixed plastic chair across from me. Her face was drawn, even paler than usual, yet her large gray eyes were glittering in a feverish way. Alice never left the Science Building except when she couldn't avoid it. If she could, she would only take science courses and never bother with any of the humanities electives. But here she was in the Arts Building.

"I got another text from Benjy," she said, her smile heartbreakingly wide. "He wants me to join him."

"Alice, no!" It was out before I could stop myself.

She looked at me, hurt in her eyes. "Dara, this is Benjy. He needs me, he says. He..." She looked back down at her phone. "He says he's looking after someone's baby, and he needs my help, because, well, you know Benjy..."

"Do you remember when we found him?"

She screwed up her face. "I haven't seen him since he left," she said. "But it's okay, he says he's staying up by the berry patch up the hill, though I can't imagine what he's doing up there with a baby. The things he gets into, I tell you."

The whole incident had been wiped from her mind, I could see, whether it was fairy magic or just her human inability to comprehend the supernatural. Yet, according to Nan Hoskins, Alice had elf-blood in her from way, way back. Why this disconnect?

The pieces fell slowly into place. We had the same story. Just as I had been unable to accept that I had power, despite the evidence before my eyes as I slipped in and out of Alt and regularly talked with Maundy my ghost, so Alice had no reason to believe she had super-natural blood in her. She must surely have had hints of it in her life, though, at some point. But perhaps that's why my friend liked science so much – in that space, you could disregard conjecture and only focus on the physical reality that could be measured.

Now my troubles were triplicated. Not only did I need to rescue Benjy and the baby, I also had to prevent Alice from going up to the berry patch and drinking the fairy Kool-Aid. Aside from kidnapping her and locking her into the cellar of Richmond Cottage, there was no way I could stop her.

And I also had the sinking feeling that if I confided in Hugh all about this additional twist he would have me packed off on the next plane out of here, no matter where it went. The Witch Kin would have no moral qualms about abduction to further their own means.

"It's raining out, and they're expecting a storm," I said. "Not a good day to go traipsing around the Southside Hills."

"What are you talking about? I know those barrens like the back of my hand," Alice scoffed. "And Benjy needs me."

"Alice, please listen to me." I leaned over and grasped both her hands in mine. She started in surprise, because despite our friendship, we rarely touched each other. It was one of those unwritten rules. "I need you to promise not to go up there without me."

"Why? You don't even like babies."

True, but I'd never let on to that with Jane.

"It's not the baby I'm worried about, it's you."

She rolled her eyes and shaking her hands free of mine, stretched her long lanky legs up on the chair beside her. "Why?"

"Fairies, Alice," I said. "Benjy is caught by the fairies. And it's gotten worse than that, way worse. That baby he wants you to look after? Well, a fairy came by Jane's last night when I was babysitting and stole her youngest, and left a changeling in its place. You just can't go up to the fairies, Al, they'll eat you alive."

I could tell by the way her jaw dropped that she thought I was cracked, yet the fact that she didn't bust out laughing meant that something was getting through to her. Maybe her elf-blood was making her see sense, I don't know.

She looked down at the little red book in front of me, the Folklore text, and pointed at it. "Hello, Dara? Are you taking all this stuff a little too seriously?"

"It's real," I said. "Do you remember me telling you I talk with ghosts?"

She hesitated, then nodded.

"And that your great-grandmother, Nan Hoskins, is the one haunting your house?"

She didn't want to nod, but I kept staring at her and at long last, she gave a quick dip to her head.

"You can't deny that is happening in your own home, can you?"

She shook her head.

"Well, all Nan's activity started when Benjy got himself lost in the world of fairies," I explained to her patiently, though I knew we had already gone over this. "Now do you remember being in the fairy hall?"

Her eyes began to water, the luminous gray turning silver in the light. "I thought that was a bad dream," she whispered.

It was my turn to shake my head. She glanced back at her phone with longing.

"But perhaps if I go up there I can help him."

"Not alone, you can't," I said. "Please don't think for a moment that you can outwit the fairies."

"But..." She stroked her phone as if itching to reply to Benjy's text.

"Don't do it," I said and tried to appeal to the logical part of her mind. "Think about it, Alice – he's been gone how long?"

"Two weeks, maybe three..."

"And he's been up on the Southside Hills all that time, and his phone battery hasn't died?"

"That is weird," she said, sitting up. "Unless he snuck down to the house to recharge..."

"He can't leave the fairy hall," I told her. "He's enslaved by them, they'd never let him go. It's fairy magic that is powering his phone right now."

She thought some more, then nodded. I was really glad to see the reasoning light in her eyes again.

"So what are we going to do, if all this is true?"

"The first thing I'm going to do," I said apologetically as I reached over and took her phone in my hand, "is to confiscate this."

She gasped, as you would. A girl's phone is her lifeline, so she tried to grab it back from me.

"No," I said, shoving it into my bag as I turned it off. "The fairies are using this to cast the spell on you, pretending to be Benjy and getting at your emotions that way, and trying to control you."

She got the seriousness of the situation now that I had taken the unprecedented step of removing her phone.

"So, what do we need to do?"

I thought for another moment. Now I had Alice on my side, even if her hold on this new reality was a little shaky and I might not be able to trust her around the fairies, I did feel better and stronger.

"I know someone who can help us," I said. "But I'm afraid I might not be able to trust him. He's a witch."

....

I needed to take some time to think before phoning Hugh, even though I had a bad feeling that every minute counted. I'd given my own phone to Alice with explicit instructions to keep in close contact with me if she saw anything weird happening. I couldn't trust the fairies not to come down the hill to her house themselves even though they knew Nan Hoskins was still there. I also told her not to answer the door if she didn't recognize the person outside.

Mark was over for supper again that night. This was odd, him spending so much time with us, and Edna allowing it. Not that I was complaining, as we were eating really well for a change. Usually she told me to forage and graze through the cupboards if I was hungry. I ate a lot of pasta with salad dressing sauce, and avocado on toast.

He'd brought Indian take out with him, my all-time favorite. I really liked this guy.

"So what's the special occasion?" I asked as I undid the bags. "Not that it's not nice to see you."

I saw the two of them exchange a significant glance, and I got a funny feeling in my stomach. My antennae went on high alert.

"Mark just... wants to spend more time with us," Edna said as she brought down three plates, and totally failing in her attempt to lie.

"Right," I said, my eyes switching back and forth between the two. "What's brought this on?"

I heaped a double helping of butter chicken over my rice, then placed a load of dahl next to it. Whatever the news was going to be, it was not going to interrupt my feast.

Mark and Edna hadn't even started to dish out their own food. This was getting really strange, because despite her reluctance to cook and nurture, Edna loved food that other people cooked and was usually the first one to dig in.

"And I want the truth," I added, at which Edna broke down.

"Your father's worried about you."

"Yeah, as if," I said. Did I roll my eyes? Maybe.

"He is," Mark said. "He called me at work today. Said you might be having a little trouble."

Dad called Mark? What the hell? My fork paused halfway to my mouth.

"He told him about your visit the other day," Edna chimed in. "And your father thinks you're into drugs."

The two were staring at me sorrowfully across the kitchen table. Drugs! Dad knew the difference. He was deliberately lying to them in order to... keep me from getting further entangled with the fairies.

"And the other night," Mark added. "That business with the baby. What was all that about, Dara? I spoke with Jane. She's worried about you, too."

He had brown eyes like an old dog who's seen everything in its day, and that soulful gaze was turned full force on me. He dug into the brief case he always carried with him and brought out some papers. Laying them on the table between us, he pointed at the photos on them.

They were the standard before and after shots of meth users and their teeth, the ones they use to scare highschool kids away from going down the road to hell.

"Oh come off it, Mark!"

"I can understand your desire to experiment when you're young, lots of people do that," he said in that very kind and gentle voice. Edna found something pressing to do at the far end of the kitchen. Her experimental stage had lasted far into her thirties and she wouldn't want to share that with Mark. "But you have to know what you're getting yourself into."

"Edna," I called out to her. "Mark. Do you really think I'm into drugs of any kind?"

"Well, Benjy Hoskins? You're not keeping the best of company," Mark began, then looked apologetically over at Edna as she came back with the salt and pepper. "I'm sorry, Dara. I'm not your father or anything close to it, but I care. I hate to see any kid go off the rails, especially you."

"I'm not doing drugs," I said tightly as I scooped up dahl with my naan. "Dad made that up."

"He said you went over to his house and were raving about fairies or something."

I could feel myself turning red from embarrassment. My father was a bastard! How could he do this to me? I looked over at Edna, who shrugged and pointed with her eyes at Mark.

She knew the truth, but no way was she going to tell her boyfriend.

"I don't even know how he knew to call Mark," she said in a lame attempt to divert the conversation. "I mean, it's not like we're married or anything."

Me and him exchanged a glance now. Spending so much time in her own little worlds of fiction, Edna maybe didn't have a deep understanding of this town and its intermingling grapevines. Mark wasn't from here, but he knew.

"Edna," I said in a very controlled voice. "Tell him. Tell Mark *why* you don't believe I'm doing drugs." This was a confrontation and I was going to make her stick up for me, or I would tell Mark all about the whole supernatural business, and she knew it.

"I know you're not messing with drugs," she said as she sat back down. "But, if you're getting into... difficulties, perhaps you should do like your dad says and get out of town for bit."

"Dad wants me gone because he's embarrassed by my existence," I said. There could be no mistaking the bitterness in my voice. "Because I'm the accidental by-product of his affair with my mother."

I stared at them both, daring them to deny this truth. Mark looked back at me with a warm pity on his face.

"Maybe there's something more to this," Edna said. "Maybe he thinks you should go away for your own good."

She gave me the wide-eye stare, the one that says 'you know very well what I'm talking about, don't make me say it out loud'.

"Why now?" I asked. "Why does he want me gone now, instead of when I was a teenager? Why didn't he send me away to some nice private school far away from anyone he knew?"

"Because I wouldn't let him," she snapped. "Okay? I wanted you to stay with me."

"Oh," I said, taken aback by the fierce look on her face. "I didn't know that."

Dad had wanted to send me away but my aunt had fought to keep me here by her side. I finished the rest of my plate off in thoughtful contemplation.

"So," Mark said, glancing between the two of us. He must have been aware he'd missed something in this conversation but he respected boundaries. "You know you can come to me if you're having any problems, right? Anything at all. I don't want you to end up as a statistic, I've seen too much of that. And whatever it is that's going on, I want you to know – you're not going to shock me. I've no doubt dealt with worse in my time."

I put down my fork. This was my opportunity, I could unload on Mark and Edna, and tell them all about the trouble I'd gotten myself into. Explain why Dad really wanted me gone, and explain why I couldn't go until I'd cleaned up my own mess.

But had Mark really dealt with these kind of troubles? I doubted it and, judging by the apprehensive look in Edna's eyes, she didn't think it likely either.

CHAPTER 15

Maybe I should have gone away like I promised Hugh, just packed off to his Hebridean island and learned how to harness my power. It would take, what, a year or two, and I'm a really fast learner as he pointed out. Then I could come back, save Benjy and the baby, undo the wrong I'd caused.

But I had a bad feeling that even one year would be too late for either of them.

In the meantime while I was hanging around in limbo not knowing what to do, there was a report in the news about another hiker disappeared off the Freshwater Bay trail. What sort of fool would go hiking alone on an exposed trail on the barrens in September when a hurricane was on its way? I didn't know if it was the fairies ramping up their activity with their newfound strength or if it was a genuine case of a misstep too close to the edge of the cliff side path. The RNC, the RCMP, and the Search and Rescue Crews were combing the hill and the waters all day – I could hear the helicopters from the house. It was really dangerous for them to be out there near the cliffs, what with the rising winds.

It was while I was biking over to Alice's later that evening that the idea came to me. I couldn't ask for help from Dad or Hugh, but there were other supernatural beings in this town, ones without an agenda to get me far away from this place and who might also have a grudge against the fairies. I decided to blow off Alice for the moment – she was okay, there had been no further attempts to lure her up the hill, so I rode my bike past her house to the old tunnels under the Southside Hills.

Some said they were World War II bunkers, used to store ammunition because if the gunpowder had blown up, the power of its force would be contained by the solid granite and slate of the massive hills. Others said the history of these tunnels was much older, that they'd started out as natural caves and had been enlarged by human activity, usually for a nefarious nature like smuggling and storing rum. One guy in the 'nineties had wanted to use them for marijuana grow-ops, but that was squashed pretty firmly by the powers that be.

In real time, most of the entrances to the ten or so tunnels were either concreted over or covered with impenetrable metal doors to prevent vandalism, hooliganism and stoned people wandering in and getting hurt.

But in Alt, these tunnels still had their original thick oak doors with the huge iron locks and metal hinges like medieval fortifications. I knew dwarves lived in some of them, or at least I thought they did. I didn't want to go hunting them up but I didn't see that I had much of a choice.

The sun had long since gone down and the moon was not yet risen. In real time, the few streetlights illuminated bits and pieces of the road, but the ambient light from St. John's downtown across the harbor gave plenty of light to see by.

I rested my bike in the scrubby bushes by the biggest tunnel, the most likely one, and slipped into Alt full on. It was dark here, and chilly at the base of the hills. The burning torches of Alt Town did not lend their light this far across the water.

My hand on the oaken door, I hesitated. Not because I felt myself to be in danger from dwarves, they wouldn't want to eat me or anything, but on the other hand they didn't much like anyone who wasn't a dwarf. I was thinking that maybe I should go away and come back when I had a plan in mind, when the decision was taken out of my hands.

The oak door swung outward on its heavy hinges, and before I could run away, I was caught in full view by the firelight inside.

No turning back now.

Twenty feet into the tunnel, lit by pitch torches placed against the walls, a dozen faces looked over at me from their dining table, a huge ancient pine plank sanded to a fine polish by elbows over hundreds of years. I had interrupted the evening dwarven meal of porridge or some such thing, served in mismatched ceramic and wooden bowls. Each dwarf held an iron spoon.

They were a funny looking crowd, even taking into account this was Alt. They dressed in woolen clothing styled from a long-ago era, each with floppy hats on their heads, and in soiled jerkins and loose trousers. Wool made sense for these beings since they lived and worked underground most of their lives, and the rock was cold and clammy deep within.

The tunnel was warm, though, heated by the large cooking fire by their table, and the working forges at the entrance which were never allowed to go out. In fact, the heat was stifling.

"Close the door, you're letting in the draft," shouted the dwarf closest to me, a querulous old guy by the looks of him. Then again, they were probably all old compared to me, for dwarves lived hundreds of years if the stories were to be believed.

One slightly taller than the others walked over to inspect me where I hovered half in, half out of their cave, still uncertain if I would flee.

"What are you?"

Now that was an Alt question if I'd ever heard one. Not *who* are you, but *what* are you, what tribe do you belong to?

"My name is Dara. I'm a witch," I said, then hurriedly expounded. "The de Teilhard Kin."

The dwarf sniffed the air, his red hat bobbing and beard bristling. "You smell like one, but I've never heard of you."

"She's not fully matured yet," another one pointed out. "She wouldn't be part of the Council."

The Council, huh? Something else to be filed away until I had a chance to digest it. A council of supernaturals in Alt Town.

He indicated I should follow him deeper into the tunnel. They all looked at me with suspicion, waiting for me to explain why I had come. The firelight cast long shadows over their faces, hiding the dozen pairs of eyes.

"I'm not, I'm not part of the Council, you're right," I said, nodding to the last one who had spoken. "I'm here because I have information you might want to know."

"*Not* here on behalf of the Council?" The closest one looked shocked.

Shit, I'd forgotten that dwarves were such sticklers for protocol. Their lives were guided by rules and ancient laws, and they would not look kindly on a renegade like myself. I decided to level with them for I didn't have anything to lose. The worst that would happen would be they'd chuck me out and report me to the Kin, and then I'd be deported and Dad would win, which was probably going to be the end result anyway no matter what I did.

Might as well be hung for a sheep as a lamb, as the old saying goes.

"I am the daughter of Jonathan de Teilhard," I said clearly, drawing myself up to as much height as I could muster and trying to arrange my face in Sasha's haughty manner. At least it was easy to look down my nose at these shorties.

"This visit is irregular," the main dwarf said, a frown creasing his already creased face.

I desperately searched my mind for memories of Tolkien's descriptions of dwarves and what motivated them. That guy sure had known his supernaturals, even if he did tend to go on and on about the boring battle details.

Greed, of course. I needed to somehow work in about the fairy gold up inside the hill above their heads. Dwarves were notoriously avaricious for anything that came from the ground, believing it all belonged to them.

"My visit is not sanctioned by the Council," I told them honestly enough. "I have been sent to request your help in settling a dispute in an unofficial directive."

"You'd best sit and join us then," he said in a grudging tone. "Make way there."

A couple of dwarves shuffled down the bench so I could sit at his left hand. A safety precaution I guess, so he could draw his short sword if I made any sudden moves against him.

The dwarf to my own left nodded as I sat. He appeared to be younger than the others, his face less lined and grimed with rock dust.

I was offered a bowl of evil smelling goo with dark chunks in it but I demurred, telling them I had already eaten. The rejected offering was dumped back into the black cauldron bubbling over the fire.

"So de Teilhard sent you, eh?" The head dwarf had introduced himself as Lucas IronArms. He went back to slurping his meal, keeping a close crafty eye on me the whole time. "What is it that is so secretive that he has bypassed the Council?"

I glanced around at the other dwarves, and he brushed aside what he thought was on my mind.

"We are a cooperative society, the dwarves," he said. "Unlike the witches and others. What one dwarf knows, all know. You can speak freely."

"The problem is ..." I started, then cleared my throat. My God, was I actually doing this, sitting down at a dwarven table and attempting to deceive them? I took a deep breath and plunged in. "Thursk is the problem."

There was much nodding and murmuring from the crowd at the table. Fairies and dwarves had never gotten along well. The dwarves lived by their Law, and the fairies, well, they didn't respect any laws.

"What has he done now? Surely any action taken against him needs to be sanctioned by Council, in proper order."

"There is a stumbling block there," I said. I was trying my best to speak as I imagined an emissary from my father would. I paused, wishing I knew more about the Council conventions and the rules regarding what supernaturals could and couldn't do. "You see, Thursk has taken some people, and we would rather he hadn't."

"That's not against Council rulings." IronArms shook his head firmly. "All supernaturals are free to continue their activity as per their innate inclinations in order to sustain the balance of nature, inasmuch as they do not disturb said balance."

"And since Nan Hoskins's untimely demise, they haven't even been keeping up their allotted quota." This was the elderly dwarf who had first spoken when I entered, the one who'd complained about the draft. He was seated directly across me, the remains of his porridge still dribbled in his beard. "So I for one would never begrudge them a couple of Nons. It is their wont, after all, and they need this intake to sustain their lifestyle."

What the witch community called Normals, the rest of the supernaturals called Nons, short for Nonsupernatural, I guessed.

"One of them is a baby," I blurted. But my words went unheard, for the dwarves had begun a long and hotly disputed conversation on the finer points of the Convention and the rules governing each supernatural community. I had to wait for IronArms to call them back into order before I could continue with my request.

"I suggest we hear her out," he said loudly. "The de Teilhard Kin would not have sent an emissary on this small fact alone. There is more to the story, I suspect."

I had to think fast, for they weren't going to buy the fact that humans were enslaved by the fairies as reason enough to act against them. I had to make something up, and prayed that my instincts were right.

"The issue is, is that one of the humans is actually part elf, from Nan Hoskins's own bloodline."

"Go talk to the elves then, it's not our problem!" This came from the back of the room and was accompanied by solid cheers. I didn't know where the elves hung out, but I would keep them in mind if this venture failed.

"Good riddance to bad rubbish," muttered the elderly dwarf. "Can't say I miss the old bat Hoskins one bit."

"Also, there is a baby involved." I pitched my voice loud and authoritative to speak over the deep murmurings. "And as you are no doubt aware, there is a move behind Council scenes to enact laws protecting the young of *every* species."

This created the buzz of confusion I had hoped for. No, none of them were aware of any proposed amendments, and as changes to Laws had to be pounded out in discussion like iron on the anvil being forged to steel, they were greatly upset they weren't being included. I heard a growing dissatisfaction also towards the Council, that changes would be considered without the input of the dwarves, for everybody knew they were the ones to consult over legal matters.

I hurried to calm these fears. "This is only in the discussion stage, of course, still behind closed doors by some factions," I hastened to add. "There is after all a growing trend worldwide, and we don't want to be seen as being old-fashioned."

"Tradition is more important than new-fangled political correctness," my neighbor across the table said firmly.

"In light of this, I was sent to see if you would be open to quietly help return the baby," I said over him as I addressed the rest of them.

"I don't understand. Was there not a changeling brought forward in place of the human pup?" asked IronArms.

I nodded slowly.

"Yes? Then we will absolutely have no part in this action," he replied and he brought his fist down on the table with a crash. "De Teilhard will certainly get a piece of my mind tomorrow, that's for certain. How dare he think he can defy the Convention? The Witch Kin are getting too arrogant."

The eldest dwarf spoke up again, his voice carrying through the hall and his nose wrinkled in distaste. "Why would de Teilhard think we would help in such an action?"

"The fairy gold," I told him quickly. "I've seen it for myself, up the hill inside his hall. A huge overflowing trunkful of gold, and I doubt Thursk is the rightful owner."

I had their interest now. "If you help me... us, we see no reason why the gold should not be returned to its rightful owners. The Dwarves."

"All things hewn from and originating from the rock are the property of dwarfdom," the one in the back admitted with a gleam in his eye.

Before the conversation could descend into the grumblings of past grudges, IronArms jumped in and addressed the eldest of the group. "You know all the histories. Was this particular gold stolen from us?"

The other shook his wizened head reluctantly, the fluffy white of his beard shaking with the movement. "No, there is no record of any gold taken from these hills," he said. "The gold must belong to another Dwarf Kingdom. I have no doubt it was stolen once upon a time, but as it is not ours, we cannot claim it. By Law."

His crafty eyes glittered towards me. "De Teilhard would not have made this mistake," he said. "De Teilhard is honorable, and would never think to set up false bribes to work factions against each other."

At this a deathly silence came over the hall and all looked towards me.

"And I want to know, why would the Kin send such a stripling to carry this very strange and irregular request?" IronArms spoke up, his voice suspicious.

"Because, because I am not part of the Convention," I said in desperation, rising to my feet. "So I'm not going against it if I don't belong to it. And thus I have certain freedoms, less restraints on me. But, I see you are not open to this, so I will bid you all adieu, and apologies for interrupting your supper hour."

A hubbub of outraged Dwarfish sensitivities followed me as I fled to the door. Dad was going to hear about this latest exploit, of that there was no doubt, but at least they weren't chasing me to bring me before him themselves. I reached the door and shut it again behind me, pausing to collect my thoughts in the fresh breeze coming off the harbor.

Before I could shift back from Alt a small sound alerted me to another's presence. It was the young dwarf who had sat next to me at the table, slipping out the heavy door before closing it softly. I paused, ready to take off at the first hint of threat.

"Wait a moment," he said. "We should talk."

He came over to where I waited and drew me underneath the outcropping of rock so as not to be seen if any of the other dwarves came out of the tunnel.

"My name is Dirk," he said.

"What sort of name is that for a dwarf?" There was not the slightest bit of boast in that moniker, nothing to tell the world about the bearer's strengths.

"I don't go for all the old ways," he said shortly, pulling himself up to stand a little taller. "I'm a modernist."

"I appreciate you offering your assistance, but the rest of them... they said no, they don't want to get involved."

He shook his head. Instead of the usual dwarf intricate braids, he wore his hair in a simple bun. Dirk's eyes burned with passion as he spoke. "They're fools, so caught up in the old ways and tradition. They don't see the possibilities."

"You'll get into trouble," I warned him. "IronArms explicitly said no."

"It's worth the risk. Think of what we could do with the gold. We could invest, become a force to be reckoned with. Why should the witches have the monopoly on wealth?"

"But it doesn't belong to your kingdom, the old guy said so."

"Does the little matter of ownership of wealth bother the witches? Does it stop them amassing whatever they can? No. We, as a collective, need to get with the times."

"You'll help me get the baby out of there?"

He shrugged. "I want the gold the fairies are hoarding. They have no use for it except to lure humans in, and they don't have any understanding what can be done with it."

"You're not afraid of them?"

"I have an iron sword," he said, and spat on the ground. "I don't fear those vermin."

I thought about it while I sized him up. He was short, but solidly confident in his stance. A dwarf motivated by idealistic greed was perhaps not the best partner for this venture, but I didn't have anyone else.

"I have to go back for Chorale or they'll miss me," he said. "Wait out here tomorrow evening after the dining hour. You'll need to stay hidden, just in case, but I'll come out when I can get free. If anything comes up, leave a note in this cleft here." He indicated a narrow slot where shale had eroded.

We took our leave, and I rode back slowly along Southside Road under the streetlights of real time. Being in Alt for such an extended time was exhausting.

I had no idea whether I would be able to make our rendezvous or not, because my actions tonight would only have strengthened Dad's resolve to get me the hell out of this town, and he would definitely be hearing about it tomorrow.

CHAPTER 16

As I got out of Alt and rode down Southside Road back towards Alice's house, her phone started pinging like crazy.

I didn't bother checking it. It was either her trying to find me, or someone else looking for Alice in which case I couldn't help them. I let myself in her back door.

"Where have you been?" She looked up from where she was sitting at her kitchen table, her face even paler than usual. "I expected you an hour ago!"

"I thought I'd see if I could round up some help."

"Your phone has been going nuts here. I didn't answer it. Your Dad's looking for you, and someone called H. Who's that?"

"No one," I said, hedging. "Just a friend."

"I know all your friends," she said, suspicion tingeing her voice. "You've got me, and that dumb ghost in your house, and Maundy doesn't phone."

"He's no one, all right?"

"Hey! You got a boyfriend? You didn't tell me about a guy!"

I'd never told her about any of the guys I'd been with, because Alice just didn't understand the allure of sex or things like that, she preferred her books. I knew for a fact she was still a virgin.

"No," I said. "Look, he's something to do with my father, okay? I think he's a friend of Sasha's. He's not from here."

"Euw, I don't like your sister."

"Me neither."

Sasha. She'd changed so much over the past few months, I mean physically, getting even thinner and so gaunt her cheekbones looked like knives. Hanging out with Seth wasn't good for her, and if I didn't know her better, I might even worry about her. But she was just an anorexic bitch.

I sighed. I needed Alice's help for Operation Benjy, seeing as there was just me and the dwarf so far. I hoped she could be counted on to grab the baby when we got into the fairy den, and not get swallowed up by the fairy illusion. It was going to be rough, though.

"Alice, we're going to try to rescue Benjy tomorrow evening. And the baby."

She didn't say a word. I could see the battle inside her between her rational scientific side and what she knew to be the truth.

"Who's we?"

"You, me ... and a guy I met."

"Is that H?"

"No, but..." Just the three of us, and Alice with no idea of her own powers, it was going to be tough to get both Benjy and the baby away, not to mention the gold for Dirk. Maybe I could make a bargain with Hugh...

"Maybe Hugh, I don't know," I amended.

"Not Sasha though?" She screwed up her face.

"No way, not my sister."

"What are we going to do?"

"I haven't gotten that far yet," I admitted. "I'm going to think about that tonight. But you'll need to be outside the first tunnel door tomorrow at six pm. Under the rock face that sticks out."

"What, the tunnels on Southside Road? They're all blocked off, and I'm not going into those tunnels at night!"

"No, we're not doing that. We're just meeting there. Can I count on you?"

"I have a lab tomorrow evening..."

"Do you want Benjy back?"

"Yes, but Dara, all this stuff," she said. "Fairies? Really? They didn't take the baby, I saw Jane today, the baby is fine, just a couple of sniffles. This is all pretty crazy, don't you think?"

Jesus, were we back at square one again? My friend, the Queen of Denial.

"Alice, the fairies are all about illusion," I said. "That baby you saw is a changeling. Trust me on this."

"And about those illusions... I don't know if I can be of much help to you, if all this is true," she continued. "When we were up the hill, in that gorgeous room under the rock, you say you saw something totally different from what I saw. How do we know I won't get swept up in that again? You say they cast spells. I have no protection against that, not like you."

I looked at Alice, looked at her slenderness and height, the wispy fine long hair that was such a light brown it was colorless. Yeah, this kid had elf blood in her. And then I remembered my own awakening, the realization of the power I held in my very genes.

"You're never powerless, Alice," I told her. I leaned over the table closer to her. "You may not know it, but Nan Hoskins told me she had elf blood in her. And you are the very image of her, so I think it's very likely that you do too."

"Elf?" Her cheeks burned red in a flash. "Are you making fun of my ears, Dara? This is hardly the time."

Poor Alice, growing up she'd always been teased about her skinniness, called a string bean and worse, so much so that she had no confidence in her physical looks and no idea of what a gorgeous woman she was now. She'd learned early on to keep her hair over her ears, because they were sort of weird come to think of it, long and sharp. Yes, she definitely had elf blood in her.

"I'm not making fun of anything," I said. "I just think you have some strain of elf in you, so you're probably more powerful than you think."

"Oh, yeah? And what kind of elf powers would I have? What do elves do, can you answer me that?"

I couldn't. "Google it."

So she did. "Oh," she said, sounding pleased. "Says here they have superior intellect."

"Sounds like you."

"Strength, speed, stamina, durability..."

"Tick, tick, tick, umm, maybe not that so much..."

"It's a Germanic word, and seems to mean *white being*..."

Trust her to ignore all the modern references and go straight into the origin of elfdom.

"But it doesn't specify what elf powers are." She looked up at me with those huge gray eyes. "It just says magical powers. How am I supposed to know what my powers are? If they exist, that is."

"No one can answer that but you, Alice," I said. "May be... maybe you don't actually have any magical powers, if you haven't discovered them yet. But you definitely have a streak of elf in you, so that's got to help. You're super-smart, super-fast and really strong."

She was silent for a moment. "So what's the plan for tomorrow evening?"

"I don't know that yet, but I'll work on it."

"If what you say is true, and I think it probably is because I couldn't see the reality of the fairies like you could, how are we going to convince Benjy to leave?"

"He may have already seen through the illusion," I said. "At least that's what I'm hoping. It could be that he knows now he is enslaved by their enchantment, so he'll go along with us. If not..."

If not, there was no way the three of us would be able to get him out of there.

....

IronArms didn't tell Dad about my visit the next morning. No, he had to pass on that juicy bit of news right that very same evening.

Dad pulled up to Richmond Cottage in his gigantic midnight blue Mercedes SUV just as I was letting myself in the back door. He almost hit the railings, he was in such a fury.

We entered the house like a couple of cats squalling.

"Just stop it, the pair of you!" Edna's hands were over her ears and her eyes squeezed together in pain. She hated noise and uncontrolled emotion, she had a hard time blocking them out. "What is going on?"

He crossed his arms and leaned against the counter. I'd never realized before what a big man he was. He was taking up a lot of space in that kitchen. "Yes, Dara, we'd all like an explanation of *what is going on*."

I slumped into my usual seat at the kitchen table. Edna wouldn't want to hear this, she preferred her ostrich life with her head in the sand.

"I'll tell you," I said, sounding as miserable as I felt. All I'd needed were twenty-four hours, and I could have saved Benjy, replaced the baby and no one would be any the wiser. One day, that's all. But now it was totally gone to shit. "But..."

I looked at Edna. So did Dad.

"Edna," he said, as he flicked his head towards the hallway. "You don't need to hear this."

And she surprised me. "I think I do," she said as she came and sat by me, taking my hand firmly in hers.

"You know what this will concern," he said. "And you are not to be a part of this conversation."

"Don't try to bully me, Jon," she said with quiet strength. "Dara is my concern, so anything you guys are going to talk about, I need to know, and I need to be here."

I was touched by the love, I really was, but I wished she would get the hell out of there. It was going to be hard enough just telling Dad who understood all about the supernatural elements in town, without having to explain the details to my aunt and having to deal with her disbelief. She knew about Dad being a witch, but had never asked for the details of other supernaturals.

I bit my lip and shook my head. "No, Edna, he's right," I said. "We can't have you here."

She looked at me and made to get up, then changed her mind.

"No," she said. "I did that before, I left so the witches could talk, and Marian disappeared. We've never seen her since. I'm staying right here, and I'm holding on to Dara. You're not taking another person away from me, Jon."

She let go of my hand and moved her arm around my shoulders and held tight, then stared back up at Dad.

He glowered at us both, his dark eyes turned to flint.

"Fine," he said shortly. "You can stay. But keep out of the conversation."

He turned to me directly and spoke, his voice tight. "You lied and misrepresented me. This is an unforgivable embarrassment."

"I'm sorry," I said. "But I told you I needed help, and you weren't giving me any. I thought maybe I could get them on board."

'They' were the dwarves of course, but we were speaking shorthand for Edna's benefit. What she didn't know wouldn't screw up her head.

"I am a well-respected member of this community," he continued. "You acted in flagrant disregard to the Convention, to *them* of all the communities, and they're the ones who wrote the bloody laws!"

"How was I to know that?"

"You could have some sense!"

"And where would I have picked up this sense? At the school you sent me to? I learned all about Newfoundland history, funny they didn't include the bit about Alt Town!"

I'd been sent to no school, of course, just the Normal public school system. It was his own fault I was in total ignorance of the supernatural conventions and laws.

"Right, that does it," he said, the sparks now flying from his eyes. He didn't like it when anyone pointed out his lapses in judgement. "You're leaving. Tomorrow."

"No!" Me and Edna both shouted at once. We looked at each other in surprise.

"You're not sending her anywhere, Jon. She's staying right here with me." She gave me an extra squeeze with her arm.

"Edna, keep out of it," he said. "You don't understand the danger she's put herself into."

Danger? My heart sank. I didn't need more crap piled on me at that moment. I was already steeling myself against the perils of making a raid on the fairy hall.

He must have seen the expression on my face, for he gave a quick nod.

"Yes, danger in spreading around the word that you're a half-blood," he said, his mouth set in a grim line, and he turned to Edna. "You heard about the young woman's body found out by Portugal Cove?"

I could feel her body stiffening. Her grasp on my shoulder was becoming painful.

"She was a mixed blood," he continued. "Not from here, but from another branch of the family who'd left fifty years ago. She wandered into town looking for her roots. Didn't understand the political situation here right now, and got in with the wrong crowd of witches. Need I say more?"

He didn't. The persecutions were starting again.

"Right then. If you're so determined to let everyone know you're a daughter of mine, you'll have to stay under my protection. Under my roof. At least until we get to the bottom of that woman's death.'

This was an added complication I really didn't need right then. That baby wasn't getting any younger.

"Can't I just stay here?" I pleaded. "I promise, Edna will know where I am at all times. You can ... you can even put a spell on the house, or me, or whatever you need to do."

He shook his head. "You really are so ignorant, and I admit, it's my own fault. I thought the best way to keep you safe was to remove you totally from the supernatural elements. Sorry, no spells. Things don't work that way. No, you'll be coming with me as that's the only way I can protect you. Go, pack your bag with whatever you'll need for the next few days."

"But I have tests coming up! I'll need to go in to school." I was searching for any out I could find.

He laughed. It was not a pretty sound. "*Now* you worry about your marks? Don't be ridiculous. Your life is far more important."

I could feel Dad's eyes on me as I slumped back at the table.

"Believe me, it's not that I want you there," he said, almost hissing his words. "You've brought this on yourself. It's entirely your own work."

Even Edna saw that she had to let go and give me up to his care.

"I want you to keep in close contact, okay?" she whispered in my ear as I was set to follow Dad out to his car. She held me tight as if she was never going to see me again.

My phone. Shit. It was still with Alice, and I still had hers.

"Look, me and Alice mixed up our phones," I said quietly as my arms lingered in the hug. "So if you need to talk with me, call her cell, okay?" I knew she had my friend's number somewhere.

I climbed up into the passenger seat as if it were into the jaws of a monster. Dad drove erratically all the way into the east end, which was not like him and just showed how upset he was. I didn't realized he'd gotten on the Blue Tooth till I heard Cate's hated voice fill the vehicle.

"Get the spare room ready," he barked. "We have another visitor staying."

"The painters are still working on the north room," she complained. "Jon, I really don't have room for another of your friends. This is the limit!"

"You can put her up in the garret, then, that's even better," he said.

"The garret? Are you mad?" Then she paused. "This isn't that child of yours, is it? Jon, I said she was not to come into my house again under any circumstances, and you know I meant it."

Great, now I had to look forward to Cate's warm welcome.

"It would be easier if I just stayed home," I remarked out loud. "I agree with Cate. And the feeling is mutual, by the way." *Bitch.*

"Shut up, both of you," he said in his grimmest voice. "This is the way it is, and I don't want any more grief."

She clicked off the line without another word, and he also said nothing else on the whole way to his house.

The private laneway was pitch black, and something small squealed as he tore up the gravel. I hope it jumped free, whatever it was, as he certainly wasn't going to stop to check if it was hurt. The mansion loomed above us.

He kept my door locked as he jumped out and came round the vehicle, then a quick click. My father opened my door himself and grasped me by my arm, hauling me down out of the SUV.

"That's really not necessary, *Dad*," I said, wishing I could make myself sound less like a sulky teenager who'd been found in an all-night bar. I couldn't shake off his grip, no matter how hard I tried.

He walked me inside the back door and through the passage into the kitchen. It had been renovated in the many years since I'd been there last, all gleaming steel appliances with everything else black and white, right down to the new chequered marble floors. It looked cold, efficient and soulless, not like Edna's run-down room with the wheezing fridge and painted cupboards and colorful works of art everywhere. Cate must feel really at home in this space.

And Sasha. My half-sister was sitting on one of the stools at the breakfast bar, the bright shiny expensive chrome ones. A sneer was already on her sharp face.

"Oh, Dad," she said. "Really? Since when have we accepted her into the family?"

"It's not my choice, believe me," I told her. "I don't want anything to do with this house *or* its inhabitants."

"Show her up to the garret, Sasha."

"What, you're locking me in the room all night? I've been bad, so I have to go to my room without any supper?"

He sighed as if the robes of villainy wore heavily on him.

"Sash, what's in the fridge? I could do with a bite too."

She shrugged. "Your supper's still in the oven," she said. "I suppose you can share it with her."

And that's all the help she was prepared to give. With a flick of her long black hair, she stalked through the kitchen door and into the depths of the house.

He turned to one of the wall ovens and opened it.

Okay, I hate Cate, right? But that witch can cook. The smell was divine, even though I'd filled up on Indian food a few hours before.

"Tetrazzini okay for you?" He asked this in a tired voice.

I nodded. He got down plates and silverware and glasses. I would have helped, but I didn't know where anything was in this house.

He took a bottle of red wine from the fridge, and cocked an eyebrow at me.

"Sure," I said. I didn't drink alcohol much, hardly at all these days, but I figured this was a good night to start. It might help me to think, because I needed a new plan, and soon.

CHAPTER 17

D ad showed me up to the garret room after we'd finished, leaving the dirty dishes in the sink. Cate was probably going to freak out at that, too, having disorder in her perfect kitchen. Good for him, I thought, stand up to the witch.

He brought me up the back stairs (yes, the old servants' staircase, making sure I knew my place, no doubt.) The uncarpeted steps to the attic level were narrow and cramped, and ended in a small landing with four doors off it, no windows.

He opened the second door to the right and switched on the overhead light. It was the round, turreted room.

Now, I had always been jealous of Sasha's gorgeous round room on the floor below. At least, back when I thought everything pink and princess was the ultimate in cool. And now I had a round room all for myself, but it was hardly as light and airy as I remembered hers to be.

Being in the attic, the ceiling was low. It held a bed with a quilt on it, a rickety table beside it, a saggy looking old armchair and a beat-up chest of drawers. That was it.

Oh, except for the bars on the window.

It wasn't decorated very nicely either. It looked more like a Seventies' half-assed renovation job – someone had attempted to cover up the old Edwardian stripes of white and yellow with the god-awful earth-tone designs of that later era. They tired of the effort mid-job and wandered away, never to return to finish the work.

I dropped my knapsack onto the old plain rug which covered most of the floorboards, and we both stared around at the unwelcoming space.

"Well." Dad cleared his throat. "It's not for long."

He looked over to the windows, the bars visible through the lights of the city far below. "It used to be the nursery once upon a time. Really, this is the last spare room we have."

"Oh, well, here we are," I said. "Don't forget to lock the door on your way out."

"Christ, Dara! You're not a prisoner," he said, towering over me with a face like a thundercloud. "This is for your own safety, can't you see that? You've been meddling in things beyond your ken, you've reneged on our agreement, and this is the only way..."

"The only way you can control me?"

"I wouldn't put it like that, but if you insist."

I plunked myself onto the single bed. The old iron springs creaked. I was confused, but he was beginning to get through to me. His actions stemmed from love, or responsibility, or something like that, not because he hated me.

"There's no TV in here," he said in a much calmer voice. "You're welcome to come down to the... family room."

"Right," I said. "Maybe I'll just stick in my room for tonight. I have an essay to finish, and studying to do, you know."

He nodded. "The bathroom is across the hall. There's always towels there. If you get hungry or need anything, just go down to the kitchen and look for it," he said. "And please, treat my home as yours."

Before he left the room, I stopped him.

"I don't suppose there's a spare reading lamp? I hate the overhead light, it's too bright."

A smile slowly worked its way across his face. "Marian was particular about lighting, too," he said softly. "Let's look in the other rooms up here, I'm sure there's got to be something."

We poked around in the other two attic rooms. They held the detritus of years, things too good to be thrown out or given away, but still not to the liking of the present inhabitants of the house.

"This is pretty cool," I noted, pointing to a heavy looking lamp tucked away in a corner. It was made to look like a huge old lantern, the kind with a glass base to hold the oil and another glass funnel to contain the flame, where the modern light bulb sat. There was an oversize shade to go with it.

Dad reached over and affixed the shade, then picked the whole thing up.

"This is a solid one," he said, grunting with the effort. "Let me bring it in for you."

He laid it on the small bedside table and plugged it in. The bulb still worked.

I looked at the layer of dust over it all, and at his shirt front.

"Uh oh," I said, pointing at the soiled white silk.

"No matter, it's only dust," he said as he brushed at it. "A trip to the drycleaners, and it'll be as good as new."

He paused at the door. "Dara," he began.

I looked up at him. The expression on his face was almost tender. "Thanks, Dad," I said. "I mean it. Sorry for... everything I did."

I bit my bottom lip. I really was sorry for the havoc, and he didn't even know the half of it yet. He would be absolutely furious when he found out.

He nodded. "I know you are," he said. "We need to talk, but there's lots of time for that tomorrow. Have a good night." He flicked off the overhead before shutting the door.

I lay back on the pillows and stared around at my new refuge. In this softer light, it really wasn't so bad. The Edwardian yellow stripes actually worked with the mustards and reds of the seventies abstract blobs, in a weird sort of way. And after a while, you didn't even notice the bars on the windows.

I could hear the muffled sounds of Dad's family in the house below me as they did their evening things, and through the closed window the faint sound of a car pulling up. I didn't know who all was home or which of the four kids were still living here, aside from Sasha of course.

There was not going to be any studying happening that night, I soon realized, as the math book lay forgotten on my lap. My head was too full of things I needed to sort out.

Like... Dad. His mention of Mom had really floored me. I took out the photo from my wallet, the one taken one summer day so long ago, years before she disappeared. She was dancing in a field of daisies, it must have been July, maybe somewhere in the fields around Torbay, and I was trailing behind her in that pink chiffon dress with the sequins dotted over the skirt. Back when I thought pink was cool and fairies were friendly.

The photographer had captured her smile and delight in life, in that moment of time. I sat up. Who had taken that picture? Whoever it was, there was a strong bond between them, you could see the adoration in her eyes as she looked their way. There were no barriers, no guardedness there.

Was it Dad behind the camera? He had spoken her name with tenderness. And... I'd never thought about it before, but he must have loved her tremendously to defy the strict conventions of his life and position, to take up with a Normal and even have a child with her.

He couldn't be the one behind her disappearance, the love and pain in his eyes told me that. Which left only one other person who could be responsible. It had to be his wife.

What had Cate done to my mother?

I lifted my head and stared at the window bars in horror. He had brought me to her house and effectively jailed me in the lair of my mother's enemy, the woman who had to be responsible for – what? Mom's death?

No. She wasn't dead, at least she hadn't been when she'd hidden the book of spells in the library book case.

Yet if she wasn't dead, why would she have left me?

I couldn't even think of what that witch had done to my mother.

And if Jon had loved Marian so much, how could he have allowed this to happen? My heart was torn between wanting to believe that their love had been real, yet seeing the evidence before my eyes, the fact that he had opted to stay with Cate even after she had removed his loved one. Had his love for Mom been that false, that shallow?

No, I couldn't believe that. My mind was racing so much it didn't know where to land. I threw myself back on the bed and shut my eyes tight and forced myself to breathe deeply.

Yes, perhaps Dad did love me, even if only for my mother's sake, but his caring actions had only made my present job harder. It was going to be difficult to get away from this prison and make my way across town to meet Dirk and Alice in time for our raid on the fairy den tomorrow evening.

And I didn't have a plan ironed out yet, either. How on earth would the three of us manage to swoop in, take what we wanted and get out without being torn apart by those sharp fairy teeth?

Alice was the weakest link, I knew. Despite the signs of her being part elf, she had no notion of what power she had or how she could use it, if she did in fact have any. Perhaps I could task her with grabbing the baby while Dirk guarded her with his iron sword. Saving the child was, after all, the most important objective.

Me and the dwarf would be able to see through the enchantments, while Alice could not. So I would run towards Benjy and unloose the bounds the fairies had placed on him and drag him out. Yes, he was a full grown man and I was smaller than him, but he would also be weak from being in the hall for so long. Even if he struggled against me, I figured I could take him on.

How Dirk would access the fairy gold I knew not and cared less, as long as I got the humans out of there safely.

A faint sound caught my awareness, a stealthy foot on the creaky wooden steps to the attic. It wasn't Dad's confident tread, and there were no other inhabited rooms up here, I'd seen that for myself. The person making their quiet way up those stairs was coming with the sole intent of seeing me.

And torturing me, I had no doubt. A sibling? Or worse, Cate herself.

I tensed, ready to jump up and attack if necessary, or at least scream the roof down.

A soft knock came at the door and I let out my breath. At least it wasn't going to be an angry confrontation.

It sounded again.

"What? Who is it?"

The ancient brass door knob twisted slowly, and the door opened.

"Okay to come in?" I heard the soft northern Scottish accent as he peeked his head round the painted wood.

"Hugh? What are you doing here?"

"Same as you," he said as he entered the room and quietly pushed the door closed till it clicked. "I'm a guest of Jon's. Cate's not too happy about having me here, either. Oh, and keep your voice down, Sasha's room is right below us."

He looked around. I scooted my legs over to allow him on the bed. The slight fragrance of his soap brought a welcome freshness to the dusty stale room and as he shifted himself back onto the mattress, the muscles on his shoulders moved against the fabric of his t-shirt.

"I didn't know you were staying here," I whispered as I laid my long-forgotten text book aside.

"Jon invited me when the first rumblings of trouble began," he said. "When the prejudice began to rear its ugly head again. He wants to open the minds of the Kin, help bring them into the twenty-first century. It's only through working together can we thrive, as a group."

He sighed. "It's an uphill battle though, I'm afraid. He's working against infighting factions and small minds."

"What's your part in it?"

"I have the blessing of the EURO's behind me," he said. "The European Union of Realtech Operations, it's a ... oh, I won't get into that. Suffice it to say, it's the formal convergence of the European witch community."

"Good luck with that," I said, remembering the harsh words given to me by my own siblings about my half-blood ever since Mom's disappearance. Their attitudes had been learned from Cate, I knew, and she was a product of her own Kin. As I said, prejudices ran high in this town. "You being a half-blood and all."

"Enough about me," he said as he turned his golden green eyes to stare right at me. "What gives?"

"What did Dad tell you?" I shrugged as I hedged.

"Little, except he was in a fury earlier this evening after a visit from a certain Mr. IronArms. He seems to have calmed down about it now."

"Hmmm," I said. Maybe Hugh didn't know about the baby. Dad would know, for the dwarf would have delighted in telling him exactly which conventions his daughter had broken, and on which page of the constitution he would find these broken rules.

"So, the dwarves." He leaned against the footboard of the old iron bedstead and turned to me, waiting for me to tell him.

"Umm." I wrapped my arms around my knees and rested my chin on them. Believe me, I had the mind blocks up full force, and I was getting pretty good at it. Unfortunately, I knew that he could sense this.

If we had Hugh's help tomorrow night, we would be assured of success, yet if I broke down and spilled the whole story to him, he wouldn't help me. No, he would work with Dad to get me on the first plane out of here tomorrow for my own safety. Never mind Benjy and the baby, they were natural collateral damage in the Rule of Law of this strange world I'd gotten myself mixed up in.

The ironic thing was, I'd secretly decided that I did want to get training for my powers, I needed it. But not yet. I would gladly leave as soon as this business was all over. Screw university – I was only marking time there anyway; it was never what my heart called for. But it was the only card I held right now.

I had to trick Hugh, but I hardly dared to form the thought in my head for fear he would sniff it out. Yet perhaps I could fill my head with another truth, and this would shine over my other, more insidious plans.

"I do want to be trained," I said. "I want it more than anything, now that I've found out I can be, that training actually exists and I can have it, me, a half-blood."

He relaxed and smiled at me, the light glowing in his eyes.

"Yes," he said. "I'm so glad you see the sense of this. Finally. You've got strong powers, and you need to develop them, learn how to use them."

"But not yet," I said. "I really need to pass this semester. I'm sort of on probation with the university right now, and I don't want to mess up my chances of finishing that degree." I peeped up at him to see how he'd take this.

"I wouldn't worry about that," he replied, waving aside my worries with a flick of his hand. "Your marks here are meaningless. Your father can use his influence to get you in anywhere you want to go. You're not stuck at the local uni, you know. You can go anywhere in the world you want to."

"Maybe I want to go *here*," I said, bristling a little. I needed this excuse to buy me time. "This is a perfectly good school. It's not Oxford or Yale, but it's fine. This is my home town, you know."

He gave me a funny look that held no clue as to what he was thinking. "Your loyalty is admirable. Misplaced, but rather sweet."

"I need to keep going to classes," I urged him. "And I have a test tomorrow. You have to help me persuade Dad to let me out of the house. I'll be safe, I'll keep my head down and out of trouble."

I silently crossed my fingers as I stared at him, imploring.

He nodded as he got up off the bed. "I'll see what I can do."

....

Thank God this family didn't go in for a formal breakfast table. By getting up early and sneaking downstairs for a quick bite, I was able to avoid the lot of them.

As I stood and chewed, I looked around the kitchen. It didn't look like my idea of a witch's kitchen – no herbs hanging from rafters, no cats sprawled before the ovens, no crooked stovepipes or crooked anything. As all my knowledge of witches and the supernatural came from books, it was no wonder I knew nothing about the reality of witchcraft and the ways of witches.

I actually felt excited about going away to learn. It felt right and good. But not yet.

First I had a fairy hall to raid, with the added complication of being grounded in my father's house.

Hugh was the key. I would somehow convince him to bring me over to the Southside Hills when he picked me up again at MUN this afternoon, and from there I could trick him into providing assistance. I hoped.

CHAPTER 18

I hadn't lied to Dad about the exam that morning, the one I was totally unprepared for. Stupid Math 1010, having tests so early in the semester. I'd breezed through this subject in highschool with Alice at the desk next to me. Not that she *allowed* me to cheat off her, of course, but she never suspected a thing. And what she didn't know had never hurt her.

And I hadn't been physically looking over her shoulder or anything, I only allowed her mind to help me with the answers. I'd never examined the process, I just let it come naturally.

But at university, Alice had sped past me easily, already having her maths component done and working now through Statistics, which I didn't intend to touch. History, English, Folklore, with a smattering of German and Linguistics – that was more my style, the courses I could bullshit my way through if necessary. But I had to take basic math, those were the rules.

Hugh convinced Dad to let me go to classes, and I hopped on to the back of his motorcycle. I could easily have walked or taken the bus from Dad's house, but neither of them were taking any chances with me. The greatest joy that morning was seeing Sasha's cranky face peering through the window as we sped off down the drive, me clutching Hugh tightly on the back of his bike. I gave her a third finger salute as we turned down the lane.

·····•·····

As if I didn't have enough on my mind, I was thinking as I stared down at the paper on the desk in front of me. Greek? It could have been. I wished I'd been paying more attention in class those few times I'd attended.

But then a wisp of an idea came to me. Alice had been as familiar as my own skin, but could I make this power work with someone I didn't know? Like, actually get inside the head of someone who knew what they were doing with this exam? I'd learned pretty quickly how to block my thoughts from Hugh, and he was a powerful witch.

A surreptitious glance around and I found my prey, that guy to my left, the one with the unwashed hair whose name I could never remember. We'd spoken a few times, hung out at the cafeteria so I already had a small connection with him. I sent out mental feelers, just relaxed and let my antennae waft in his direction. I didn't have a clue how this worked, but this was a good time to learn.

And the trick, I found, was not to try and not to think about it. I set my pencil at approximately the same place on the page as he was at, and I let it flow. Whatever this was, it was working. I was channelling the nerd.

Sort of hard to explain how I was doing this. It was just that, in the moment right before he wrote on the paper, what he intended to write flashed through his mind and so in to mine, and I could see the letters and numbers and copied them down as fast as I could.

This guy was smart! We were done in record time. After he left, I spent a few minutes trying to figure out the first equation. I didn't try too hard, as no one expected a perfect test result from me.

With this hurdle out of the way, I now had the whole day to figure out the evening's plan and who I was going to get to help me. I had seriously considered Hugh, I really did, but on second and third thought I acknowledged that there was no way he would ever lend assistance. He was a stickler for rules, and going to the fairy den to steal back Benjy and the baby would be absolutely verboten in his eyes. Not to mention Dirk's plan to help himself to the fairy gold.

The only other witch I knew was my sister, the one who hated my very existence. Oh man, this was not going to be easy, but I didn't have much choice, did I? I just hoped I could find her without Seth being there.

I think I said before, Sasha and I had gotten along pretty well in the few times we'd been together as little kids, before Cate realized what was going on and put the kibosh to our friendship. I had actually felt really at home with her, I remember feeling like I belonged.

We had played magic games in my garden at Richmond Cottage, little kids learning to stretch and develop our powers. It had come to us as natural as running and tumbling down the steep slopes, learning balance and how to fall.

These memories were only coming back to me recently, I must have put them away when Edna told me to, taking my cue from her fear of all things supernatural and related to my father. But we *had* played with magic, having competitions like who could shoot the blue energy from our fingertips the furthest, or who could lift the heaviest object without touching it. How could I have forgotten these things?

We hadn't been very friendly in the past few years, but I was confident I could call on her for help in this time of need, perhaps appeal to the kinship we had once shared. Never mind I was a half-blood, for I was beginning to rediscover that I did in fact have magical powers, and the witch blood in my veins was the same as ran through hers. Surely that must count for something?

Still feeling rather smug about my success with the exam, I did the stupidest thing imaginable. I walked into the lion's den.

I deliberately chose to seek out my sister in to the Arts Building cafe, the one at the top of the atrium that the Kin crowd had long ago claimed as their own territory. Of course Sasha would be surrounded by her friends here, and that was my first mistake.

It was a spacious yet cozy room, with tall ceilings and windows looking east over the campus and down into the glassed-in space at the heart of the Arts Building. This was the perfect place in which to feel like you were on the top of the world, and the Kin students treated it like their own private sanctum. Outsiders were not welcome. And despite my genetic heritage, I was still an outsider in their eyes.

The large airy room became deathly quiet as I strolled up to the counter, everything silent except for the hum of the refrigerators. I could feel twelve pairs of eyes on my back, then the low buzz of whispers growing.

With coffee in hand, I turned around to face the room. My eyes met those of my sister, widened in surprise at my daring, with a little horror thrown in too. She was sitting by Seth, of course.

"Hey, Sasha," I said, and nodded in her direction.

She quickly turned away to her companions. I'd gone to school with most of these kids, known them half of my life, all except for her boyfriend. They were the 'perfect' crowd, all of them beautiful and clever and entitled, for Kin were always so much more polished than the rest of us, as if their wealth ran them through a machine which honed all their brilliance before spitting them out into the world. Or maybe it was their magic which gave them the extra glamour.

Sasha was, of course, looking hot today. Her long black hair shone like a stream in the sunlight and her black and white print dress was perfectly fitted to her form, not showing cleavage but still way more sexy than any student had a right to be. Her lacquered nails were a tasteful red and the whole ensemble was set off by her matching red suede heels.

Yet her face was pale beneath that perfect complexion.

I straightened my shoulders to allow my own hoodie to hang gracefully on my body, but yeah, I couldn't help but feel like a frumpish teenager in my rumpled jeans and scuffed sneakers. With a flick of my unbrushed hair I ignored her ignoring me and boldly took the table by the window overlooking the inside of the building below, my back to the lot of them.

Frig them all. This half-blood witch was claiming her rightful place in society, and they were going to have to get used to it.

I took out my notebook to set out my plan for the evening because I've always found it easier to write when I'm thinking. No sooner had I put pen to paper than the pages riffled as if in a breeze.

Sasha's false tinkling laugh sounded over the buzz of conversation.

"Stop that," she said in a teasing scold to one of her companions.

Then I heard the words 'her father's bastard' whispered loudly, reverberating around the room.

The coffee in my cup began to shimmer and shake, and in mere moments small perfect waves were forming on the top. The paper cup itself didn't move a millimeter as the tiny storm grew and coffee began to slosh over the top and splash onto the table.

A burst of laughter sounded behind me. I continued to ignore my sister and her pack of hyenas. I merely wiped up the spills and set back to writing. I glanced up to the cafeteria worker, to see if she had noticed anything out of the ordinary, but she had her back firmly turned to the room. There was no one else in the cafeteria to witness these strange happenings.

But my pen was suddenly working against me, and the words I wrote were not my own.

Half-blood! Half-blood!

The accusation stared up at me. I tried to control the pen physically but just ended up with a huge gash down the middle of the page, the nib cutting through to the paper below.

"Noah!" But whatever else Sasha said to him was lost in the screams of laughter from her friends.

I shut my book, laid down the pen and turned in my seat to confront them. I couldn't fight them on their own grounds. Not yet, but that didn't mean I was powerless.

"Hey, sister," I said, with nonchalance in my voice.

She winced slightly at my direct attack.

"You're no sister of mine," she said, darting a quick glance at her companions. "You're an accident of nature. A freak."

"You might not want to be drawing attention to yourself," one guy drawled. He wore a purple shirt with large white polka dots on it. He could get away with it because it was silk and obviously expensive, and his hair was all quiffed up. His face looked like it had been photoshopped.

"Half-bloods are dropping all over the place," another noted.

"Like flies."

"And the air is becoming... pure." This was said by the largest guy, who leaned back in his chair in his pressed white linen shirt and a menacing smile on his lips, leaving me in no doubt what he meant.

My heart literally skipped a couple of beats. Were they claiming responsibility for the murder of that poor woman, Tracey, the half-blood witch? Suddenly I felt very small, vulnerable and exposed.

Sasha shifted uncomfortably.

"Oh, run away home, why don't you?" This in a bored voice, but then she caught herself, no doubt remembering that my home was now, albeit temporarily, hers. The venomous look she threw me dared me to bring that up.

"Of course, she's going to be exiled soon enough," she added to her friends. "And sent far away, out of our hair."

"The sooner the better," one girl said.

"Perhaps we should round up all the half-bloods," White Shirt said. His lips were thin and mean. "Send them out to colonize some island off the coast."

"What, like Alcatraz?"

"That's far too hospitable," said Polka Dot Quiff. "Kolyma in the Siberian Sea might do better."

"A gulag, no less!"

Ten voices laughed and cheered. Seth had not made a sound the whole time I'd been there, but his eyes hadn't left my face, and I could feel the hungering start. It was just magic, I told myself. See through the illusion, don't allow him in like the other day. Don't let that happen – I'd get eaten alive here in the witches' eyrie.

Sasha brushed imaginary crumbs off her skirt, then looked up at me impatiently. "Just go, would you?" She spoke in a low, urgent voice.

"I came up here to speak with you," I said, far more bravely than I felt. "Do you mind?"

She shrugged, not meeting my eyes. "I doubt we have anything to say to each other."

I stood up and moved over to where she was sitting. "I need to speak with you, in private."

Her friends laughed amongst themselves, still openly mocking me. Sasha was turning red in the face.

"In private," I hissed again.

She glanced towards Seth, and he nodded slightly still with his eyes on me, and a small smile formed on his lips. I don't know, but it looked an awful lot like my sister was asking permission to speak with me. What the hell? The Sasha I knew had guys dangling from her fingertips like puppets; always in control and uber-confident.

If that's what love looked like, I wanted nothing to do with it.

We took the table furthest away from everyone, right in the corner under the supersized spider plant and I sat right next to her.

"Look, I know you don't like me..." I began, speaking in a low voice.

"What are you doing here?" she broke in with a harsh whisper. If I didn't know her better, I'd say she was nervous, but nothing had ever fazed my sister. "Why can't you just... stay under the radar, like Dad told you to do?"

"What's going on with you, Sassy?" The nickname from childhood slipped out. "You've changed, some-thing's bothering you... I'm not interested in your boyfriend, you know, if that's what's bugging you."

She gave me an incredulous look and drew herself together, smoothing the skirt of her dress. "Tell me what you want to say and then go."

"I need your help."

"I can't help you with anything," she almost spit at me. Her face was taut and showing how tense she still was.

"I've gotten in over my head," I continued, still keep-ing my voice to the barest minimum, and motioned her to come even closer. She reluctantly bent her head toward me.

In as few words as possible, I told her everything, all about Benjy and the fairies and the baby and the dwarves and the evening's plan. Her eyes grew wider and more horrified with each sentence.

She glanced over to the backs of her friends. Seth was now staring off into space, his smile grown to a full blown sneer of triumph.

"Just drop it all," she almost mouthed the words. "Do not get involved. I advise you to call Hugh right now and ask him to come get you."

"I can't do that, can't you see? I'm meeting Alice and Dirk this evening, and I need you to come help me," I said louder than I meant.

A susurration began around the room, the whispers echoing off the high ceiling. I couldn't tell which of the Witch Kin were speaking or who started it.

"Alice."

"Sweet Alice."

"We'll help you, Alice."

"Come play with us, Alice."

"Alice of the half-blood elf-blood."

A chill ran down my spine. Sasha stared at me, the skin around her lipstick almost white.

"Get the hell out of here!" My sister screamed at me. "Leave me alone. Get out of the country while you're at it!"

"While you still can..." This last whisper danced around the dusty sunbeams streaming through the sky-lights.

If I'd known what was happening, what was really afoot, if Sasha had had the decency to take me aside and explain, just a couple of words would have sufficed, I would have grabbed Alice and taken off to the safety of Hugh and Dad and confessed everything, let them put me on a plane to anywhere at all. Never mind Benjy or the baby, frig them both, Alice was my true family and the most important person in my life and I was endangering her.

If I had but known how serious the threat was.

But I didn't, so I chose to cover up my fear through taking the offensive. These fascist bastards had made no secret of their prejudice against half-bloods or that they were cheering on the deaths of my kind. Dad was going to love hearing about the sentiments expressed by Sasha's fine friends. Maybe I wouldn't be the one sent away, after all.

"I'm going, but I'm sure we'll have a lovely chat over the dinner table. *Daddy* will want to know how my day went. And what I've learned about your friends."

I turned and left, but not before I noticed how quickly she stiffened and how quiet the room suddenly became. Damn right I was going to spread the news to Dad and Hugh that this little nest of vipers might be single-handedly responsible for the deaths of innocent people.

Vipers? I did snakes a disservice. They were more like bored, indulgent cats looking for the thrill of torturing and killing for their own amusement, pushing people out of their way like a cat clearing a tabletop the better to stretch out for its own comfort.

I shivered and exited the building to head for the library. I needed to deepen my research into the supernatural and perhaps what I might be capable of, for tonight was getting ever closer and I still didn't have a workable plan to free Benjy and the baby.

CHAPTER 19

I found a reference to an old court case from 1880 that looked promising, a man suing his boss for lost wages due to the fact that he'd been taken away by the fairies on his way to work and thus unable to show up to his job. It was pretty cool that none of the people involved – the judge, the boss, the lawyers for both sides – not one of them questioned the likelihood of the existence of fairies, they only quibbled about making up the lost time. However, the report didn't explain how he got away from the fairies, so that didn't end up helping me.

Using new search words on the library computer, I stumbled across a source I'd never heard of before. This got me excited and put the whole run-in with the Witch Kin students out of my mind.

My Life Amongst the Fine Folk, and How I Escaped Theire Clutches was a small book from the early 1700's, purporting to be one man's tale of his trials with the fairies and how he managed to get away from them. It sounded like it would be really promising for information on how to defeat those supernaturals, and I needed all the ideas I could get.

It was stored in the Rare Documents section of the Archives, way down in the basement and far removed from the dangers of dampness and sunlight. I didn't mind going down there, it was just an unpleasant route along the long, empty corridor. A very ill-lit corridor.

My sneakers made little sound on the concrete floor, yet I could hear echoes of steps in time with my own. I looked back, and I looked ahead. I could see the whole hallway, and there was no one else with me. And yet, I could hear whispered giggles reverberating all around, and soft rustles as if children were playing games, hiding in the door jambs and behind the walls. And I could almost see them from the corner of my eyes, small flashes that danced just out of sight of my vision.

My hackles rose, but I forced myself to carry on. Sweat was gathering on my back in this cold underground space.

I almost fell through the glass door leading into the harsh fluorescent lights of the Rare Books Archive, and must have looked a sight to the woman behind the desk, flushed and panting and crazy eyed. Pausing a moment to collect myself, I sent a quick mental feeler all around the room. Apart from the leftover vibrations from the ancient books and papers, I could sense nothing, and there was nothing here to be afraid of.

The librarian was still staring at me. I smiled to put her at ease, trying to act normal. After showing her two IDs, she reluctantly verified me as a legitimate student and had me sign my life away before she fetched me the book and a pair of cotton gloves for my hands. She made me sit where she could keep a close eye on me, right in front of the desk.

You'd think a book as old as this would have been digitized, or at least on microfilm by now, but I guess it wasn't considered a high priority for the library's limited resources. It was a small book, barely fifteen pages long, with a brown leather cover. It had no publisher's marks or ISBN of course, and was probably an early version of vanity publishing. The print inside was tiny.

The author had a loquacious and poetic style, telling the reader all about his early life which had nothing to do with the promised story. He was a travelling minister, a man of God he pointed out frequently, and had scoffed at the tales of little folk and supernaturals.

I quickly scanned his words till I got to the part about where the author was out walking one day and passed a fairy ring, a circle of mushrooms growing on the moors of Cornwall. He stopped to watch the fairies dancing.

I settled in to be enlightened, but despite the claims in the title, this author had not gotten himself mixed up with the fairies after all. He had watched the Fine Folk at their games, but when he realized they had seen him he threw the bread from his pocket at them and ran away. He lived to tell the tale.

What a letdown. Fifteen pages of tiny print that was a lot of blethering about nonsense, nothing concrete that would help me. This was no use to me at all, except to remind me to bring bread to distract the fairies when I invaded their home to steal away the baby and Benjy. Like that would be a big help.

I yawned and stretched, then shivered into my hoodie. The basement room had gotten noticeably colder in the short time I'd been there. They must have the air-conditioning up on bust. Looking up, I saw that something else had changed.

The dragon lady librarian was no longer standing over me with her hawk eyes. There must have been a change of shift, for the only person I saw was a student worker, a girl with long blonde hair who had her back to me.

I was getting pretty hungry by this time, having abandoned my muffin in the Arts Building Cafe, and I returned the old book to the counter. The gloves were giving me a bit of warmth, so I kept them on. The girl ignored me, continuing her busy activities.

"Thanks," I repeated in a slightly louder voice. "Do I need to sign something to return this?"

She stopped what she was doing and looked at the entrance, gave a small nod. Without even turning around to me, she walked through the door into the depths of the archive storage. It softly closed behind her.

"Okay," I said. I admit I was a little put out by this. Did she want me to sign it back or not? Frig it. This was pretty lax security, and I bet her boss wouldn't be happy to hear about it. But I had no plans to steal the book or get her into trouble, so I left it on the counter and turned to go.

That's when I became aware again of the whisperings and laughter that I'd heard in the corridor outside the room, only they were louder now, not coming from anywhere in particular but reverberating through the large reading room. I was instantly on high alert, for my senses were telling me this wasn't the air conditioning system. There was something unnatural afoot.

The fluorescent lights began to flicker, giving off a static electric sound, buzzing like something from a horror movie. The air was charged all around me and the whispered laughing grew in pitch becoming frenzied and hysterical and echoing through my head.

I clamped my hands over my ears and shrieked in pain. And then the lights failed entirely with a final clap and I turned towards where I remembered the exit to be. Fumbling, my head roaring and my knapsack half off my back, I found the door and pushed through it into the black corridor outside. Which direction? Right, I had to turn right. I saw the exit sign gleaming red far away.

Then cold hands grabbed my shoulders and pulled me roughly aside.

CHAPTER 20

The noise was so loud in my head it was painful, but that was forgotten as I struggled against the very physical grips on my arms which hauled me out of the Archives and into the pitch black corridor. But no use fighting, for my abductors were far stronger than me.

I heard a door open, then I was thrust inside a tiny space and just before they let me go, a whispered voice rose above the clamouring, so close to my ear I could feel the warmth of the breath.

"This will teach you not to poke your nose in where you're not wanted," he hissed, then I was given another thrust and thrown against something hard and sticking out, my shoulder taking the brunt of it. A door slammed behind me. All was quiet now, my head no longer reverberated.

Dazed, I sank to the floor, scattering unseen objects on my way. A wooden stick fell against me, striking me on the head before clattering away.

The place smelled like chemicals. Cleaning fluids, that harsh ammonia-like odor which creeps in your nose and stays there, no matter what perfumes might be added to cover it up. And underneath that there was the lingering smell of dirty mops abandoned while still wet.

I was imprisoned in a janitor's closet. How frigging humiliating. I kicked out and a metal bucket rolled and rang hollowly.

Those had been human hands on my shoulders, of that I had no doubt, strong fingers digging into my flesh as they forced me into this cramped space. Malice aforethought, definitely, and I was pretty sure I knew who my abductors were. Those bastard Witch Kin, for I had recognized Polka-Dot-Quiff's aftershave.

The second Archive worker, the one who had ignored me, she must have been one of their friends.

Right. I was going to get them back, I vowed as I lifted myself up carefully from the floor. Later, after I'd rescued Benjy and the baby, they would feel the force of my wrath. After I got out of here.

I found the doorknob, but it wasn't turning. My hands felt all around the door – yes, there were the hinges, there was the outline of the wood, but it wasn't moving, not even when I banged against it with all my might. The door should at least have been shaking against its jamb, but nothing, it was as solid as if it was nailed into place.

Fumbling with the handle again, I felt for the unlock button but there was nothing there, just a smooth ball of metal. No need to have an inner lock on a broom closet, right?

They had magicked the door shut. It had to be a magic spell keeping that door closed, and I cursed the father who had refused to let me develop my innate talent. It was his fault I was stuck in here powerless, unable to help myself against the malicious actions of the Kin.

I had (sort of) joked with Dad that he was going to cast a spell to keep me barred in, and he'd replied that it wasn't that simple. Well, it turned out it was, as long as the spell caster wasn't bothered by minor things like ethics.

But even in the midst of my fright, I took off the cotton gloves to be sure, and yes, I could feel the spell just around the door handle – like a little itch on every third nerve of my fingertips, like tiny shocks along the hairs of my forearm. This was what magic felt like. I remembered this faintly, from the games played with Sasha and my other siblings in my childhood. Too bad I'd never been taught to properly work this energy.

I shoved stuff out of the way with my feet and sat on the floor cross legged, my elbow leaning on the overturned bucket and I tried to think my way out of this situation. It was pitch black in here, so either the corridor lights were still off or the spell had sealed the door so completely nothing was getting through.

There wasn't a lot of traffic outside at the best of times as the library staff would use the inner staircase. Patrons had to use the elevator or go down the concrete staircase through the basement corridor, and not many people frequented this out of the way spot, not so early in the semester.

I felt for my knapsack and with a sigh of relief found it in a corner where it must have slipped off when I was tossed inside. Okay, first things first, because I was starving by now. But no luck in that department, I hadn't been bold enough to make myself a lunch in Cate's kitchen, and there were no crumbs of chocolate or cookies in the depths of the bag, no matter how hard I searched. Crap.

But Alice's phone was there, I grabbed it and pressed the button to make it come alive. It was now almost one o'clock; Hugh wouldn't be looking for me until after three when my last class finished.

I found him on the contacts and pressed dial, but nothing happened at all. Looking closer, I saw there were no bars, no reception way down here in the bowels of the concrete library.

The glow from the phone illuminated my prison, even without the flashlight app on. It was a creepy little space in this twilight, the thin sticks of brooms and mops crisscrossed in the shadows, their heads hovering above me. The metal of two industrial shelves glinted in the faint light, loaded with plastic bottles of chemicals and paper towels and a forgotten Tim Horton's cup from last spring's Roll Up the Rim contest, the rim unrolled and evidently a loser.

Closer to me on the floor was a dustmop and buckets and an old pair of rubber boots. The corners of the closet were blurry with accumulated dust underneath the spartan industrial sink. Not a great place to spend an afternoon.

I kept my ear opened for someone passing by, anyone, but no one came. The time was long and my thoughts drifted to the unfairness of my life, as this wasn't the first time I'd been bullied by Witch Kin kids.

At my elementary school, St. Mary's, I hadn't experienced much trouble. That was a tiny school crammed between Waterford Bridge Road and Topsail Road, saved from the inevitable budget-driven closures by dint of the rich people whose children attended it. If it had been located up in the projects it would have been shut down long ago and the poor people's five-year-old kids bussed up to Mundy Pond. But wealthy educated folk sat on the school board, and their kids were staying in their own neighborhood.

Quite a few Kin kids went to St. Mary's, it being located near the huge old houses along the river, the homes that stayed in wealthy families for generations. They kept to themselves, for they were a tight-knit group although we all shared classrooms.

This was long before the new movement against half-bloods started. Back then, we all just accepted our differences, apart from the odd scuffle in the playground which is just normal little kid behavior.

It was only in highschool when it started to get rough. Edna wanted me to go to Holy Heart of Mary in the center of the city because they offered so much more there in the way of music and art, not that I was talented in either of those. But she had dreams for me I guess, back then, and she drove me and Alice there and back every day.

Holy Heart was where all the Kin kids went too. Imagine Sasha's horror when she saw me there on the first day of classes. Being a year older than me and the legitimate offspring of our father, she was of course far too superior to acknowledge my existence, despite those few sunny days we'd shared as kids. But that didn't stop her and her gang from pulling some mean tricks.

The sneering and the name-calling I could handle, but when they began messing with my locker I learned to keep my eyes open. Somehow they must have found out my combination and for a while, every day there was a special new treat inside for me. Their favorite was to pile all my books on the top shelf so everything came crashing down as soon as the door opened, but there other things too. The dead rat in my lunch bag was the worst. I learned to tread very carefully in that school, and found all the quiet nooks to hide in. The positive side was that I met a lot of interesting nerds that way.

I didn't realize back then that Sasha and her friends were witches, or that I was too. I just thought she was mad because of our dad.

Edna put it all down to teenage bullying, the usual crap that kids pull on each other, and maybe that's all it was. But it was enough for me to spend the next four years going out of my way to avoid my brothers and sisters. I became very adept at this, and this made my actions that morning in the Arts Building all the more unusual, the boldness with which I'd entered their eyrie as if I belonged.

You'd think she would have gotten over the whole father thing by now, I thought as I listlessly kicked a mop in the dark. But she had been scared this morning too, beneath the anger and spite. Was her fear on my behalf because I'd trespassed into the Witch Kin den? Had she known they would get back at me by playing silly tricks like this?

Or was it for Alice?

The more I thought about it, the colder I grew. What could they want with Alice? And they had known, oh God, somehow they knew about her elf blood. I needed to warn her, about what I didn't know, but she was in some kind of danger from the Witch Kin, and I had done that to her by my meddling.

It was long past three o'clock by now, and Hugh would be furious with me. He'd squared it with Dad, insisted that I was to be trusted in being let out of the house, and now that was totally screwed up. I had no way of letting him know where I was or what had happened, and for sure Sasha wouldn't be telling him.

How long was this enforced captivity going to last? A joke was a joke, but this was a bit over the top and now I was beginning to seriously worry about the evening. The dwarf would not be happy to be stood up, not when he was going out on a limb to offer assistance like that.

Alice would worry, too.

And that baby wasn't getting any younger in the fairy hall. It was all my fault and I was helpless to fix it, stuck in the closet like this.

I must have dozed a bit even in the state I was in, because when I next looked at the phone it was past seven o'clock and I'd missed my appointment with Dirk. There would be no second chances with him, I knew, even with the lure of the fairy gold. Dwarves are known for holding grudges for any perceived slights, I think it comes from spending so much time underground. So now not only did I have the baby and Benjy to worry about, the Witch Kin kids were after me, a dwarf was totally pissed and Hugh and Dad would be sending me out on the next flight to the Outer Hebrides off the coast of Scotland. And then there was Alice.

Standing, I gave the door an almighty kick from pure frustration, and it rattled in its jamb. The spell was off! I felt around the doorknob, and yes, no tingling, so I turned it and pulled, and almost fell out into the harsh white fluorescent light of the corridor.

The archive directly across from me was closed, the room pitch black through the glass door and no one around, though the main library upstairs must still be open. I took the stairs not the elevator, because I'd had enough of small enclosed places for one evening.

I tore through the main entrance like a bat out of hell, and into the coolly lit night outside. The air was bracing, true, but so good to draw into my lungs to chase out the stale chemicals I'd been breathing for the past what, six hours? Those bastards. They would pay for this.

A rattle of rain started as I headed out the door, the force of it almost driving me back inside. I realized I had to make a decision – get the bus or walk back to Dad's? Then again, perhaps I'd be better off avoiding them all together and cutting directly across town and trying to get Alice and the dwarf back on my side. A cab would cost about fifteen dollars, I figured, and I had just about that amount on me.

As I quickly set off across campus in the general direction of the Southside Hills, my phone began pinging like crazy with messages and missed calls. Alice and Hugh, of course. Well, he would have to wait, especially as I read the latest text from my friend.

We'll meet you up there.

Alice and the dwarf were going up to the fairy den themselves? This was suicide on her part; she didn't have the strength of mind to resist the enchantments. Christ, what had I gotten her into?

I began sprinting through the rain, the hard pellets were almost hail despite the unseasonal warmth of the night. I didn't even pause to phone a cab, thinking there would surely be one cruising along.

Bursting out onto the crosswalk of the main road I took my chances that any cars would see me and slow down, hanging a left down Elizabeth Avenue rather than take the shorter route across town because by now I was praying for a taxi to show up. Just at the entrance into the enclave of posh new houses I was stopped and almost run over by a car pulling sharply in front of me.

If I'd had the head-space in which to think and wonder, I would have been blown away by this vehicle – it was the Batmobile come to life, or at least it looked like that in the dark rain, a sleek black sporty car screeching up to the curb, the rain beading on it as if it had been freshly waxed.

But it wasn't Batman who jumped out of the car and began yelling at me. "What the hell are you doing?" That unmistakeable Scots accent was not happy. He rushed over in front of the car to confront me. "Where have you been?"

"Get out of my way." I was breathing hard from the run as I tried to push past him, but he had a firm grip through my by now soaked jean jacket. "Hugh, leave me alone."

"Get in that car," he roared as he not-so-gently marched me to his vehicle. With his free hand, he opened the door and pushed me inside, knocking my head against the low jamb. After the door slammed shut behind me, he stood for a moment with his finger pointed at me, daring me to move.

He needn't have worried. I was so hungry and out of my mind by this time that the warmth in the car broke my last defense, and I just sat there waiting for him. Hugh was my only hope right now.

I let him fume and sputter as he put the car back into gear and pulled away back down Elizabeth Avenue, heading east, but before we reached the intersection of Allandale, I put my hand on his arm, pulling the wheel towards the south.

"Don't bring me back to Dad's," I begged. "Not yet. We have to get Alice. She's gone up to the fairy den with a dwarf, and she's no match for them. You have to help!"

He shot me a look that would have burned me if it could.

"Up on the Southside Hills in this weather? I don't think so." But at least he headed down towards the center of town, past my old high school and then over to the Tim Horton's parking lot, all without saying a word.

"We don't have time to stop for coffee!"

"We're stopping for an explanation," he said, his voice grim. "And to feed you. You're as pale as a ghost."

After ordering a hot chocolate and sandwich for me and a tea for himself at the drive through, he parked the car overlooking Harvey Road. Across from us, way past the city and the harbor, the Southside Hills were invisible in the drizzle. Alice was up there somewhere.

He sat and waited.

"Where do you want me to begin?"

"What happened to you today? I promised your father on your behalf that you would go straight home after classes. You made me look like an idiot."

Chicken salad on a croissant had never tasted so good, and as I ate, I told him all of it except for the cheating on the exam bit. About how I had stupidly gone up to the cafe, knowing my presence was just taunting the Kin students, and how I'd asked for help from Sasha and she had screamed at me. About how creepy her friends were and how they'd locked me in the janitor's closet with the door affixed by a spell.

His face grew darker and darker as I related the tale.

"And Alice? What's this about the fairies? How the hell did she get mixed up in this?"

So I told him that too, a quick version, right from the beginning. How Alice was desperate to save her brother. About the baby and the changeling. And then about the dwarf who'd promised to help.

Finally he looked over at me and shook his head. His eyes looked tired and his face was drained. "This is all wrong on so many levels."

"I know, right? So that's why we need to go up and get Alice," I said. "I just couldn't bear it if I lose her on top of it all."

"We'll not be doing anything of the kind."

CHAPTER 21

The windows inside the car fogged up as we sat there, for the night outside was warm and wet. Hugh opened his window. We could hear the breeze rustling through the trees but further away, the sounds of sirens filled the night air, coming from all directions as if bouncing off the granite hills that surrounded the old downtown. A smell of burning was on the rising wind.

I took off my sodden jean jacket to give my hoodie a chance to dry out.

"So let me get this straight," Hugh said as he stared across at the hills across the harbor. "First, you broke all sorts of conventions by invading the fairy den."

"I had no idea there were rules against that," I retorted. The meal had returned my spirits. "I was just trying to save Benjy."

"Hmmm," he said. "That's assuming he's worth saving. But then you allowed the fairies to steal a baby in your charge. Or so you believe."

"They switched her out for one of theirs," I defended myself. "I didn't invite them in, they ran into the house and upstairs before I could catch them."

He shot me a dirty glance for interrupting him.

"In *your* charge," he continued. "Then you royally offended IronArms by fraudulently claiming to be a representative of your father."

"It was a misunderstanding."

"But you managed to convince one dwarf to assist you."

"Dirk."

"Dirk," he repeated with distaste. "Who is abetting you because...?"

"I promised him he could help himself to the fairy gold," I mumbled. Even as the words came out of my mouth, I realized how Hugh would view this.

"Dirk is helping you because he wants to steal from the fairies," Hugh agreed in a very patient voice. "And what do you think the consequences of *that* action will be?"

"Thursk won't be happy," I admitted.

"No, Thursk will be extremely unhappy at losing his gold to his neighbors, the dwarves. IronArms will also be extremely unhappy at Dirk bringing shame onto their Dwarfdom. The best outcome would be that Thursk would demand an investigation into the whole sequence of events. The worst, and by far the more likely, would be that Thursk and his band would take matters into their own hands, causing war within Alt Town."

I hung my head and had no reply to this logic.

"And, pray tell me," Hugh was on a hot streak now. "How exactly did you plan to exchange the baby? How would Jane react to having two infants all of a sudden? Or were you going to break into her house, do the switch, then gaily run up to the fairies and give them back their sprog? Without the fairies killing you?"

"I hadn't gotten it totally figured out," I said sullenly. "I thought we'd come up with a plan between the three of us on the way up the hill."

My words were met only with silence. Hugh really knew how to make someone feel like crap. The wind outside was picking up even more, it was warm, from the south. A hurricane wind. I could see smoke coming from downtown now, just a haze in the strong wind. It smelled like ancient wood and tar.

"They're just hill fairies," I burst out finally. "They're rotten vermin, and horrible and cruel!"

"That sounds like prejudice to me," he answered in a dangerously calm voice, the soft burr in his voice becoming more pronounced. "And we all know where that kind of thinking can lead to. They have the right to live as their natures dictate."

He had me there, didn't he? The sole reason he was supposedly here in St. John's was to fight against this very sort of thinking for the benefit of half-bloods like myself. I slumped down into the bucket seat of the sports car and watched the wind dance in the wires.

"So, what? We're just going to let them keep the baby and Benjy, and..."

"And what?"

"And I'll never get a chance to undo what I've done. What more can go wrong?"

"You've also now made an enemy of Dirk, for what that is worth," Hugh pointed out, not being helpful. "He'll be annoyed that you've gone back on your promise. Dwarf dignity and all that, they can't stand to be disrespected."

I stared across at the Southside Hills. The wind had increased steadily, blowing away the rain and allowing the almost full moon to bathe the downtown below us in a harsh silver light, yet those hills remained shrouded in a heavy blanket of fog. How could anything remain in this rising wind, why wasn't it being blown out to sea?

"Alice is up there," I said softly.

"Where?"

I nodded at the hills. "Up there. The last text I had from her said they'd meet me up there. She's with Dirk."

Hugh swore softly.

"I know," I said. "That's my fault too."

"Call her."

Why hadn't I thought to do this already? I took out my phone and pressed my name. The ringing went on for twenty seconds which felt like two minutes, then cut to a busy signal.

"There's something wrong with the phone," I said, and dialled again. This time it immediately went into the short staccato beeps of disconnect. I held out the phone so Hugh could hear.

"Right then." Hugh started up the car and put it into gear. It was a stick shift, of course.

"Don't take me to Dad's, not yet," I begged him. "I need to find Alice, make sure she's okay. I promise, I won't even bother going up the hill to the fairies, really, if you just let me get her."

He drove to the exit onto Harvey Road. "Is there anything else you're not telling me? Anything I need to know about the whole situation?"

"Aside from the fact that I cheated on my exam this morning, and I think Sasha's crowd are a bunch of fascist pigs, no that's about it." I sat back in the seat, finally defeated.

"What?" He paused before turning on to the road, unmindful of the cars behind him.

"I used my powers for bad," I confessed. "I hadn't studied, and I just don't get this math stuff."

"No, not that. Sasha's friends..."

I quickly debated if I should tell him my suspicions, then I remembered how they had taken up the chant of Alice's name. My blood ran cold. "I think... they may have something to do with the killing last June."

"At the last solstice."

"Yeah."

"And tomorrow night is the fall equinox."

"Shit."

"And Alice is not answering her phone." He took the time to stare at me, as if not believing how dumb I really was despite the evidence.

"Please can we go look for her?"

His face was grim. "That's exactly where I'm headed. Which is the fastest route across the harbor?"

"Oh my God, thank you," I said fervently. "Hang a left here, we can avoid the worst traffic lights."

The tires peeled off the pavement as he cut across the evening traffic. He almost missed the turn down Garrison Hill, I swear the outer wheels left the road as he took that sharp right at the last moment. I've never sped so fast down the length of Queen's Road. Thank God there weren't any drunks wandering into our path.

As we raced down the hill past the end of Duckworth, I witnessed the source of the sirens and the smell of smoke which filled the air. It was Zeta's store, flames licking out of where the plate glass window used to be. Fire crews and police had the street blocked off.

"That's the magic store burning," I said, straining my neck to watch in horror. "Zeta must have left the candles lit or something."

"I think you'll find that's not an accident," he said grimly. "She's another casualty of the prejudice which won't die in this godforsaken backwater."

I sat back in the bucket seat and braced myself again. I was shaken to my core. Such evil in my own home town, it was hard to conceive.

The coin in the basket. I hadn't thought of it since that day in Zeta's when she sold me that stupid useless unmagical spell. That slim disc of metal had been the only thing with any power in her whole store, but it had been dark and grief-stricken and I had longed to take it with me. Would it be destroyed in the conflagration?

The car swerving brought me back to the present. Just the one traffic light that turned unexpectedly green a split second before Hugh roared up to it, and then a moment's hesitation as I directed him down Job Street, then rescinded when I realized it was a one way street.

"No matter! You can take the left up there, down Brine Street!"

We passed the tiny old houses of that road, then Deanery Row and without even pausing for the stop sign we were past the church and headed back down to the main road. The sleek black car wove through and passed the other vehicles on the road as if it were made of water itself. Again at the intersection of Leslie Street and the road up to Shea Heights the light turned green, this time with the arrow to allow Hugh to turn left without slowing down, and then we were across the river and flying by Alice's house on Southside Road.

"Where were you supposed to meet her?"

"Further along, by the overhanging rock, just outside the dwarves tunnel." I pointed up ahead.

He screeched to a stop, and we looked around. No sign of Alice or Dirk here. I hadn't expected to see them.

"Wait here."

As I sat in the car and watched him cross the road, I realized there was something very odd happening here. All around was pitch dark except for the light of the moon with no electric lights anywhere, just like in Alt, yet *I was sitting in the car*. How could this be? It was as if the veil of Alt was nothing more than a gauze curtain and the two worlds were intermingling.

I watched as he leaped across the road and pounded on the thick oaken door, then slunk down in my seat when IronArms appeared, not wanting to be spotted by that giant of a dwarf.

A quick and terse conversation began between the two, but it quickly deteriorated into a shouting match with much flinging of arms on the dwarf's part. I don't think they were fighting, dwarves are just loud like that. Their voices were muffled through the closed car windows. Eventually IronArms looked over his shoulder into the tunnel and roared something out.

Dirk was the next player to show up on the scene, head drooping down and feet shuffling as he tried to look casual. Finally, he began speaking and gesticulating up the road, and up the hill while shaking his head. He spoke for a long time, and it looked like he was confessing all. After IronArms had clouted him over the head twice, once with each hand, and yelled some more, the two disappeared back into their tunnel.

Hugh let himself back into the car and sat staring at me for a moment his brows drawn.

"So Dirk came back," I said hopefully. "Does that mean Alice gave up on it too?"

He shook his head.

"Dirk claims they got lost up on the headland, before they even reached the top of the hill. He said Alice was pushing him to continue, but he didn't feel right."

"As in, he realized he was doing wrong?"

Hugh shook his head again, his eyes now looking out to sea, at the full moonlight on the water. Despite the wind which was now building to a crescendo, the ocean was as flat as glass. The whole scene was discordantly set. It didn't fit together.

"No. He says there's something afoot up there on the hills, and it's more than the fairies."

CHAPTER 22

I shivered.

"What's worse than fairies up there?" I was whispering.

"They couldn't find the fairy den," he continued, ignoring my question. "And then he says he came back down."

"You mean Alice is alone up there? In the dark with the fairies?" I shot up almost out of my seat and fumbled with the door handle of this unfamiliar European sports car. "How do I get out of this?"

He put his hand on my arm. "Wait," he said. "She came back down, too."

"What? Then why isn't she answering the phone? Hugh, what's going on?"

"Dirk said she met with some friends at the bottom of the hill, they were parked waiting for her as she and he came off the track."

"That's not right." I shook my head. "Alice's friends would never be hanging around Fort Amherst at night. They're nerds, they're not into night hikes."

"Unless they were Benjy's friends?" Hugh looked at me.

I shook my head again. Even less likely. Something didn't fit. "Dirk wouldn't know who they are, I suppose?"

"Try her again," Hugh said softly.

I tapped my name on her phone, but it rang only once before starting that harsh pulse of disconnection.

"I don't want to worry you, but I don't like the sounds of this," he said. "She's not answering the phone, you can give that up."

"Sal," I told him. "I'm calling Alice's sister, she'll be able to tell me if Alice is home."

Sal was home, but didn't want to get off her bed to go in search for her sibling. Instead she bawled out her sibling's name as loud as she could.

"I don't think she's here," Sal told me in a bored voice. "Would you mind getting off the line now?"

I hung up and shook my head at Hugh. "Nope."

He drummed his fingers against the leather covered steering wheel.

"What are we going to do?"

He shrugged. "We're going to go home. To your father's house, anyway."

"We can't! Alice is out there somewhere, we have to find her!" I was adamant.

"And where do you propose we look?"

"You're a witch!" I said. "Why don't you try to find her telepathically?"

"Why don't you?" he retorted. "I don't know Alice. You do. Go find her, now."

I stared at him. My mouth was probably open in surprise. "I'm just a half-blood, I can't..."

He raised an eyebrow. "No? How was that exam this morning?"

I shut my mouth. I had boasted about that, hadn't I?

He put the car in gear. "Tell you what, we'll go up to a physical vantage point, and I'll give you some pointers on how to go about searching."

As we sped back along Southside Road, I admit to feeling a little excited despite the seriousness of the situation. Finally! Some education on how to use the gifts that had lain dormant for much of my life.

We made it from the bridge right up to the end of Duckworth Street without hitting a red light once. I wanted to learn how to do that, too. To be able to direct all the traffic lights in my favour – well, that alone would be worth getting my driver's license for.

At the top of Signal Hill, Hugh parked facing the city. He nodded out to the expanse of St. John's below us, stretching off for miles west and north.

"Where is she?"

"I thought you were going to show me how to look?"

"You have to find your third eye first," he said. "Come on, you've done it before. Don't tell me you've never cheated off Alice in tests over the years? Similar thing. It's just a matter of adjusting your focus."

I grinned at him. Yes, I was quite familiar with the inside of Alice's head. Then I shut my eyes and sent feelers out, down and all through the city, trying to get a sense of the feeling of my friend.

I shook my head and opened my eyes. "Nothing's happening," I said. "I can't pick anything up."

"It's not a radio signal," he said, then thought a little more on the matter. "Well, perhaps it is rather like that. But at any rate, you need to go slowly. Let's get out of the car, into the air, that might work better. But first – do you have anything belonging to her? That will help."

I took her phone out of my pocket. "Sure do," I said, holding it out for him to see.

I climbed down the short hill to the path by the reconstruction of the old fortifications, and stood on a bench. The wind was still rising, now so strong it threatened to blow me off altogether. I gripped the rough wooden fence and stared ahead of me.

The city lights spread out before me. Somewhere, Alice was down there. She had to be. I closed my eyes and I could still picture the scene before me and I sent my feelers out.

For a moment it felt like I was flying! I gasped and opened my eyes, turning to look at Hugh who was by now just standing a few feet behind me. He smiled.

"Yes," he said so softly I almost didn't hear him. "That's it. Keep on doing that, you won't fall. Your body is still here. I'm with you."

I drew a deep breath and turned back to the busy streets below me. Looking down made me dizzy, and I stepped back a little.

"I don't know," I said. "I ... I..."

I was scared. It felt like jumping off a cliff into unknown waters, or taking the first leap from the Marble Mountain zipline on our trip to the west coast last summer. I'd climbed to the landing stage and all I had to do was step off into the vast space before me with nothing but a wire keeping me from crashing onto the rocks of the waterfalls below, but that was a huge step for the mind to accept.

"Alice," Hugh reminded me.

I shut my eyes and let myself go, pretending to feel safe in the knowledge that Hugh was right beside me. He was my wire over the falls.

I pictured Water Street again, and then I was there, hovering over the slow moving cars and past the pedestrians, some of them drunk already this early in the evening, weaving and singing their way along the ancient streets.

It was exhilarating! I found my wings and swooped down low, I could hear the words of the song as the crowd of students left the Black Sheep still roaring out their early Christmas tribute to the Pogues. I let myself rise again, and travelled further west to George Street. I could see the lights from the Rocket Cafe, and inside the windows people were sitting over coffee and cakes while a single bearded young man strummed his mandolin.

Dancing back up into the air, I set my sights towards the north and east and up the steep hill of the old town. There were the churches and the Cathedral and the Basilica, all the old monuments to Christianity which had held sway over the land for so long. I could finally look into the blank stone stare of John the Baptist, instead of merely peeking up his skirt from the ground.

"Alice," Hugh's voice reminded me again, whispering through my mind. I could feel him beside me, the warmth of his presence in my head.

I paused mid-flight, sending my mental feelers out in search of the familiarity of my friend, but the city lay black and void of her beneath the bright lights. I pictured her, tall and willowy and fair, but found nothing.

"Go further afield," Hugh's voice whispered. "She has to be somewhere."

I was tiring fast, even though I had not physically moved an inch. Pushing myself, I headed for the east end, around the dark waters of Quidi Vidi Lake, then back up New Town Road all the way to Dad's house set back apart, surrounded in black acreage, a single lamppost marking the driveway. Was there something there? I was feeling a whisper of my friend.

No, it was closer to downtown, over by Bannerman Park. A slight tinge to the air in the form of Alice. But what would she be doing in the park, or by the Colonial Building? I dropped in closer over the trees, almost exhausted and panting by now, but it must have been a trick of the light, for there was no feeling of Alice there now.

I crumpled onto the bench, my head almost striking the splintering wood of the barricade and I forced myself to sit, and catch my breath.

I looked up at Hugh, who was staring at me in the reflected light of the city, his face unreadable.

He came and sat next to me, putting his arm around me to allow me to lean into him. He was strong and solid. I laid my head on his shoulder, the black leather cool to my cheek, and I hid my face from the wind.

"You did great," he said softly into my ear.

"Could you see me?" I lifted my head in wonder.

"I was right behind you, all the way." He gave a deep low laugh. "You used to peek up the skirt of John the Baptist?"

I spluttered, releasing the tension in my body. He really had been there, beside me and in my head. It hadn't been my imagination. "Could never see anything, though. He wears a loincloth."

I had flown, in my thoughts at any rate. I sat for a moment further, remembering the feeling of the wind and my flight.

"That was beautiful," I breathed. "I want to fly again. Is this what witches do?" His body was warm and smelled of leather and spices. I felt him nod slowly, but could tell his mind was elsewhere.

He stood, pulling me up out of the shelter of the fence. The fierce wind whipped my hair in every direction, stinging my eyes. I almost fell, overcome with a sudden exhaustion.

"We have to go back now."

"But Alice! I didn't find Alice," I raised my voice weakly over the wind.

He shook his head. "You need food again, and rest," he said. "After what you've just done. I shouldn't have allowed you to do so much."

"But..."

He looked down at me.

"I want to try it again, but in Alt."

His eyes widened. "I don't think so!"

"In Alt, I'll be able to see more, get a sense of if there's anything... supernatural that has her. Dirk said it was witches, right?"

"No, no, no," he said, shaking his head. "No, not a chance am I going to be responsible for that." He led me back up to the Batmobile and clicking the little box in his hand, my door swung open. He made sure I was belted in before shutting the door and returning to his own seat.

We went back to Dad's house, Hugh firmly insisting that he wasn't letting me out of his reach again despite my protests that I wanted to sleep in my own bed that night. After my experience in the library that day, I didn't want anything to do with Sasha, didn't want to risk seeing her all smug and sneering in Cate's kitchen, because I might just have to kill her. Even after I told him this, he still refused to bring me home.

Fortunately, my sister was making herself scarce.

He rustled up some roast turkey and other leftovers, heating them up in the microwave. I watched him putter about the cold space.

"Why don't you just, I don't know, magic it hot?"

He turned to look at me as if he didn't know what I was talking about.

"Instead of wasting electricity on the microwave oven," I said. "Besides, aren't those rays supposed to be harmful to food?"

"You think ingesting magical energy is less harmful?" He set the plate in front of me and I began to eat, surprising myself by how ravenous I suddenly was again, despite having eaten not so long ago.

"First pointer about magic," he said as he sat himself across the island from me. The overhead pendant light shone on his dark hair and made the gold specks in his eyes glitter. "It is not to be used indiscriminately or for fun. You have to have a damn good reason to use it."

"But it's so much easier," I objected, between mouthfuls.

"Magic energy accumulates," he said shortly.

"Sasha's friends were using it on my coffee this morning, after my exam," I said. "They were making waves in my paper cup."

He set his mouth grimly. "They are foolish, then, ignoring the basic laws of the craft. If they'd been trained to respect the power, they would never do such a thing. It can accumulate, as I said, and come back to haunt them. This is another reason all witches should receive proper education. I fear your local educational system leaves something to be desired."

I shook my head. "They all got sent away during summers and for finishing school," I said. "All the local ones from here, all the friends she's had for years anyway. I don't know about Seth, though. He's not from here."

"Who's he, then?"

"You haven't met her boyfriend?"

Hugh's eyebrows rose. God, that man had the best, finest, thickest brows I'd ever seen.

"I'm not surprised," I said. "From how she's been looking at you, I think she has a crush on you. And Seth, he's only been hanging around the past year or so, off and on. I don't think he's even a student at MUN. But he's sort of creepy... I don't know if he's really good for her." I was not, *not* going to tell Hugh about my experience in the library with those two sitting across from me.

He became very still, his eyes watching me closely. "Seth," he repeated.

I paused before the last bite of turkey made it to my mouth. "Did I say something wrong?" My heart was sinking, for I felt I'd put my foot in it somehow.

He hurried me off upstairs after I'd finished without answering my question.

The bed was softer than I remembered, more welcoming than the night before, or maybe I was just plain worn out. Before I dropped off though, Hugh's reaction to the mention of Seth was bugging me.

I wondered what Hugh's real reason was for coming to St. John's, and staying at Dad's house. He'd said he was here to investigate prejudice and something, but... I wondered.

Dad and Cate's families were traditional in that they always had arranged marriages for the scions of their houses, carefully considering bloodlines and political power structures before a choice was made.

Was Hugh here to be vetted as a husband for Sasha? Was that why he went all quiet at the mention of Sasha's boyfriend?

But the Scotsman claimed to be a half-blood and surely to God Cate would never allow her daughter or her future grand-children to be tainted in that way. Yet, he was here in her house as a guest because he was in town for official Witch Kin business. Something didn't add up.

What did he have that allowed him to cross the chasm of prejudice? Who was Hugh Sabiston?

CHAPTER 23

The weather hadn't let up by the next morning. If anything the wind was even stronger. As I looked out the kitchen window to the north, I could see clouds scudding across the otherwise blue sky.

I'd hoped to be getting back to our search for Alice because she still wasn't answering my calls. Sal was refusing to pick up my calls too, but that was probably just fifteen year old cussedness. However, Hugh was not interested in finding my friend today.

"Later," he said. "It'll all come together later. Right now, I have to check something out, and I'm afraid I have no choice but to bring you with me."

I really needed a change of clothing, for there was no way I was going to ask Cate about her laundry facilities, so Hugh agreed to bring me home. We took Dad's big midnight blue SUV this time.

"We're going off-roading," he said, when I asked.

"So I take it I'm not going to classes today." I was okay with that, really I was.

He'd taken a right to go down Warbury Street, when I spotted Jane up in the distance with her kids all around her.

"Stop here," I said to him. I had to find out about the baby. He made no move to slow down.

"Oh come off it, Hugh," I said. "I'm not going to make a run for it! I need to see how Jane is, and apologize for the other night."

I got out of Dad's vehicle and approached my ex-friend with caution. The kids saw me and squealed with joy as they began running towards me.

A curt word from Jane stopped them in their tracks, and they looked back at her with guilty eyes. She stared at me, her eyes narrowed into tiny mean slits.

The baby was in one of those old-fashioned prams with the big hood protecting her, the kind English nannies used back in Edwardian London.

"Hey Jane," I said. "How's the baby?" I edged closer to her, trying to peer over the hood.

"Get away from us," she said, pulling the handle so the pram turned. "The baby is fine, no thanks to you."

A weak cry sounded from the depths of the pram. That didn't sound good – that infant had had the finest set of lungs on her before I'd gone and let the fairy into the house.

I came up next to her and quickly looked into the pram and got a fast glimpse at the redheaded cherub. Our eyes met, and I swear I heard an evil chuckle. It may have been gas.

Jane elbowed me out of the way. "Leave us alone!" She stalked down the street, forcing the kids to hurry after her.

I mumbled my apologies yet again and got back in the vehicle where Hugh waited.

"Is it a changeling?"

I shrugged. "I'm pretty sure it is, yeah."

He silently drew up to our back door.

"I'll just be a minute," I said. "Unless you want to come in to keep tabs on me?"

He shook his head. "We may have to hike for a bit," he said. "Wear jeans and running shoes."

"And by running shoes you mean sneakers?" As if there was anything in my wardrobe but. "Don't think that'll be a problem."

Clean underwear, along with a fresh bra, t-shirt and jeans, even socks too, for it looked like summer was good and over despite the unnatural sultriness of the wind. I put on the same hoodie and over it, Mom's jean jacket which had now dried out from the night before.

We headed back in the direction of Dad's house, but he sped right by it and on up Portugal Cove Road. Soon we were past the airport and Winsor Lake even, right outside the city limits. I didn't often go this far out of town, having no call at all to go beyond my tight circle of Alice's house, downtown and the university. There were a lot of trees and fields out this way, but it was a civilized country and had been habited for a long time, not like the unfriendly barrens on the top of the Southside Hills.

Going down the steep hill towards the cove, Hugh took a sudden right hand turn up a side road, and then a left a few moments later, up a gravelled track. I saw now why he didn't take his Batmobile, for that low slung car would have bottomed out on the first of the many sizable potholes. Even the SUV was having a hard enough time of it.

The lane, if you can call it that, went on and on till eventually we came to a bog, the wet reeds showing lushly green in the autumn landscape. Other tires tracks led past this, but Hugh pulled off and parked over some blueberry bushes. "We'll walk from here," he instructed, finally speaking.

He started along the path without waiting for me to catch up.

I couldn't hold back anymore. This silent treatment was getting on my nerves.

"What's the matter?"

He turned to look at me as if he'd forgotten I was there. "What are you talking about?" His face was blank, whether on purpose or not I couldn't tell.

"You're mad at me," I said, deciding to get it all off my chest. "What is it? The baby? I told you that wasn't my fault and besides, I want to fix it. Or is it Sasha and Seth – is that what's got you worried?"

Hugh stopped in the middle of the track, avoiding a puddle where vehicles had worn away the topsoil and rocks. "Dara, has anyone ever told you that you have too much imagination? If you must know, we're going to a murder scene."

It was my turn to look startled.

"Is this the woman who was killed? Oh my God. Yes, Mark said it was behind Portugal Cove, this must be it," I said in a rush. I was talking too much, I knew, but I was really relieved that he wasn't mad at me. "Holy shit, are we allowed back here? And why did she die, was it because of witch craft or devil worship? Mark said there were all sorts of weird symbols all over the place?"

"You're surprisingly well informed," Hugh remarked drily as he began walking again over the rough path.

"Edna's boyfriend is part of the investigation team," I explained as I leaped over a small stream. Hugh didn't even break his stride. "Not that he usually talks about his work, mind. It's just that this had him so puzzled, and he was also trying to warn me against going outside at night by myself."

"She was a half-blood witch, we've determined," he said. "By the name of Tracey. I'm coming out here to see if there is any residual energy at the scene. This could give us a hint as to who was responsible. We couldn't read anything off the body."

"Mark said she was burned, as if by lightning," I replied. "Is that ... could it have been magic scorching her?"

"I've seen the corpse. It was definitely magic. Now I have to find out who did it, and why."

He had seen the woman's dead body. So was Hugh working with the cops? I couldn't get my head around this.

"But she died months ago," I said. "Will there be anything left to sense around there?"

"She died almost exactly three months ago," Hugh said, nodding his head. "If I'm correct, three months to today and on the night of the Summer Solstice."

By now even the old cart road had ended and we took a sharp turn, plunging into the tracks left by the passage of recent utility vehicles.

My mind did a quick start. Today was the equinox, and from what I'd read in fiction, the two solstices and equinoxes were important times in the witch's calendar. I'd learned from experience it was dangerous to delve into Alt Town on those dates of the years, especially if they happened during full moons. Some weird shit could go down then.

"Hugh, why are you here? In St. John's, I mean. You said you were looking into the prejudice that's rising up, does this woman's death have anything to do with all that?"

"This, and other things," he replied. He sounded almost grudgingly, as if he didn't want to tell me. But I was going to get it out of him, for my mind was leaping and I didn't like where it was going.

"Does... does this have anything to do with the weird symbols and graffiti around town?"

"Perhaps."

"So today is the equinox, the day is equally long as the night. You're saying this woman died at the solstice," I continued, hurrying to keep up with him. "God dammit Hugh, turn around and look at me."

He stepped up his pace and I raised my voice to holler after him.

"Do you think there might be something planned for tonight?"

He had stopped answering me.

I yelled at his back. "Does this have anything to do with Alice?"

That made him pause. He waited until I caught up to him, his hands huddled into the pockets of his leather jacket.

"Does it? With what Dirk said..." My voice had grown suddenly smaller, till it was a bare whisper. "Witches? What would they want with her?"

Had they been waiting for *me* at the bottom of the hill last night? Tracey, that unknown victim, had been half witch, and had been sacrificed in some sort of weird ceremony.

Was I the next intended victim? And not getting me, they had taken Alice. Oh dear God what had I done?

Hugh reached out his arm, as if to hug me and give me solace, and I braced for the rush of tears this sympathy would draw from me, but it didn't happen. Instead, he patted me roughly on the shoulder.

"Bear up, Dara," he said. "The worst hasn't happened yet."

"Yet?" I screeched over the wind. We were now out of the stunted woodlands and on to the barrens proper. Conception Bay lay blue before us in the morning sun, with Bell Island sticking out of the water like the prow of a giant old steam ship. "What do you mean, *yet*? You frigger!"

He stopped short just as I caught up to him. Peering from behind his bulk, I saw the yellow lines of police tape flapping in the breeze. Below us, the mountain dipped into a hollow.

Usually small dales like this in the midst of granite outcroppings became ponds, places where the water collected, unable to escape through the rock. Over time, these tiny stagnant lakes would fill with silt and organic matter to become bogs, and eventually peat. Yet this was a simple scoop of the rock, perhaps thirty feet wide and ten feet deep, and the bottom was just plain grass.

A perfect small amphitheatre, naturally hewn from the surrounding rock. You wouldn't know it was here until you stumbled over it. And unless someone came right to the lip like we were right then, you could hide a small army down here without being seen.

There were no police there anymore, and nothing to show the presence of human beings save for the faded chalk outlines of symbols on the gray rock faces.

Hugh lifted the yellow tape up and indicated for me to cross it with him.

"Keep your mind open," he said softly. "Try to sense magic, or the things which passed here."

"See into the past? I don't think I can do that." If I could peer into the past, I would have done so long ago and known what had happened with my mother.

"Just..." He shook his head and moved ahead of me down the steep slope of scree.

When we'd reached the bottom of the pit, he stood motionless with his eyes closed, moving only his head as if trying to hear faint glimmers of the events gone by on the lessened breeze which made its way down here.

I followed suit. It came to me slowly, then quickly and so intensely I had to back off. It was just like trying to find a radio station on Edna's old boom box with the volume way up high. Turning the dial, looking for a connection but all I could get was static, static, static until boom! Like an assault to my ears the announcer's voice broke in from the stratosphere.

Only it wasn't a human talking on these wavelengths. It was the entire ceremony of that dark night, the pitch torches strung up around the bowl of rock, the costumes of those who participated. The strange chanting, the terror of the person held in the middle, drugged so her body couldn't move or escape. Though her body was relaxed through the potions, I could feel the surge of emotions running through her, I could see the fantastical forms before her. I knew how, despite her terror, she also yearned for them to come upon her.

And I could feel the blood lust of those who closed in, steadily, like a pulsing beat in their heads it took over their minds until all they could see was their prey.

Like being hit by a bolt of lightning, I fell to the ground, colors dancing on the sides of my visions and the smell of her scorched flesh in my nostrils.

"Dara, are you alright?"

He was bent over me, fear in his green eyes. I nodded slowly.

"Sorry," he said. "I'm sorry. I shouldn't have subjected you to this, knowing what I knew."

I sat up. The bowl was as quiet and brightly lit as it had been, with the shadows of clouds as they passed through the sky. No hooded figures, no fire light. No victim in the midst of terror and longing.

"Did I see..."

He nodded. "I'm sure you did."

After a pause, he spoke again, but hesitantly this time. "I don't suppose you could tell me exactly what you saw?"

He took a bottle of water out of his knapsack and opened it, offering it to me.

"I'd rather not talk about it," I said after chugging, a cold shiver running down my back.

"But you must."

"It was only a split second, I think, though it was so intense," I began.

He stiffened beside me. "Intense, in what way?"

"I could see everything in the firelight," I said. "There were torches lit, five of them." I looked around. Sure enough, there were still two sturdy branches sticking out of the ground, the ends burnt to charcoal.

"Five. The pentagram," he said, nodding. "What else?"

"The woman in the center," I said. "She was drugged, so her body was all relaxed, but she was awake, and she could see them coming towards her."

"Did she know the identities of the people who brought her there?"

"No..."

"Think, girl." His voice was stern as he command-ed me to use my brain. His Scottish accent was the strongest I'd heard it yet. "She must have given you some hint. Go back inside her mind."

I closed my eyes for a moment, not that I was going to go back into that place. But I tried to remember, when I was her, what else had I noticed?

"She was scared," I whispered. "But she couldn't move. And one part of her wanted ... it, whatever this was. And that scared her even more. She'd thought they were her friends, her family, and she thought this cere-mony was going to lift her up and give her the power she sought..."

"Who were they? Did you get a picture of them from her memory?"

"No," I said. "Just the picture of them in their hoods, and how scary they now looked to her."

"And from your own experience, did you get a sense of them?"

"Only..." I stopped and looked up at him. "Just the feeling from them, and I felt it too."

He waited, his eyes on mine.

"I... we wanted to... to ravage her," I said. "And that word isn't enough, it doesn't convey, the feeling in my blood as I joined them. I don't know if I can tell you how..."

I couldn't go on, for it was bad enough that I'd admit-ted aloud the hunger I'd glimpsed deep inside me and the horror that I could feel like that.

"It wasn't you," he said, gently. "Not you. You just picked up on the mass hysteria of the spell they were all under."

"But who was responsible for this?"

"That is why I'm here," he said. He helped me back to my feet, and we walked toward the scree slope.

"Hugh." I hesitated but plunged on. "The woman? She was a stranger to me, I really think. She wasn't... Alice."

"No."

"But, could she be Alice?"

He thought a moment, then shook his head. "I really don't see it," he said. "Your friend is not a witch, or even a half-blood witch? You would have told me if she was."

"Not witch blood, no," I said. "But I suspect she might have elf-blood in her. From Nan Hoskins's line."

He stopped halfway up the slope, his back stiff.

"But it's pretty diluted after all those years," I hastened to add. "Besides, why would they care about elves? Surely they're only concerned with witches?"

I was growing greatly confused by all this.

He waited until I caught up with him, then he placed his arm around my back, helping me up over the steeper parts of the hill.

"If there are supernatural powers to be used, they will take them, no matter what the source," Hugh said in a low voice.

I grew cold, even in the warmth of his protective arm. This was Alice's life he was talking about. Where was she?

CHAPTER 24

He started up the SUV again. ""So. Alice."

"Yes."

"Who are those people who've taken her?"

I was met only with silence. He put the vehicle in gear and turned it around in the narrow space. I could hear the bushes scrape the bottom, then we bounced as the right rear wheel rolled over a rock. Slowly we made our way back down the track.

"Do you think it's the same ones who did this... this thing?"

I turned to look at him as I did up my seatbelt.

He nodded, slowly.

"Why?"

"You know why," he said. "You felt it, that evil back there."

"Not *why* are they doing it," I said with a shudder. "I mean, why do you *know* that?"

"The timing," he replied. "It's the Equinox coming up, this marks a time of power, when the forces are heightened. The halfway point. It's important in witch lore, even if it's only because it's believed to be important."

"So this woman was killed on the Solstice, another important date for witches?"

He nodded.

"We have to find Alice. Before they do that to her." I was fretting, of course I was. Not only was she my best friend, but this too, was all my fault, for Alice would never have been hanging around waiting at the foot of the Southside Hills at night, if I hadn't gotten her mixed up in all of this. If we didn't get to her in time, I couldn't bear to live.

"You know what we haven't discussed," he said as he continued down the rough lane. "Why did Alice get in the car with them?"

"She wouldn't go with strangers! Oh my God, why didn't I think of that before?"

"Does she know any witches?"

"Only..." I almost couldn't say it, but forced the words out. "Only Sasha."

He said nothing but the SUV picked up speed, bouncing from pothole to pothole. I held on to the overhead strap, not trusting the seat belt to keep me from jolting off the roof.

"And Sasha knew we were going to the fairy den, and what time we were meeting," I said. "I'd asked her for help, and she laughed at me, and then..."

And then her friends got even creepier and began talking about Alice. Oh shit. Alice's abduction and possible sacrifice, they really were my fault.

·····•·····

Arriving at Dad's, Hugh jumped out of the truck without even waiting for me, and ran to the back entrance, the one off the driveway. I followed close at his heels.

"Sasha!" The roar could be heard throughout the mansion.

Cate appeared at the door from the sunroom, a mug in her hand.

"Hugh," she said pleasantly enough till she saw me tailing him, then her face soured as if her coffee had turned to vinegar.

"Where's Sasha?"

"Really Hugh, what's this noise about?" Cate came into the room, managing to turn her back on me at the same time and exclude me from the conversation. "I just made coffee, sit and have a cup with me."

"Cate, where's your daughter?" This was said through tight lips. It was the first indication I'd seen that Hugh didn't like the woman, and my heart warmed to him yet again.

She waved her manicured hand as if to say she couldn't be bothered keeping tabs on all her offspring. "I haven't seen her this morning," she said. "I don't think she even came back last night."

"Think, woman! Where could she be?"

"Good Lord, Hugh, why the rudeness? She's twenty-one years old, how am I supposed to know where she is at any point in time? It's hard enough to get the family together for Sunday dinner once a week."

He took a deep breath and continued in a more reasonable, socially acceptable tone. "Did she mention any plans for the equinox this evening?"

"She usually comes to the Gathering at the Temple, the Kin always have the service and social afterwards. I told her she needed to come this year, especially with... you know, you being here, a representative from an international house and all. Can't it wait till then?" She turned a magnanimous smile towards him, forgiving him his ill manners.

"No, Cate, it can't," Hugh said tersely. "Where's Jon?"

"Oh, squirrelled away in the office, as usual, anything to get away from his family." This was said lightly, tossed off as a joke, the bitterness only coming through in the appearance of a finely drawn net of wrinkles on her top lip.

Hugh disappeared into the depths of the house, leaving me alone with the woman who hated my guts. I busied myself pouring a coffee, anything to avoid her glare, yet I could feel her loathing like dark slime dripping down my back.

"Be sure to wash that mug well when you've finished," she snarled. "And listen up, you little mongrel..."

My head snapped up and I whirled toward her, the liquid splashing from my mug onto the pristine black granite counter top. Those were fighting words. I wanted to throw the cup at her, coffee and all – hell, I wanted to throw the whole gleaming stainless steel coffee pot at the bitch and wipe that hating off her face.

And I would have if I wasn't so intimidated by her.

"Why are you still hanging around here, anyway?" Cate took a cloth in her hand and approached me menacingly. I took two steps back as she viciously swiped at the coffee spill.

"Don't think just because he claims to be a half-blood that you're his equal," she hissed, jerking her head to the interior of the mansion. "They operate by an entirely different set of rules over there. Hugh's line can be traced right back to the Roman times – he's no more Normal than I am. Don't even think of aligning yourself with him."

I could feel my cheeks burning red with anger. She probably thought it was embarrassment, for she pushed on with her abuse.

"And don't get in the way of my daughter," she hissed. "Or I will crush you like the bug you are."

"Like your daughter is going to crush my friend?" I found my voice. "Like Sasha and her friends crushed that woman in Portugal Cove, because she was a mongrel like me?"

Her eyes widened slightly. I thought I saw a hint of recognition there, possibly. Did she know what her daughter was up to this evening?

"What do you know?" I leaped across the room and grabbed her by the folds of her silk dress. "You goddamn bitch, you better tell me."

She shrieked her husband's name, that shrill voice echoed throughout the house, and I knocked her to the chequered marble floor. I wish I could say I heard her head crack against it, but no such luck. I grabbed her by the shoulders and tried to shake the life out of her, I did, I admit. The fine fabric ripped in my grip. I was taken over by rage and the frustration built up over the years, and the anger at this woman who must have had something to do with my mother's disappearance.

"Bitch! Bitch!" I was yelling over her cries. "Where is Sasha? Where is Alice? And my mother – what did you do to her? I'll kill you!"

The fabric of her dress slipped out of my grasp as I was lifted through the air and slammed against a glass-fronted cupboard, breaking it into a thousand pieces which rained on my head as I was dropped hard to the floor again.

Cate leaped up with both her hands aimed at me as I lay there, unable to move in the paralysis of her magic grip.

"What the hell's going on?" Dad burst into the kitchen with Hugh right behind him. They summed up the situation in one glance.

"Cate," Dad commanded. "Stop it now. Let her go. You will not use magic against another being in my house."

"That cur attacked me, physically," Cate said as she dropped her hands and dismissed me. She turned away from me, fingering the torn shoulder of her dress. The cords of her neck were taut. "Remove her from my home. I can't abide this intrusion any longer. Bring her back to the hovel where she belongs – just get her out of my sight."

My eyes met those of Hugh, and I could have sworn I saw a flash of sympathy wash quickly over his face before he stepped forward and took my arm. He nodded.

"We'd best leave," he said.

"She knows," I hissed at him. "She knows something about all this. About Sasha and the murder..."

Both men stilled at these words, and looked toward Cate.

"Don't be ridiculous," she said, affronted at the question in their eyes. "Murder? Sasha? Are you talking about that pathetic creature who died last June in Portugal Cove? How can you even think that our daughter could be mixed up in anything like that, how can you say such horrible things?"

"That's enough Cate," Dad cut in, his voice flat and tired. "Hugh, take Dara out, somewhere, anywhere. We've got too much to do and not enough time."

"But Jon, we need to..." Hugh began, but my father cut him off.

"We're not going to be able to do it right now," Dad said. "That much is obvious."

"What we *need* is to start preparations for the Gathering tonight," Cate said as she gathered herself together, her voice icy. "It's my Kin's turn to host, and I require both of you by my side."

"On second thought," Dad said, totally ignoring his wife. "Hugh, I can't do this without you." He turned to me, despair written on his face. "Go up to your room."

"It's not *my* room," I stormed. "And I'm not staying a moment longer under the same roof as ..."

"Cut it out, and do as I say," he replied flatly. "You're really not helping the situation."

Hugh nodded quietly and flicked his head towards the door. "It's for the best. I'll be up in a bit," he said, in a much kinder tone than that of my own father.

So I withdrew with as much dignity as I could find and headed up the back stairs to the turret room, burning all the way.

If I had been properly educated, I could be of use right now. But instead, I was stuck up here out of the action.

I was going to take Hugh up on his offer, later, when all this was over – if it ever ended. I was going to learn to harness my powers and go anywhere I liked in the world, anywhere as long as it was away from this shit town with all its prejudices.

I turned the chair to face out the barred windows and looked down on the town, then above the trees across the way to Signal Hill and on over to the Southside Hills where all this began, at least where it began for me.

My sister was a murdering bitch, and her mother approved of her actions. She was going to be responsible for the cruel killing of my only real friend in this world, and I was banished to an attic room like some toddler.

How the hell had Sasha turned out so rotten? Aside from the fact that fifty percent of her genes came from Cate, of course.

But what exactly were Sasha and Seth and them getting from this ceremonial killing? I didn't understand how supernatural powers could be transferred over. I understood so little back then.

The Southside Hills jeered at me across the harbor as they peeked out behind the downtown office towers. The fairies were up there, going about their business, Jane's baby weakening by the day and Benjy... well, I hated to think how he must be doing by now. Alice abducted by the Kin, soon to be the next victim of some twisted ideology. Of course, I'd been trying to call her off and on since the morning, but still nothing.

With her phone in my hand, I sent loose feelers out over to the hills, but there was no sign of her, no feeling, no taste of Alice.

A thought hit me. If I could do this for Alice, could I not do it for Sasha? They were probably together. We had a long history, my sister and I, and we did share blood. I would look for Sasha. And maybe that's how I could find Alice.

For this, I needed to get something of my sister's, something she held dear for Hugh had said that made the search easier. I slipped down the winding twisty attic staircase to the second floor.

There were no sounds coming from the rest of the house.

Once there, I hesitated. Yes, I'd been in Sasha's room before, but that was years ago and I'd forgotten the lay of the land in this large house, was no longer sure which was the tower room on this floor. I prayed I wouldn't happen on Cate by mistake.

I realized I might be able to cut down on the search time and dangers by letting my nose lead me to Sasha's room. Closing my eyes, I envisioned her, her smell and her presence and sent feelers out to each of the doors.

It worked. The first door I opened was hers, it had to be, a room decorated like something out of a magazine these days, all shabby chic done very expensively, a *fin de siècle* Parisian boudoir in St. John's. The artworks on the walls were originals, or at least expensive crap from Winner's anyway. The *en suite* bathroom (of course she had one) was tiled all in glass, and was airy and filled with light, while the walk-in closet was massive. She must have taken over the adjoining room in order to create this whole apartment for herself, this shrine to Sasha.

It smelled like her, and that really wasn't a bad scent, sort of floral and lemony. I remember back when she had gotten into the hippie look when we were teenagers, all her floaty gauzy clothes that she bought in New York City. Those clothes suited her better, the sister I remembered all those years ago, than this hard, sophisticated witch with the dragon red claws that she had become. A witch just like her mother.

I looked around the artistically arranged jumble in Sasha's room, looking for one object that would serve my purpose. Her makeup, her jewellery box, the hand-made cards from her last birthday – none of it seemed suitable. I was headed towards her desk drawers in search of a favourite pen or her IPod, but glancing up at the mirror, I saw exactly what I needed.

It was just a gaudy pressed-tin locket, a heart shape on a cheap chain, hanging amidst a bunch of other me-mentoes. I remembered winning it at the Regatta that year when I was ten and she was eleven. It had been the last time we'd been together as sisters.

The game of chance I'd played and won was long forgotten, just the memory of the locket being passed to me by the scruffy barker and our mutual delight in it. On impulse, I'd given it to her and in return, she pressed on me the fluffy pink lion she had won elsewhere. For that moment in time, we were truly sisters of the heart.

I'd forgotten that summer till now, but the pink lion still sat on a shelf in my own bedroom, too.

The metal was cold on my fingers as I lifted and disentangled the chain from the assortment of jewellery and beads hanging by the side of the mirror.

Quickly, I ran back up the way I'd come and sat in the saggy armchair facing the Southside Hills. This was it. I was going to find my sister, that evil fucking bitch.

But I had no more luck with that search than the one for Alice. I could feel no hint of her over the wide city, nothing at all.

The only thing left to me, the only weapon in my very limited arsenal, was to go into Alt and find her there. Hugh had told me not to do it, but I didn't really have any choice by now, did I?

Yet, I couldn't do anything in this house, this prison, because Dad and Hugh and even Cate would know immediately that I was slipping into Alt, at least I suspected they would be able to sense it and I couldn't take that chance.

And what was my plan when I'd found either Sasha or Alice? I had none, but that didn't stop me.

CHAPTER 25

It was easy to escape from the house that afternoon. There were at least five entrances to the huge mansion and only two guardians, because Cate wouldn't care if I left or not. Once out, I ran for my life even though no one was chasing me. Down the private lane way under cover of the overhanging trees, and across New Cove Road. Hugh had said this was best done from a high place, so my mind was working furiously as I tore across the road, unmindful of the midafternoon traffic. I knew I needed to find high ground, and quickly.

As I came to the corner, I suddenly knew exactly where to go. Somewhere high overlooking the city, and somewhere that was unlikely to have dangerous properties in Alt. Behind Gaspar Corte-Real, the statue of the explorer given by the Portuguese sailing fleet who had for centuries come over the ocean to fish for cod off the island, there was a large green space, hardly ever used, that had always been farm land. I headed up Gooseberry Lane to those fields below the present Confederation Building, placed so the first Premier could keep a watchful eye on the city below his feet.

A pathway, there's always a path somewhere, and I found it, leading to the sloping green below the Parkway. Yes, this was the perfect spot.

I sat myself under the shelter of an old tree and looked around. This was high enough up for my purposes and the space was totally free of people as usual. The roar of the traffic up the hill behind me was steady, a lulling sound and the uncut grass of the fields below me swayed in the fierce wind. Although the clouds were gathering fast, there was no rain yet. It was peaceful and quiet in this tiny vale, sheltered from the storm which was approaching yet still not upon us in full.

Despite my misgivings, despite Hugh's warning not to do it, I closed my eyes and willed the switch into Alt. And when I opened them again, the air smelled sweeter and the forest was closer.

I heard a snuffling sound very close by, and almost leaped out of my skin at the feeling of hot breath on my neck. But it was just a curious cow come to check me out, and when I laughed it wandered away again. Just a regular cow, nothing magical or supernatural about it. Settling back onto the grass, I saw there were fields all around me. No sound of traffic, either. I looked behind me and where the Confederation Building had stood was now a single farmhouse, the white paint half peeled off.

I was sitting in an orchard of apple trees.

Was this actually Alt? There was none of that creepy supernatural feeling that I usually found in the other land, this place was pastorally pristine. Yet it wasn't where I came from, for there were no office buildings in sight, no Southcott Hall sticking out like a sore red thumb by the lake, no glittering snake of late-season tourist cars lined up Signal Hill to see the sights.

The tower still stood there up on the hill overlooking the city, but instead of a parking lot I could see the roofs of buildings behind it, perhaps the old fever hospital and soldiers' quarters, stuck way up on the top of that inhospitable lump of rock.

No Battery Hotel looming off the cliff over the downtown either. In fact from this new perspective I could actually see a corner of the ocean at the Narrows where Signal Hill met the Southside Hills.

There must have been moisture in the air, for both hills looked close enough for me to reach out and touch. Without the gargantuan oil tanks scarring the side, the olive green of the Southside Hills looked peaceful.

I shivered, for the wind was continuing to rise. The weather was the same here in Alt as in the real world. What was I doing, and what did I hope to accomplish?

Alice's phone was still in my hand, lifeless and useless of course, here. It was twenty-first century magic that didn't belong in Alt.

I concentrated on her, on the feeling of Alice, on my love for my friend and everything she meant to me. I also kept Sasha's locket in my other hand, for I knew the two had to be in close proximity to each other. And then I sent myself out into the wind. Alt Town was much smaller than the city of real time, the crooked wooden houses hemmed in by fields and streams which had disappeared in the modern landscape. I tried to do what I did the previous evening but without Hugh at my side I faltered, because I could sense bad things in the atmosphere the closer I got to Alt Town, as if there were noxious currents in the very air itself. An idea struck me, and I bypassed the town itself and headed over to the Southside Hills.

Benjy was in Alt, he had to be, for that's where the fairies dwelt. I had a loose idea that if I could prove that, then maybe somehow I would find a clue as to where Alice was, for the witches were supernatural too, right? Like I said, this wasn't a fully formed thought, more of an intuition really.

Anyway, even though I hovered over the crevice leading to the fairy den, I found no sense of Benjy at all. His red bucket was still there, glowing in the dried grass like a beacon – as to why the pail showed up in Alt, don't even ask, for I have no clue as to the workings of this strange place, what stays and what doesn't. At any rate, I wasn't going to go looking for him in the fairy hall. I had more pressing matters.

For I realized right then what this meant – I couldn't sense Benjy, got no hint of him at all beneath the heavy boulders on the barrens, even though *I knew he couldn't have left the hall*. And that's how I knew that Alice must be imprisoned underground. Somewhere in this vast land in a cellar, or in a cave, somewhere surrounded by thick stone which I couldn't get past with my sensors.

At least that narrowed it down a bit. Unfortunately, I didn't know if her prison was in Alt or not.

I turned to head back when my eye was caught by something else, a strange configuration in the landscape. I hadn't noticed it when I passed straight overhead, but now I could see off to my left, a dip in the hill just like the one where the dead woman, Tracey, was found. The half-blood witch. Like the dell behind Portugal Cove, this had straight sides almost all the way around save for a scree slope and it was bare except for grasses growing at the bottom.

I gave a shiver but before I could head back to my body I felt a stinging whip on my left ankle like a snakebite. I shook my metaphysical leg but the biting itchiness remained, and when I looked down I saw a rope of blue light winding around me, reaching up and growing and encasing me till it met around my middle and stayed fast. It hurt, as if something had kicked me in the stomach and took my breath away.

I faltered in the air, but knew I had to make it back to relative civilization. Yes, I was still out of body at this point, but the pain I felt was real and physical, and something was stopping me from breathing as if all the oxygen had been sucked out of the atmosphere.

So, Hugh had told me not to do exactly this, astral travel in Alt, untutored as I was. He told me I didn't understand the dangers of Alt, let alone flying in Alt, and he was so right.

The blue light girded me like a belt, and it was pulling me into the heart of Alt Town. The more I pushed against it the more pain it caused, until I gave up and allowed it to take me over the water, through the sea of tall wooden masts of the boats that lined the harbor four deep in places, steadily losing altitude the whole time. How was I going to make it back to my body high on the hills overlooking the town? More to the point, why couldn't I? I tried to will myself back to that field, but of course I didn't have a clue what I was doing.

Can an astral figure vomit? For it felt like I was about to upchuck from lack of air as if my lungs were bursting.

And then it loosened its hold on me, enough for me to gather my energy and head slowly back to the field where my body sat. I reached me and sank gratefully into my corporeal self again.

Yet the blue tether remained around me and held me fast. I tried to slip out of Alt – usually it was so effortless! But I remained stuck in that apple orchard. The line of energy which bound me stretched off into the distance towards Alt Town, and I was alone, even the cows moved away from that fearsome magic, their mournful lows echoing my despair.

"Help me!" I called out towards the old farmhouse, but it remained dark, no lights within. The late afternoon was growing into dusk, unnaturally so, and the wind continued to rise.

I remained like this for an hour or more, the pain dulled to a roar, until I felt the faint gallop of a horse's hooves through the turf below me.

Dara? Can you hear me?

"Hugh!" I looked all around me, over among the apple trees and the cows then above in the sky but saw no sight of him. "I can't see you, where are you?"

No matter, I can see you.

"Is that you on the horse? Did you do this to me?" I asked the air. The hooves were pounding louder. "Why, Hugh? Do you know how much it hurts? Untie me right now, you shit head! I'm sorry, okay? I did what you told me not to do, but I really think this is a bit extreme!"

Shut up and don't move from that spot. I'm on my way.

Don't move, he said? As if I could.

Through the dusk, I could see the other end of the blue rope racing towards me, held by a dark shape on a black horse. I tried to stand but the light strand held me fast in place, and the more I struggled the tighter it became. I was fuming at Hugh, ready to stalk off and leave him, but couldn't.

The rider grew closer, a cloaked figure on a coal black horse. They were almost upon me before they pulled in, the horse whinnying loudly with his eyes rolling. It was a huge beast. I cowered as close to the tree as I could so that it didn't step on me.

And at last I saw that it was not Hugh who held the reins, but Seth. The tormenter, the outsider. How could this be?

"Oh, oh, what have we here?" As he reined in his mount, he wore a smile but it wasn't friendly. The look in his eye was hungry and covetous.

"If it's not the treacherous little half-blood sister," he said as he swung himself down off the horse. "What are you doing in Alt?"

I stayed mute. Hugh was on his way, he'd said he was.

Seth moved closer to me and laughed. "Looks like there might be two for the service tonight."

My heart sank. It was true – he had Alice and planned to, what? Sacrifice her on his altar to his dark gods? I remembered Mark's description of the torture the other woman had undergone, and I shivered.

But then Seth stopped being so cheerful, and he yanked on the magic power line. It hurt like slivers of glass pulled through my skin. "How did you get here?" He leaned in close to me. "Who taught you how to switch into Alt, little mouse?

"Not going to answer me, eh? No matter. I can get the information I need." Seth stood back, stroking his clean shaven chin. I could feel him probing inside my mind and clamped my eyes shut, the better to close my thoughts from him.

"I'm impressed," he said at last, and he really did sound it. "A power like yours, and in a half-blood no less! Too bad you're not better trained.'

Next time I would listen to Hugh, I promised myself, when he said not to do something. If there was a next time.

"Hugh, eh? Can't say he did you much good, only half teaching you like that," Seth moved closer. "He didn't teach you to cover your tracks, you know, and he could have. Should have. I saw you up there spying, leaving the magic exhaust behind you like the vapor trail from an airplane. Totally unnecessary. I could teach you properly. Why not let me be your tutor, little mouse?"

He squat down beside me and began gently stroking the hair out of my eyes. His hand wandered down my cheek to the tender skin on my neck. My skin tingled where he touched me, oh so lightly, but it felt like burning as if he were igniting my very atoms. I couldn't move, and I'm not sure I wanted to.

"I can teach you to do things you only dream about," he whispered, his cold breath in my ear, then he took my chin in hand and gently brought my face up to his. "You could be my apprentice. My own little half-blood helper."

I couldn't take my eyes away from his. I felt like I had been thirsting without knowing it all my life and was now able to drink in the aqua vitae that only Seth could offer, drinking him in like he was the source of life itself. The black depths of his eyes were fast becoming the world to me as they mesmerized me, and I felt stirrings deep inside me, as if a light glowed in a dark pit I'd never known was there. He shifted his cloak to envelope me, to shield me from the rising wind.

And then he kissed me. Can I tell you how it feels to be kissed by a witch with his power? Can you comprehend the spell he was placing over me, weaving around me? I was transported by the promise his lips gave me, ready to throw it all to the wind.

And even betray Alice, for he whispered to me what we could do in his ceremony, how my powers would be made tenfold, and how I could reign by his side. The dark power surged through my very bones, filling me with him. He planted a seed inside me then, by awakening a hunger in me, a need for more and more. I was ready to surrender anything, everything, if only he would take me into him.

But far off in the distance of another world, I heard a car door slam and a deep voice call my name.

....

Seth must have relaxed his grip on my tether, secure in the knowledge I was in his power, or perhaps he also felt the power of Hugh coming close to us, heard him striding through the underbrush another world away. In an instant he had let go of me both physically and magically, loosened the bonds and tossed me aside into the ether, not caring which dimension I landed in. I hovered between the two worlds like a ghost for those few seconds. It felt like a lifetime, not being of one or the other.

I opened my eyes to see Hugh running towards me in real time and although I was free to move again, I couldn't summon up the energy it required. I could sense Seth slipping away over in Alt.

"Seth," I coughed out as Hugh neared. "He's in Alt..."

Hugh's outline wavered in the dusk as he flipped then solidified once more. He shook his head. "He's on a horse," he said. "No way to catch him. Not right now."

"But Alice..."

"It'll have to be later," he replied, his voice grim.

He held me in his arms as I caught my breath and we were firmly in this world, even though I sensed he wanted more than anything to get into Alt and stop whatever demons had had hold of me over there.

Finally he held me back from him and searched my face. "What happened?"

"I did what you told me not to do," I confessed, meeting his eyes reluctantly. Could he see the mark that Seth had left there in my mind, the burning on my skin where it still tingled from his touch? Could he see the searing Seth had left on me deep within? "I went looking for Alice in Alt."

"Jesus," he breathed, and held me close again. "You bloody idiot."

"I couldn't find her," I said, my voice muffled by his chest, then I slowly told him everything that had happened on my foray into Alt.

He stepped back to allow me to speak.

"But I think they may have her underground somewhere," I said. "Because... I also couldn't get any sense of Benjy over there either. And he's in Alt, in the fairy den below the surface. Am I right?"

Hugh nodded slowly. "So this means..."

"Yeah, we have to find out which cellar or cave she's in." I looked around the trees and at the city which was now quickly disappearing into the dark in this unlit field. Seth had not followed me out of Alt, there was not even a glimmer where he could have been. "And quickly, because Seth is having his... thing... tonight."

"Somewhere underground, in Alt or here," he repeated, then shook his head. "We won't be able to search for her. We don't have the witch power."

We were both silent till he spoke again. "The best we can do is to return to the ceremonial site and stop them there. That's the only way we can be prepared enough."

I didn't question that he was right.

CHAPTER 26

No one was at home at Dad's house; they must all have been busy getting ready for the evening's events. Hugh led me into the study with him as he literally wasn't letting me out of his sight, and he said he had things to do before we went to lay in wait at the site high over Portugal Cove.

"I need to do some searching," he said softly after he had me sit in one of the deep leather armchairs. He stood over me with his hands on his hips and stared down. "Can I trust you not to move? Please don't try to follow me."

I nodded mutely. This half-blood wasn't going anywhere, especially not into Alt, not with Seth on the go. I'd learned that lesson.

Behind the desk, Hugh was sitting very still, his body barely breathing. Meanwhile, I was still trying to process what had happened in that lonely field in Alt with Seth.

What did it mean, that darkness he had opened up deep inside of me? I was still shaken at what I'd found inside myself – that willingness to join him, to sacrifice Alice if need be, in order to quench that black thirst for power, to fulfill my hunger for Seth. I tentatively probed that place inside of me, but quickly backed away before I could get into the heart of it when I realized I didn't want to see into that part of myself.

For distraction, I looked around Dad's study. The few times I'd been in here, I had never been free to just sit and gawp. Two walls were covered floor to ceiling with leather-bound books old and new, all looking very important and severe and nothing there that you would read for fun. Covering the heavy coffee table between the two armchairs was a large, spread out paper. Hugh had told me not to move an inch, but I figured it didn't count if I kept my bum in the chair and was really quiet about it, so I shifted my body over to examine it more closely.

It was a map, I saw as I twisted my head round and leaned over it. A map of the Avalon Peninsula, the oddly shaped eastern end of the island of Newfoundland, the bit that had floated over from Africa all those millions of years ago when the earth was still young and defining itself.

There were some streets marked in, some communities, but it was old and very out of date. It was also topographical, that much I could figure, with the high points on the landscape indicated by concentric circles. No highways crisscrossed the barrens or connected the tiny communities strung along the coast like random flotsam washed up on the shore. I reached out to bring it closer and as I touched the paper, I felt the tingle that spoke of the magic in this document, and I realized it was a map of Alt.

I caught my breath in excitement, and quickly darted a glance at Hugh, but no problem there. He was still in his trance or astral travel, whatever he was doing. The paper was about three feet by three feet square.

There were lines drawn all over it, sort of like the latitude and longitude lines on a regular map, but instead of a grid pattern these lines intersected at weird angles like a math problem. Alice would probably make better sense of what it conveyed than I could. Some lines started in the middle of the topographical circles, some petered away off the map in all directions.

Hugh stirred in the chair across from me. My movements must have disturbed him.

"It's a map of Alt with the ley lines charted in," Hugh said.

"The what lines?"

"Ley lines," he repeated. "In the Normal world, they're thought to be magnetic influences in the earth. In Alt, the best way I can describe it is they're seams of magic."

He had to dumb down a lot of explanations for me back then. My finger found the location of the natural bowl in the mountain behind Portugal Cove, and followed the line where it met a bunch of other lines passing through Pippy Park, the huge wilderness area donated to the city years ago, which in recent time was becoming surrounded by new builds. The park stood on the highest point of land over the town. "What's this intersection here?"

"That's where many of the local lines converge, one of the most important locations for us as witches," he said. "It's like a power source for us, and where the Kin built the temple."

"Temple? In the middle of Pippy Park?" I asked. "I've lived here all my life and never heard of a witch temple."

"It was constructed with buffers," he replied. "It's not in Alt, but it might as well be for all Normals can see of it."

"Sounds religious," I said after thinking about that for a bit. "Do witches worship God?"

"A little more complicated than that," he replied. "But the same sort of idea, yeah. The Holy days are celebrated there."

I traced the line past the location of the temple where it ended on the Southside Hills, near the end overlooking the ocean, again at the highest point, and shivered.

"We haven't a lot of time." Hugh broke in. "But I want to teach you something you'll need."

"What, like spells?" I brightened, for although he had shown me how to do stuff, and use my power, he'd never gotten into the nitty gritty of spell casting.

"Spells?" He looked incredulous. "Dara, you read too many fairy tales. There's no such thing as *spells*."

"But, then how do witches do their magic?"

"They... *We* do our magic through using our powers," he said. "Our own power, we don't call on some outside force to do the work for us."

He actually rolled his eyes at my ignorance.

"Well, excuse me," I muttered.

"Never mind," he said. "You picked up on how to block thoughts quickly without any instruction, so this should be easy enough for you to do."

He came and sat across from me. "Now you need to learn how to hide yourself."

"Be invisible you mean?" I liked the sound of this.

"Not as such, it's more like camouflage," he said, considering his words carefully. "Like blurring your edges so that you blend into the background."

I looked at him doubtfully. "How do I do that?"

"The same as you do anything else," he said. Was that impatience in his voice? "You picture yourself doing it, and just do it. Come on, give it a try."

"I don't think I can do that," I said. "I can't picture it."

"Well, you can't do anything if you tell yourself you can't." Yes, he was getting exasperated. But as I looked, he began to... not disappear, no, more like exactly what he said it was, as if the chair he sat in was becoming more visible than him, not that he was growing smaller, but that the outlines of him were turning armchair color, so to speak, and it was hard to tell where he ended or the chair began.

"Like this," he said. "Imagine it first, then relax into it."

And I tried to get the feeling of it. I could do all right with the imaginings, but the last bit gave me a little trouble until I realized how the relaxing was supposed to go, like a widening of myself, starting from my back hips and shoulder blades, and allowing it to move through me like a wave. Looking down, I was pleased to see my jeans blurring at the edges.

"Not great," he remarked. "But good enough for now. Let's get ready."

He led me into the hallway, where he gave me the once over. Reaching into the hall closet, he handed me a black cotton hoody, an old one which might have passed through all three of my half-brothers. "Try this on."

It was big on me, oversized, the way a hoody should be. My white sneakers were already grubby enough with grass stains and scuff marks, so I passed his inspection. He exchanged his leather jacket for a matching hoody in a larger size. It didn't really suit his look.

"The leather will catch the moonlight," he said, noticing the shake of my head.

"There's no moon out there, Hugh," I said. "It's too cloudy."

"Believe me, there will be where we're going," he said.

Outside there was no moon in sight, like I had told him, but the wind had risen even more, gusting and catching at the leaves still not turned color but ripped from their branches regardless. We took the SUV again, travelling out of the city at speed. I looked around at the hurricane happening all around us. Parts of the city were blacked out already, the result of old tree branches cracking off and bringing down power lines, no doubt, yet still there was enough reflected light to see the clouds racing over the city towards the ocean.

We went back up to the wilds of the mountain behind Portugal Cove, the highest point on this eastern shore of Conception Bay, and we battled our way across the barrens to the site of Seth's ceremony. I walked behind Hugh in order to shelter from the terrific force of the wind and even still I had to hold on to him to avoid being blown off the high ground. As we stood on the lip of the bowl, the wind was cutting through the thick cotton I wore, and I wrapped my arms around my body to conserve what heat I could. We looked down, and there was nothing to be seen except loose pebbles rattling through the tall grasses. No moonlight. It was still hidden by the clouds.

"You sure about this?"

He shook his head. "They should be in mid ceremony by now," he said so softly I almost didn't hear him above the wind even though we stood shoulder to shoulder. He brought his hand up to his mouth. "Bloody hell."

"Do we have the right night?" But I knew we did. Seth had said so not hours before.

Shoulders bowed against the force of the gale, he put his arm around me. "Let's go," he said. "Sorry, but I'm going to have to bring us to the temple. We're going to need backup. We haven't got a moment to spare."

He took the SUV on a twisty path on gravel roads I hadn't known existed, around Winsor Lake and up the back side of Pippy Park. The temple was located in a small clearing of the boreal forest of this hillside, an ancient untouched woods at the edges of the city. As we breached the top of the hill ready to go down to the spot, I glanced across the landscape. From way up here, you could see straight across St. John's right to the Southside Hills. Or where that mountain should have been.

"Hugh," I said, my hand reaching out to his arm. "Wait. Look over there, across the harbor."

A huge fog bank, or was it low cloud cover? Whatever, it completely obscured the hill from the midpoint up and even the white oil tanks weren't visible through its murk. Despite the hurricane force winds, that miasma was not stirring.

"The ley lines," I said. "Don't one of the ley lines end up there?"

"It's a meridian," he said. "From Portugal Cove through the temple to, yes, right there,"

"I know where it is, the ceremony," I said excitedly. "I saw it earlier, a bowl shape just like the last one where that woman was killed. That's what Seth meant when he accused me of spying over on the Southside Hills."

Without questioning me further, he put the SUV back into gear and continued past the clearing, deep down into the city again, intent on reaching the Southside Hills.

"We don't have a lot of time," he said grimly. "And... I'm afraid we won't make it there before..."

I nodded. "But why don't we astral travel or whatever you call it? We could be there in seconds."

"We need our physical bodies present to effect any change, to intervene, even if they're in Alt. It's better this way," he said. "Now, to the best of your knowledge, what's the quickest way up to that spot?"

I quickly did the calculations of geography in my head. "Most people would take the trail by Fort Amherst," I said. "And along the top of the barrens. But..."

"Yes?" We were crossing LeMarchant Road already and headed down Patrick Street. Once more, all the lights were in our favor.

"Behind Alice's house, there's a path that should lead up to Nan Hoskins's berry patch," I told him. "I've never been up it, but it'll be a short cut and could save a lot of time. I don't think the bowl is far from the fairy den.

We'll be coming up the back side, too, and Seth wouldn't expect anyone from that direction."

Hugh didn't even look to see if traffic was coming from other directions as we raced through the green lights and over the bridge.

"I hope you're right," he said as he pulled up beneath the overpass and parked behind the huge concrete pillars across from Alice's house. We exited the vehicle and looked up the hill, but it was still shrouded in that unnatural mist.

"Shouldn't we have others with us?" I asked, starting to get nervous as I looked into the blank thick wall of fog.

"As in?"

"Other witches? The dwarves?"

"Jon is already working with us," he said. "And the dwarves won't intervene in an interspecies dispute. It's against the Convention." He pulled the hood over his head and tightened the drawstrings so only his eyes, nose and mouth were visible.

Alice's house was dark. Had they noticed she didn't come home last night? We crossed the road against the wind. A real-estate sign torn from its moorings bounced and bobbed down the narrow road headed straight for Fort Amherst, the North Atlantic Ocean, and then perhaps on to Ireland if the gale held strength.

It was more sheltered by her house, yet as soon we reached the back yard and the stone steps leading up to the hill we found our way blocked by a wall of cold air, solid yet invisible.

"It's an old woman," Hugh whispered.

I narrowed my eyes to allow a little Alt in, and there she was, as real and skinny as in the physical life she had left twenty years before. She looked in pain, as if forcing herself outside her familiar environment was costing her a lot.

"Nan Hoskins! What are you doing outside the house?"

"Never you mind my business! What are you up to, you and that witch? What have you done with my Alice?"

I quickly explained, and with that she turned her back and started up the steps.

"Follow me," the old harridan said as she sneered. "You'll never find the path through the berry patch, you're not of my blood. I know the bowl, never went there in life as there's no berries can grow down there, dirty with magic as it is, but I can lead you to it. The likes of you would never find it otherwise."

"Nan," I panted as we hurried to catch up with her. "Thank you!"

"It's not for you, but for Alice," she said and she spit a ghostly phlegm on the ground at our feet.

We were climbing steadily and entering the fog bank by now, and a colder, clammier environment I would never want to experience. Even Nan Hoskins was wheezing as the air itself clawed inside our lungs.

Finally after what seemed forever and a day, we broke through the fog to a perfectly still night. The moon glinted off the tops of the granite bedrock where it broke through the sparse covering of topsoil and bushes, and in the hollows the mist remained, curling around like a maleficent presence.

There was no wind up here. It was as deathly calm as the Sargasso Sea. Away in the near distance I could see a glow of a ring of firelight, the edges of the hollow where Seth and Sasha were fulfilling their deadly ceremony.

Nan Hoskins had been steadily diminishing during the whole climb, the further she got from her home, but I hadn't noticed till now as the fog had been so thick.

She lifted up her hand and pointed. "Pray to God it's not too late," she whispered, then petered out altogether till she was just a cold spot on the barrens.

Hugh and I looked at each other.

"What's the plan now?"

"Put on your camouflage," he said. "And keep your mind open to instruction from me."

I nodded.

"Oh, but keep it clamped down from anyone else."

I started. How the hell was I going to do all three at once? That would be like juggling balls of fire, something would have to give.

"I trust you can do it," he said. "After all, Alice's life depends on it."

CHAPTER 27

W e crept up and leaned over the lip, camouflage in place. I looked over at Hugh and could barely make out his shape against the backdrop of the dark bushes. He had been right to choose black as our clothing, for the lack of color helped the camouflage process by taking on the shades of our surroundings in the moonlight.

Down below us, the ceremony was going full tilt, lit by five pitch torches set equidistant around the bowl. The shadows of the hooded black figures leaped as if they were dancing in the flames which surrounded the altar of stone, a heavy piece of slate atop two boulders with Alice on top of that. She wasn't bound by physical ropes, but sat up, her legs dangling as she watched the scene around her. The slackness on her usually bright face was the only outward sign that she had been drugged.

Seth was in front of her, chanting, while the others crowded behind him, echoing his words. His eyes were on hers, burning into her and she held his gaze. I could see the longing in her eyes, deep within, past the languor. No, Alice! I wanted to scream. I had been there where she was and I knew the lure, the lust for power that she was feeling. I knew what he was promising.

I felt Hugh look over to me.

Can you get inside her mind?

But Seth is right there next to her, I told him silently.

So do it without him feeling you.

It was alright for him to say that, being a fully trained witch and all, but I was just learning this stuff. Jesus. I had no option but to try. Seth had now turned his back to address his cohorts, so it was the perfect opportunity.

Alice, I whispered in my head as I stared at her. *Alice*.

I saw her perk up a little and cock her head, but her eyes were still hungrily on the witch.

Don't react, I continued. *Don't let him know I'm here.*

I felt the question in her mind.

I'll explain it all afterwards, I said. *But I need you to know that what you're feeling, what he has put in you, it's not real.*

Her mind was drifting back to the power lust Seth had offered her.

He's lying, I told her silently. *He wants to kill you and take what power you have for his own. Like a vampire on your blood. Like the fairies with Benjy.*

I could feel her mind fighting to get through the haze of drugs and magic at the mention of her brother.

Be careful, I said. *Don't let him see.*

She became very still once again as Seth turned back towards her. He stopped and stood stock still as if sniffing the air, but she turned her gaze on him again and parted her lips, shifting her hips like an invitation.

Through the depths of his hood I could see the glint of his white teeth in the firelight. Seth raised one hand and a chain of blue light fizzed from it, just like the one which had chained me to him earlier in Alt. He drew his hand down her arm, letting the string of light trail. She flinched and cried out. I felt that pain too, that tingling warmth like a lightning embrace, and I could feel the longing grow within her again.

All the while his black French eyes burned into hers, mesmerizing her under his influence.

Alice, are you still there?

Yeah, I felt her say, but dimly. I was losing her.

He's about to move in for the kill. She needs to be ready to throw herself aside, Hugh silently told me.

She's just about paralysed from the concoction he gave her, I objected.

She has to! When I give the word.

I put Hugh's message into her head, but she gave no indication she understood, or even agreed to do it. I was left with only a prayer in my heart.

The witches behind Seth increased the tempo of their chant. He stepped closer and whipped his hand across her face, not touching her physically but the blue stream flicked across her cheek.

She cried out again, louder this time, and a reddened scorch mark remained. The power surged in him, I could almost taste it from where I sat above them.

What is he doing to her? My anguished cry rang through my head.

"He's invoking an ancient rite," I heard him slowly whisper aloud. We had no need to speak only in our minds now for it was as if an unseen orchestra of strings sounded as the chanting of the witches rose in tempo and strength. It was the thrumming magic in the air all around and Seth turned to face them again like a conductor of a mystic choir, urging them on and further on. "It's a blood ritual more ancient than the druids, banned long ago."

Blood. It didn't sound good.

"What's going to happen?"

"He's gathering her energy," Hugh replied in a low voice, not taking his eyes off the scene below us. "When the blood is released and he bathes in it, he will have consumed her life energy for himself."

"Stop him!" I said under my breath.

"Only Alice can stop this." I barely heard Hugh's voice. "He has burned a connection between them. With her permission, he can strip her of her energy. Her very life."

"How can she give permission? Look at her, she's not right in the head. She can no more give consent than her grandmother over at St. Pat's could. Besides, I don't think I'm getting through to her anymore." I turned to him as I hissed these words. Only his eyes glinted in the firelight, the rest of Hugh had faded against the blackness of the night.

The chanting was soaring to a crescendo and Seth turned to face her again with his arms in the air. The lightning crackled between his hands, fingers taut as he strove to control it and his hood fell away from his head with the effort. His eyes were burning and sweat poured from his forehead and triumph lit his brow.

An acolyte reverently handed Seth a knife, the short sharp blade flashing in the firelight. He lifted his other arm high and I could see Alice's rapt face in the glow of the magic in the air.

Now! Hugh said, once again silently.

But I didn't pass the signal on to Alice because her mind was no longer present. I'd lost the tenuous connection with her, and Seth had totally filled her head with his own presence.

So I used Hugh's words as a call to action for myself. I could see she wasn't going to be able to stop the rite because she was too far gone. This wasn't an act of bravery, it was pure panic.

Standing up, I let the camouflage fall away from me as I challenged Seth with my stare.

With one hand about to plunge the knife deep into Alice's chest, he wavered and locked eyes with me.

In that instant, there was only a terrible anger in his gaze at the interruption of his ceremony, but then when he recognized me, the greed rose in his eyes, the greed for me, for my power.

This was the moment, I'd diverted his attention away from my friend, but now I had no idea what came next. I'd jumped off the deep end and was going to have to learn to swim with the sharks and would have to somehow use that greed against him. And I knew I would have to put on an act, pretend to throw my friend away in order to gain his trust.

The worst of it was, the bit I could hardly admit to myself, it wasn't totally an act on my part, for I too hungered for the taste of power he had shown me in that field in Alt.

And the jealousy – where did that come from? The envy of my friend, knowing he'd chosen her when he could have chosen me – even if it was for death. I couldn't look closely inside myself at that moment.

"I'm taking you up on your offer," I said, looking down at him. I held my arms clenched tight to my side to stop myself trembling. I just wished I could trust that I knew what I was doing and yes, I was scared shitless, because I was juggling with knives here.

So I acted, and I was good at it if only because it wasn't totally an act.

I could feel Hugh at my side, but ignored the spate of questions and orders coming from him.

The blue energy from Seth's hand abated as he folded his fingers, as if he'd put the force on pause.

"Dara," he said, a slow smile beginning on his face. It wasn't a pleasant sight, and my stomach dropped right to my sneakers. His hood was back and he gave me the full power of his glamour and those black eyes.

I took a deep breath and plunged in. "I thought about what you offered me, back in the field," I said, pretending a nonchalance I didn't feel.

I didn't know if it would work, I wasn't even sure I knew what my plan was. I didn't want to offer myself to Seth or become his partner, every atom in my being fought against it, but I could not let Alice be taken by him. The sight of that sharp dagger hovering over her chest, the knowledge of the pain which would be inflicted – I couldn't allow it. I had to give her a fighting chance. For once I was acting selfless and thinking of another, but I didn't have time to pat myself on the back.

And I couldn't allow myself to even think about it in case Seth could smell those fears, even though I had my blocks up as far as they would go. I scrambled down into the bowl as gracefully as I could. I couldn't risk looking back at Hugh. Had he disappeared into his camouflage or had he taken himself elsewhere?

Seth glanced at Alice and then over to me. "Come join me." He pointed the blade at Alice and smiled again. "Come claim your power."

His words gripped me with horror, yet at the same time I was also conscious of a stiffening in the figure beside me. It was Sasha, it had to be, because although the hood covered her features, I could feel the force of her sisterly glare.

Seriously – did she really think I wanted her boyfriend?

The French witch lifted his hand and directed the chanting to resume until it again reached the crescendo he needed to ignite the dark magic in the air. He unleashed the blue light from his hand again, his eyes never wavering from mine the whole while.

I felt dizzy, like I was going to disappear into the depths of that burning stare.

"It works better with two witches," Seth said softly, ignoring Sasha, though she pushed herself up to us. "One to wield the magic power, and the other..." He smiled again and handed the blade to me.

I stretched my mouth into a rictus of a smile, hoping it covered up the dread and shock within, even as I accepted the killing tool. Seth really thought I would shed the blood of my best friend for him, to augment his personal power? The arrogance of the man astounded me.

During this short exchange, all Seth's attention had been taken from Alice and without the force of his mesmerization, she was starting to come to. I could feel a soft, Alice-sized movement in my mind. She was wondering if I was here to save her, as I stood above her with the knife in my hand.

I swallowed hard and shut her out of my head. I couldn't afford to let Seth get a clue as to my hastily formed real intention, which was to disable or stab him before the power exchange could happen. It was either him or Alice.

Or me.

CHAPTER 28

At the same time I had to fight the dark that was rising inside myself, that dark lust for power and magic he had awakened in me. I wanted that yes, I wanted to be a full witch and exercise my magical abilities, but not this way, not through taking the life of my dear friend.

Yet it could be the easy path to all my dreams. I looked into Seth's eyes and saw that what he was promising was true and within my grasp, an instant solution to all my woes. I could finally be a more powerful witch than my sister.

He lifted his hand higher and the followers upped their chanting, holding the ring of power all around us so that the magic in the air pulsed with a life of its own. I stood over my friend with the blade poised as she blearily rubbed her eyes and looked at me, puzzled. Just as the crescendo hit its peak, Seth brought his hands down sharply and shouted "Now, Dara!" and I plunged the blade.

But not at Alice. I swerved the trajectory to aim right at Seth and my aim was true but I did not connect with his heart.

At the last moment though my arm was pushed out of the way, pushed further out, it was Sasha, coming in at the last moment as if she had second thoughts about taking Alice's life and wanted me to do in Seth. So he was spared, the blade only slicing only into his shoulder. I felt the sharpness cut him like butter, stopped only by the grating on bone.

With Sasha's unexpected action, the blue power which was dancing in his hands, primed and ready to absorb the magic of Alice's blood, was also sent off course. Instead of pulsing to the point where Alice's blood would spray from her heart, it was interrupted by the steel of the sword which sliced directly through its new path and like a mirror deflected the magic back to its source.

My eyes were blinded by the blue of the light trail but I sensed movement from Alice, I couldn't tell if it was by her own will or the result of the magic gone awry but she fell, rolling off the altar of stone and dropping heavily onto the ground at Seth's feet.

Seth stood for a moment, absolutely still as the light travelled back through his arms with no prey to stop its path, then he arched his back and let out an ungodly curdling, unending scream.

The smell of burnt flesh singed the air.

All motion in the bowl was suspended, the chanting stopped, the hooded figures petrified as if turned to stone. A wisp of smoke curled up from Seth before he collapsed heavily on the ground beside Alice.

I felt the first tendrils of the wind rising now, playing with a strand of hair around my face, and from the corner of my eye noticed the fog above the clifftop hollow lifting, twirling, dissipating as the power which had bound it was loosed.

Of the magic which had moments previously thrummed and roared and flashed in the air, there was no sign. It was now a normal, cloudy, windy night at the top of the Southside Hills. A fox barked further down the mountain, calling to its mate, and the wind susurrated through the scraggly bushes above our heads.

A movement from the floor of the hollow. One of the figures brushed back its hood and stood looking about, dazed.

"Fuck me," said Polka Dot Quiff as he shook his head and looked all around him. "What the hell are we doing?"

Another figure walked slowly to Seth and knelt by his side. It was Sasha. She put her hand to her mouth as if to stem a flow of upchuck, but she didn't succeed, and ended up throwing up the contents of her stomach to the side of her boyfriend, just missing Alice's inert body.

I saw Hugh emerge from the blackness above the bowl. The camouflage was off and all eyes were now on him as he made his cautious way down the scree slope with Jon de Teilhard at his side. Dad was staring at me hard, but didn't say a word. Shit. I was probably really in for it now. Life was so unfair.

Scuffling the loose pebbles under foot, I leaned over Sasha and nudged Seth's inert body with my toe.

"Is he dead?"

She shook her head and moved aside so I could see. Tears were still wet on her face, but she was already getting color back in her cheeks. Seth wasn't dead, but he would wish he was when he awoke. The beautiful face was now reddened and scorched, the skin bubbled in places. One hand lay across his chest, and that too was a mass of blisters.

I silently passed him and knelt by my friend's side.

"Alice," I said softly, looking for signs of life.

"Alice!" I grabbed her shoulder and shook it hard, and finally she stirred. I threw myself down next to her and held her tight. She opened her eyes, and weakly pushed me off.

"Don't crowd me, Dara," she said.

I looked deep into her eyes, where the ravages of Seth still remained, and then I hugged her again to get him out of her.

We all climbed silently back out of the bowl. The wind had returned to full force around our heads, but I could hear the wail of sirens coming along Southside Road far below us. Hugh carried Alice, and two of the Kin brought Seth down the hill as gently as they could, considering his burns.

Jon had already called for reinforcements of the Normal kind, the comforting arm of the legal and health emergency systems. He had a bit of explaining to do to them, but he knew how to handle it. An equinox prank gone wrong, he said, it backfired hence the burns. No, he hadn't been part of it, he had come on it at the last moments. Much of what he told them was true, I guess. He had only lied in omission.

CHAPTER 29

It was now almost October. The events of the equinox felt long ago as regular life crept back up on us all. Hugh got Dad to agree to let me go to the Outer Hebrides after Christmas to learn the basics of the craft – Jon could hardly refuse the request after what he'd witnessed that night. I think more than anything he just wanted me far, far away and out of his hair. The catch was I had to pass this semester at university, and without using magic on exams. Bummer, but how would he know if I cheated, just a smidgeon? I did have a lot of catching up to do, though.

So I was lying on my bed with Edna's boom box turned up on blast with the Eurythmics, trying to catch up on the stupid Math 1010 but it wasn't really working for me. Sweet dreams, indeed. That late afternoon with Seth in the field still played on my mind, I couldn't get it out. Even though I'd been scared shitless the whole time, I had yearned for him to enter me, to take me with him, to open me to the dark possibilities only he could offer. That witch's power to seduce was incredible magic, and dangerous too.

But his promises were all lies, I had to keep telling myself that. Despite being impressed by my powers, he didn't want to nurture and teach me, no, he wanted to suck my energies out to make himself even stronger.

I knew he had gotten to Alice in much the same way, I could sense it from her, that leftover longing for the allure of Seth.

While I was lost in this musing and the music, my door opened. It was Sasha. She stood on the threshold hesitantly, unsure of her welcome.

"Hey," I said, sitting up and reaching over to mute the sound.

"Dara," she said. "Edna called out to get you to come downstairs, but I guess you didn't hear."

I hadn't expected to see my sister, not in a million years, not after she'd been responsible for bringing Alice into the clutches of Seth. I didn't want to see her either, but she was here, for the first time in many years. She was looking healthier than she had for the previous few months, I had to admit, less fashionably pale and thin, more herself.

She walked on in to my room and sat on the bed next to me. I shifted over and drew my knees into my arms and waited for the bitch to begin. She had a lot of explaining to do, and we both knew it.

"I'm... I'm sorry." That was all she whispered, looking down at her lap.

That was it? She was going to have to do better than that. That measly apology didn't even begin to scrape the surface off my anger, and I prepared the guns for my assault on her.

"Do you mind clarifying what you're sorry for? Is it the bit about being prepared to sacrifice my best friend for your boyfriend? Or is it about the murder of the half-blood last June, huh? Or, God forbid, maybe you're apologizing for torturing me and making my life living hell for the past few years? Which part exactly are you sorry about?"

I wished I could have planned this better – I'd rather have been looming over her in a threatening manner as I gave my sarcastic speech. Instead, I was still sitting next to her on my bed so I held myself as stiffly as I could. The pink elephant from all those years ago lay dusty on the shelf before us.

"All of it?" She sighed deeply. "And more."

I waited, not wanting to make anything easy for her.

"Seth was..." She let out a deep breath of air. "How can I explain it? He was like a madness which took hold of me. From the moment I first saw him, and he saw me, it was like I became blind to anything else in my life."

I did know, and Alice knew, what enchantments Seth had been able to cast, but that didn't excuse her behavior. Murder? No, she could have stopped it. I didn't think of my own willingness to sacrifice Alice for the power Seth promised to share with me.

"I became engulfed by him," she continued, her eyes on her lap as she fidgeted with the frayed edge of my patchwork quilt. "He told me I was special.... and we would rule the world. Just like he told you."

She laughed bitterly at her own stupidity. "So... I can't make it up to you. I can only offer my heartfelt apologies to you, my sister."

Once upon a time I would have swallowed this whole, believed her and been full of hope for us again. But too much had passed between us, and as they say, that ship had long since sailed. I knew her too well.

"Dad made you come here, didn't he?"

She nodded. "He's downstairs with Edna. This is part of my penance, I'm supposed to offer you the olive branch, welcome you into the folds of the family. And invite you to dinner tonight."

"Gross. The last thing I want is to see Cate over the supper table."

Sasha laughed. "Yeah, she's not too happy about it either."

We sat there on my bed for a moment more in silence, till I turned my head a little to look at her. "So we're supposed to hug and make up?"

She put her head to one side and considered, looked down at me in my scruffy sweats. "Let's not and say we did, huh?"

I was cool with that, but before she left, I needed an answer from her.

"Sassy....It's just... Alice? Come off it, Sasha, how could you let him choose a friend of mine?"

She was silent. "That I am really truly sorry about. It seemed like a good idea at the time. Seth knew somehow, that she's a virgin, and that got him all hot and excited, and the way he put it... the way we all were thinking was that half-bloods weren't really important, weren't really people like us. It was crazy, I know this, and I can't understand how we could all be influenced *en masse* by him like that."

"And after I confided in you, you went to collect her," I pressed on. "Did you know that I was locked up in the janitor's closet by your friends?"

She raised her fine brows in surprise.

"No, I didn't," she said. "I wondered why you weren't there with her. I was sure you wouldn't get in the car with us and that it would turn out okay, that's why I told him."

"Because you knew why Seth wanted Alice."

She nodded. "But you weren't there."

"And you allowed him to abduct Alice. Where did he keep her that night?"

"In the house he's looking after, the one on Circular Road. It belongs to some Kin who are travelling. They have their basement finished as a home temple, it's all magicked. We would hold private ceremonies there. And orgies, well, they sort of went hand-in-hand."

My eyes widened at this, but I didn't want to know the details. "That's why we couldn't find her."

I thought a moment longer. I needed answers and this might be my only chance. "So, did you know he almost abducted me?"

It was her turn to be surprised. "No! He wouldn't dare!"

"You think?"

"Hugh had, I don't know, sort of adopted you or something. Seth wouldn't have risked getting Hugh involved, of all witches."

"Why do you say that?"

"You don't know about Hugh, what he does?"

I shrugged. "He works for some European organization, yet he's a half-witch like me," I said. "But why would Seth be afraid of him?"

She made as if to answer, then shook her head. "Never mind."

I looked at her with narrowed eyes. I'd get to the bottom of that some time, just not right now.

"He did, though," I told her. "Seth caught me in Alt, spun a web around me like a spider, and almost ate me whole. So, I did get a taste of what you went through, all of you. One part of me hungered for his lies."

She looked a bit put out. "He didn't mean any promises he made you," she assured me. "He despised you for being a half-blood."

"I know," I said, and I had known it at the time. "So what happened, with Seth, I mean, afterwards?"

Sasha took a deep breath. "Well, the Kin all got together and had a big pow wow. They decided not to turn him in for the manslaughter of Tracey."

"Manslaughter? It was murder!"

She shrugged and flicked her raven-black hair off her face. "Well, we didn't realize it was going to end up like that, and by the time it did, it was too late," she said. "We were all in it too deep. So, they didn't turn him over because that would have meant dragging us all through the muck."

By *us* she meant the offspring of the wealthy Kin houses. Jesus. Some things would never change in this town. Cover ups were a way of survival when you held the reins of power. I almost couldn't believe that they would go as far as to hide the facts of the murder from the authorities, but then again, this was the Kin, and the sad thing was it wasn't all that surprising that they hushed the whole thing up.

"Anyway, they've exiled Seth back to Montreal with the expectation that his own Kin there will take appropriate action."

"I hope we've seen the last of him.'

She nodded halfheartedly, then changed the subject. 'So, you're going to learn to be a proper witch, huh?"

I pulled myself up and set my shoulders straight. Only my sister would know the buttons to push for greatest offense.

"Sasha, I *am* a proper witch," I said and quoted Hugh. "It's not the genes, it's the magic in the blood. I'm just going to catch up with my heritage, learn what I should have been taught when I was younger. Like you guys were."

We didn't have much to say to each other after that, and she left, obviously relieved to have it over with.

··········

I'm sitting on the edge of the wharf with my feet dangling over the murky water of the harbor where me and Hugh sat that day, the first time we met. Feels like a long time ago, but less than three weeks have passed. Looking out at the Southside Hills across the water, that whole time is like a dream half forgotten. The fall sun is still warm on me as I sit in this sheltered place, although the days are fast getting shorter and the night frosts are turning the leaves their brilliant reds and yellows. The hills are quiet now.

But I *am* excited about learning how to be a proper witch, despite what I said to Sasha. I really am but I'm dreading it too in a way, because well, it's a lot of responsibility, and I know it's going to change me.

Hugh agreed with me when I told him that, pointing out that I'd been too comfortable in the little rut I'd dug for myself, dressing like a kid, acting like a spoiled brat around Dad and enjoying my own pity party all the time. He said it was time I got over myself and began to fulfill my potential. He's only six years older than me, you know, but you'd never say it because he acts so grown-up and pompous all the time.

Zeta didn't get hurt in the fire, by the way. She looked fine as she was interviewed on TV, grabbing what attention she could, claiming the fire was started by jealous witches who didn't want her opening up the craft to outsiders. I know she doesn't have much magic in her, but she's probably not wrong in her statement and I somehow think we haven't seen the last of her yet.

Oh, and Benjy showed up not long after one morning down on George Street, looking like the leftovers from last night's party, only more strung out and greasy than usual and ranting about his time with the fairies. I was the only one who believed him. He told me how he woke up by the red berry bucket, and how he'd had this fabulous time with the Gentle Folk and he couldn't wait to go back there again. My guess is they tired of him pretty quickly and kicked him out after they'd had their fun. So I did all that for nothing, after all, the worrying and the scheming, I should have known they wouldn't want the likes of him around for long. He brought the bucket back with him, but now he's over at the Waterford Psychiatric Institute as they try to dry him out.

Speaking of all the trouble I caused – well, the baby. I've seen Jane around a bit, and the kiddies always run up to me still hoping for a bit of chocolate, but their mom keeps a pretty sharp eye on them. Is the baby a changeling? I may never know for sure. Maybe I imagined the whole fairy visit to her house, maybe the evil glint in the infant's eye when she sees me is just gas and not a warning to keep my mouth shut. Perhaps. She should know I can never say anything, because too much talk about the fairies would get me locked up in the room next to Benjy at the Mental.

Alice came out of her ordeal okay, I'm happy to say. From what I gather, Sasha and Seth showed up at Fort Amherst that night waiting for us, and Seth turned on the glamour to enchant her, to lower her guard and convince her to go with them, despite how much she hates my sister. She still yearns for him deep inside, I can tell, although she's in total denial about the events of that whole twenty-four hour period.

Of course, she doesn't tell it quite like that. Alice hints that she was Seth's lover, and she totally accepted Hugh's explanation to the Normals that the whole night was just a prank gone bad. The burns on her arms and face are healing well, especially with the help of a salve from Hugh that the doctors don't know about.

My friend has also firmly turned her back on the supernatural. All that shit that happened? Well, she says it didn't. Nope, because she's a scientist and she knows it's not possible. I should be writing fairy tales, she tells me, like my Aunt Edna, and she won't entertain the possibility that she has elf-blood, not even after I made her sit through *Lord of the Rings*. She just cannot see any similarity between herself and Arwen, even though Alice is the spitting image of her.

Edna and Mark don't know about the events of the equinox as Jon had that covered up pretty damn quick, and Tracey's death is fast becoming a cold case for the police. Hugh told me that the Kin have all gotten together and are finally admitting that the prejudice within their ranks is unacceptable. They're going to open their Kinship to any who have magical blood, not just the ones born in to the right families. This is providing the half-bloods can show the proper credentials of course, and you know they're not going to advertise this publicly. Maybe things will change here, slowly.

So, I didn't end up rescuing Benjy or the baby, but I did put Alice in deeper danger, but then got her out again in time, thank God. I still avoid the dwarves, because those guys have long memories and are famous for holding on to grudges long past the sell-by date. At least we got Nan Hoskins quieted down and she's no longer terrorizing her family. I guess that trip up the hill must have taken the good right out of her.

And Mom. I'm no closer to finding out what happened to her, or why, or who did it. But I know I'm going to, once I'm a fully trained witch.

The biggest thing I've taken out of this? I learned that power isn't given to you from an outside source. It doesn't come from knowing the right words to a spell, or because someone else says you have it, or even from being born under the ideal circumstances. Real power can only come from within, and I think I've found mine.

My fingers absentmindedly play with the paper bag still in my hoodie pocket. Zeta's spell. I smile as I take out the sachet, lift it to my nose and breathe deeply of the oregano and cumin within the cotton. These spices won't scare off ghosts or do anything at all except add taste to a meal. Spells and potions and all that gobbledygook? Hugh says their only power is to help you focus your thoughts and desires and intentions in order to help the real magic come through.

I open up the sachet and let the contents drift through my fingers into the water below as I think of my mother, remembering how her presence felt, sending mental feelers out into the world, where ever she might be.

Mom, I'm going to find you.

....

*Dara's story continues in **An Arrogant Witch**, Book 2 of The Witch Kin Chronicles. Available for purchase through Liz Graham's shop or from your favorite retailers.*